A Chance for Us

- special edition

NEW YORK TIMES BESTSELLING AUTHOR
CORINNE MICHAELS

A Chance for Us

Cover Design: Sommer Stein, Perfect Pear Creative
Editing: Ashley Williams, AW Editing
Proofreading: Michele Ficht, ReGina Kay, & Julia Griffis

dedication

For Jan and Pang. Thank you for loving Oliver enough to push me to write his story. If it weren't for you, this series would have never happened. You were right, Oliver Parkerson is pretty amazing and deserved to find a love for the ages.

one

OLIVER

"Two weeks, Oliver! Two freaking weeks and we're not even close to ready! Again! You did this to us again! I could kill you. I could wrap my hands around your neck right now," my sister screams as she signs a sheet one of the construction workers hands her.

I give Stella my signature grin as the worker walks away with wide eyes. I'm used to her going off the rails about things. However, I've always got it under control.

Well, that's not entirely true here. I don't have this handled, but I'm not going to let them know that. I'm actually freaking the fuck out.

The wedding we had planned a few months ago we had to cancel and refund all their money because we weren't ready to open. It was a big blow to the resort, and even though I managed to book another wedding for our new projected soft opening week, we're still not ready.

"It'll be fine, Stella."

"No, it won't. Do you see this?" she asks, pointing at the ground.

"Yes."

"What do you notice about this?"

I shrug. "It's gray."

"I hate you. I swear to God, I hate you. How about the fact that it's concrete? Are the floors supposed to be concrete?"

"Foundation is often that."

She groans and throws her hands up. "Lord help me!"

I take pity on my twin, tossing my arm around her. "Relax. It'll be fine. The flooring will come in, and we'll get it installed before the guests arrive."

The look of utter hate she sends me would make most men cower. God, she's mean. "You don't know that."

"No, but I am not going to worry about it. Maren knows that the resort isn't even open. It's why she got the place for less than fifteen thousand dollars."

"Yeah, a fucking wedding for fifteen grand, another brilliant idea of yours."

"I thought so," I retort. I'm in charge of all the special events, pricing, and adding all the little details to make something go from affordable to profitable. I never really thought of myself as a sales guy, but I'm pretty charming and was able to prove myself. One of the few talents I have, other than annoying my siblings, is planning. I see everything as a puzzle, and I'm going to use that to make us a lot of money.

At least that's the plan.

This issue might be a bit out of my reach.

"It wasn't. You booking a wedding as our soft opening was stupid."

"Go big or go home," I repeat our estranged father's motto and instantly hate myself for it.

"Really?"

"It slipped," I admit.

Stella sighs. "I can't help but think we bit off more than we could chew."

"We might have, but we'll do the best we can. If we have to put down temporary floors or spin some bullshit that it's all part of the rustic décor, we'll do it. No one will know but us."

"As if the floors are the only thing not done?" My brother Josh enters the room. He opens his folder, running a finger down a page as he reads. "Delay in the kitchen sinks, chef just fired the entire kitchen staff for being idiots, furniture leg broken on the sofa in the lobby, electrical issue in the upstairs left wing, the lighting wasn't what we ordered for the guest rooms . . ." He lifts his eyes to me. "Should I go on?"

"I don't know what else you'd like me to say. I booked it weeks ago and they're paying. In order to secure the loan, we needed to show we'd have actual revenue, and booking all the rooms did that as well as allowed us to hire the chef who isn't happy."

"We could've done a wedding after we had a better plan and knew what the kinks in the resort were." Josh pinches the bridge of his nose. "It's just with Delia and the baby, Grayson busy with his kids, and Stella sneaking off with Jack constantly—"

I groan at that image and start to fake gag. "Gross."

"I am not sneaking off with Jack," she defends herself. "We're newlyweds who like the . . . forest."

"You like nothing about nature," I remind her.

"I like wood."

I deadpan. "Get out."

She laughs. "Grow up. I'm married and have a kid. Jack and I want another, and I'm ovulating."

"Seriously, can one bleach their own ears?" I ask Josh.

"I sure as fuck hope so."

Stella rolls her eyes. "Brothers." Then she turns her attention to me. "There's nothing we can do about the delays and issues, but we have to have a plan. By us having to move the deadline up to accommodate this wedding, it cost us a lot in overtime fees. I know your intentions were

3

good with wanting to help your friend and needing to secure the loan, but it really wasn't good business."

Maren called me in the hopes I was still working for my father, needing a place to get married. Time wasn't something she had an ample amount of, so I did what I could to help her out and with the income loss from the previous wedding, this seemed like a win-win.

"I get it, but she'll be here tomorrow and I'm not going to tell her or her fiancé that the venue isn't ready. We'll tackle whatever we can this week, and I doubt she'll complain."

"Maren and Oliver might not complain, but the people actually paying for the wedding will," Josh adds on.

And that is the issue we're all worried about. A soft opening is a great chance to work out the kinks and make sure that everything is in order. I know this. I've been a part of an opening several times. Doing a wedding is a whole other thing. It's going to be a complete shit show. I never would've agreed to this, but there was something in her voice that I couldn't ignore. A sadness that I felt deep in my soul. I had to say yes to her, regardless of the outcome.

She was desperate, and I could tell she had been crying before the call. At first, I brushed it off as her being happy to be engaged, but . . . I don't know.

Stella grips my forearm as I start to walk away. "Wait, the groom is named Oliver?"

"Yes . . . as much as I like to think I'm one of a kind, there are other men with that name."

"I know that, jackass. You just never mentioned his name or had her fill out the wedding sheets I asked for so I could order things I needed."

Stella and her spreadsheets. It's no wonder she and Jack are so perfect. He's just as crazy about his paperwork. "I didn't think we needed more sheets."

"Yes, well, you didn't run The Park Inn here. You know, the one that was featured in bridal magazines. I did. I was the one who handled it, and while I know you're smart, I do have some experience too."

I give her the smile that usually dazzles everyone. "And you will make a perfect assistant to me."

Josh chokes a little and then steps in before our sister can beat the shit out of me. "Let's make a list of what else needs to be done in this room so we can move to the next."

"A few of the guests are friends from college," I say, hoping to steer the conversation in a better direction.

Stella laughs. "Like your ex."

She couldn't resist.

I grumble. "Yes, Devney is the maid of honor."

"That won't be awkward," Stella says with a grin.

Josh snorts and shoves me. "Maybe that'll make up for the fact that you're an idiot to agree to this. Having to watch your ex with her husband."

"Yes, we'll call it penance," I say with exasperation.

I need to move this conversation away from the woman I thought I'd marry. It's not that I am still in love with her two years later, because I'm not, it's just that no one wants to see the woman they loved married to another man. I'm glad she's happy. I really am. Her heart was never mine, and I accepted that—begrudgingly. However, my heart was hers, and it broke the day we ended things.

"I heard Devney had a baby," Stella says as we move through the room, each noting things that are wrong.

"Drop it, Stella," I warn.

"I'm not being cruel, Ollie. I'm just saying that I saw it online. There was a picture of her and Sean . . ."

I huff, turning to look at her. My sister is concerned that it's going to be bad for me. Well, it'll suck, but I'm a big boy and can handle it. "I saw it. She's married to him, so I assumed they'd have kids too. I'm not worried about seeing her if that's your concern. We ended things so she could be with him."

"Doesn't mean that your heart isn't going to hurt."

"My head hurts, that's for sure," I counter.

She smiles, her hand resting on my arm. "I just love you. That's all."

"I love you too, but I promise, Devney is the least of my concerns. I'm glad she's moved on and found what she wanted."

Stella sighs deeply. "Good."

We head through the next two rooms without talking about exes or weddings. When we get up to the front, a car is there, and my fucking heart stops.

Not beating, just hovering in my chest.

The air leaves my lungs, and I can't force myself to inhale.

She's gorgeous.

This woman who just exited the driver's side is absolutely stunning.

She's an angel, blonde hair flowing around her. I don't move as I watch her turn and move toward me. Her long legs and slim body make her appear as if she's floating rather than walking.

The passenger door opens, and I look away for the briefest second and realize the woman who slides from the car next is Devney, which means the angel walking toward me is Maren.

Holy shit.

It's been years since I last saw her, and I don't remember her being this arresting. She was always pretty, smart, funny, but I never really saw her. Until now.

She smiles as she reaches me, but there is something in her gaze that stops me from speaking. "Hey, Ollie, it's good to see you."

I swallow, hoping I remember how to speak. "Yeah. Hey, Maren."

She looks toward the car where Devney is lingering. My ex lifts her hand to wave, and I return the gesture.

Maren turns back to me. "It's been a long time."

Yeah, no shit, and time has been really good to her. "It has. How are you?"

Her gaze goes to the ground before her big, green eyes meet mine. "Well, not so good. I . . . I have a problem, and I think you're the only one who can help me."

I blink. "Me?"

I'll do anything for her. No, wait, she's getting married— here. In two weeks. What the hell is wrong with me?

She nods.

"How can I help?" I ask, trying to slip back into business mode.

Maren bites her lower lip before speaking. "I need you to marry me."

two

MAREN

~Forty-eight hours earlier~

"**A**re you excited about the wedding?" Mark, my boss, asks as he walks into my office.

"Yeah, I'm just stressed. So much is going on, and Oliver is still on that mission, which I haven't forgiven you for sending him on."

My fiancé and I both work for Cole Security Forces.

We've only been together a short amount of time, but we clicked the moment we met. It was fast, fun, and now, I'm going to marry Oliver Edward Kensington III. Well, I will if he gets his ass home in time for the wedding at the resort that my friend from college, who is also named Oliver, owns.

He raises his hand. "Hey, I didn't tell you to get married with, like, three weeks' notice."

"Well, I appreciate your agreeing to step in to be our officiant."

Mark grins. "That is my specialty. Plus, you gave me a reason to dust off my license and expand it to cover the entire fifty states. I'm an excellent minister."

"Natalie and Liam would beg to differ."

"And yet, here you are, begging for my services."

I laugh. "I don't recall that part. I believe it was you who said it's tradition and you'd do it for free."

He waves the comment off and then sits in the seat in front of me. "Were you able to workup some options for the team going out next week when you're on your destination wedding and honeymoon?"

I grab the file and hand it to him. "Of course."

I work as an analyst for one of the most elite security firms and assess risks and possible outcomes before my team goes out and executes the missions. I see angles and issues and possibilities, and I'm always two steps ahead of them.

He opens it and studies the contents. "These are good."

"I wouldn't leave for two and a half weeks without making sure the guys were taken care of."

"I didn't think you would."

"Now, if you could get my groom home . . ."

Mark shrugs. "I have no control once they're gone, but at the last check-in, they were wrapping up. All will be fine."

I really hope so. This wedding, while being as close to shotgun as a wedding can be, matters to me. With my father's cancer treatments and the constant complications, this is the only chance I have to make sure my dad gets what he's always dreamed of—to walk me down the aisle.

Even though he's never met Oliver, he's beyond happy it's finally happening.

My phone rings and my father's name flashes across the screen. "I have to take this."

"No problem. I'll go annoy Natalie."

I laugh and then swipe the video call.

"Hi, Daddy." I smile as his face fills the screen. Some days, it's easier for him to video call since it hurts to talk and I can usually read his face allowing him a respite from trying to speak.

"Hi, Princess."

I smile at the nickname. "You look handsome."

He grins. "Always look your best. Are you . . . all . . ." He struggles to speak. "Ready for your big . . . day? I can't wait. And Linda is excited too."

That last part is a lie. My father, the most loving and caring man I've ever known, is married to a vile human who I call Satan's sister. Linda is, well, the worst. She's a bitch who believes that nothing other than her feelings matter. Not that he was married before, has siblings, a daughter. No, none of that is relevant in her mind.

I loathe her, but she's the gatekeeper to my dad, so I pay the fees, which means I have to be nice to her when she gets on the phone and then poke a voodoo doll after the call.

"I can't wait to see you." I leave off the other person intentionally.

"Same."

"What's wrong?" I ask, sensing a hesitation in him.

Daddy sighs, which sends him into a coughing fit. After a few seconds, he gets it under control and he clears his throat. "Today we got some news."

"Oh?" I sit up straighter, pulling my chair in closer to my desk.

"The doctors said there's not much more we can do."

My throat goes dry, but I push the words out. "I don't understand. I thought the treatment was working."

"I wish that were the case, Princess, but it's not."

My mind immediately starts to go through scenarios and options. "Then we find another doctor. We can . . . we can go to that specialist in New York who is having a lot of success with a new combination of chemo."

"Maren . . ."

I shake my head, not wanting to listen to whatever he's going to say. "I read about it online and it seems promising. Or maybe you just take a break for a month or so . . ."

"Maren, stop. It's been years and years of fighting, and I'm tired."

I know he is. God, I know he's exhausted and has been

11

at this for longer than I ever would've been, but I'm selfish and want my father. I need my daddy, but right now, my daddy needs me not to fall apart.

So, I stay silent, not trusting my voice.

"I'm just so tired, and when the treatment was working, it was worth it, you know?"

I nod.

"I wish it weren't the case, but it's time. It's time to let go and live out the rest of my time."

I want to wail, to scream at him to keep fighting, but I won't do that to him. I can see the pain and fear in his eyes. "I hate this," I say.

"Me too. The doctors say it won't be long, and I meet with the hospice team tomorrow."

That is a word I hoped never to hear. It was a silly hope, one that I was aware would never be fulfilled, but still, a girl can dream.

I had dreams of him being a grandpa and loving my kids, taking them horseback riding or teaching them how to build things. I wanted that for him as much as for myself. Now, that time won't ever come to pass.

Whatever time he does have left, I want to spend as much of it with him as I can. "Why don't we cancel the wedding, Daddy? Oliver and I can come down to Georgia and be with you."

My father's face turns red. "Absolutely not."

"Why?"

"Because . . . you will not give up your wedding because of this."

"It's fine, Daddy. We can wait."

"No, it's not. You have no idea what this means to me. To be there, at your wedding. To know that you'll be loved and that you found the man you want to spend your life with."

I do know. He told me that exact thing a few months

ago. I cried so hard that night, knowing that I might never give him that peace.

Thankfully, Oliver understood, and he proposed a week after that call.

"But you're sick and you need to be home where you can rest."

"What I need is not to stay in bed. I am sick, and that won't change. But this is what I need. To be able to give you away to the man you love, well, it's what every parent hopes for. To know their child is . . ." He gasps and then swallows. "I want a happy memory for us, Maren. Don't take that from me. Don't let cancer be the reason I don't get to see my only child marry the man she loves. I want to be there for you. To see you start your lives together."

My chest aches. "I don't want to make this worse for you."

"The only thing that would make it worse is . . . if you . . ." He struggles for breath. "Cancel it."

I lean back in my chair and look out my office window, feeling dejected and sad. "If you say so."

"I do. Now, do you have everything ready?" He chokes out the words before gasping.

Even now, while he can barely speak, he's worried about me. I've always known he is wonderful and I'm lucky, but it's never been quite so obvious before. He wants this for himself, yes, but I also think it's for me. So I can look back and know my father was at my wedding. I've already lost my mom, and . . . well, he would always talk about my wedding.

I will make this wedding perfect for everyone. He'll get to be there, and I'll get to give him a memory that will allow him to rest.

I force a smile onto my lips and give him whatever joy I can. "Almost. I did find my perfect dress."

He laughs. "Most important . . . part."

"Well, and the father of the bride, right?"

Dad's eyes brighten. "You're the important one."

13

"I think you're pretty high up there."

The bright green eyes that mirror mine are pooling with tears as his lower lip trembles. "I'm so happy, Maren. I have prayed for this."

My heart falls to my stomach. I don't know how I'm going to watch him die. How do I make it through my wedding, knowing that we may not have the chance to make any more memories? I can't. I can't lose him.

"Dad . . ." I start, but he lifts his hand, coughing hard.

"I'm okay," he says after a few seconds of what sounds like excruciating chest heaving. "Just a little setback."

Those four words have been his constant saying. No matter what life threw at him, it wasn't more than just a little setback. He would fight. He persevered and tried to look at the obstacles as just that—things to overcome.

Now, there's nothing he can do but let his body fade away.

And pray to see the things he wants.

"Your setback sounds bad."

He scoffs. "You don't worry . . . about me."

"I always worry about you."

My father wipes away a tear. "You are giving me everything. Everything," his voice cracks at the end. "I'll see you in a few days."

"Okay."

My heart crumbles and so does my resolve. Tears break free and I cry at my desk because I'm about to lose the only man I really love.

three

MAREN

Devney and I are getting ready to head to North Carolina. I have cried more than any human ever has, but I'm not going to cancel the wedding. Daddy sent me an email, which he does when speaking is too hard, reiterating how happy he was. So, I'm going to put on my brave face and give my dad what he wants.

A wedding.

"I am so, so sorry, Mare," Devney says as she loads her last piece of luggage into the trunk.

"He just . . . I don't know. I just really thought he would be fine. I know that's crazy, but I wasn't ready."

"Are we ever really ready?" she challenges.

"Probably not, but it's been fifteen years of him being in and out of hospitals for treatment or surgeries. Now, they're no longer trying, and he's going to die."

That's what is killing me. The loss of hope.

"And how is your evil stepmother with it?"

I shrug. "Who knows? She called me three times, but I couldn't answer."

She flinches. "You'll pay for that later."

I know it. "She'll call again. It's like clockwork. Every hour until—" Like the demons alerted her my phone rings.

Devney's eyes go wide, and I flash her my screen so she can see the ID. "No way."

"I told you, Satan's sister," I say. "She's something like Beetlejuice when you say her name, she appears."

"Hey, Linda," I answer with as much pep as I can. Lord knows if I'm not nice enough, my father will hear about it.

"Your father really doesn't need to be making this trip to North Carolina."

And so it begins.

"You approved it when we booked it, and he has been adamant I not cancel."

"Yes, but it's a great inconvenience to me. You don't understand what it's like to have to travel with him. He's not a well man, Maren. We have a lot of appointments and things I have to shuffle about in order to make this . . . event . . . work."

Event. I roll my eyes. "It's a wedding."

"I'm aware."

She just doesn't care. "I understand the inconvenience it is to you and the stress you must be under, but I offered to cancel, and he refused to even hear it."

"Of course, he would refuse, but I'm just informing you of the difficulties we face. Had you done what I asked and come to Georgia and got married in the church here, your father wouldn't be suffering. He's dying, and instead of spending his last few weeks comfortable, you have him trekking up to North Carolina. Do you know what this does to me?"

The last thing in the world I want is for my father to suffer. I would give anything to keep that from happening. He never once complained about going to North Carolina. In fact, he told me to get married wherever I wanted and he'd move heaven and earth to be there. Oliver is atheist and I'm Catholic, so getting married in the church anywhere couldn't happen. Besides, I wanted my dad to get out of that damn house for just a bit.

16

I stay silent, biting my tongue until the metallic taste of blood reminds me to ease up. She can only upset me if I let her, and so far, she hasn't said anything outside of her normal repertoire of selfish and narcissistic talking points.

"Anyway," she says, "I am packing things now, and I wanted to inform you that I'm going to wear a cream-colored dress because it's all I have. I don't have the time or inclination to find something else."

She's such a bitch.

"You're going to wear cream?"

"Don't worry, no one will care."

Right. No one will care that she's wearing the same color as the fucking bride.

Fifteen years of anger, frustration, and headaches from dealing with her bubble up. Fifteen years of listening to how I'm not good enough, I don't do enough, or visit enough, and how it's all on her. She seems to have forgotten that she *chose* to move my father from Virginia Beach. Had they stayed here, she could have had an army of family surrounding him, caring, helping, and loving him. No, she is the perfect martyr.

Well, I'm not. I'm over her nonsense too. "That's fine, I'm thinking of wearing black instead of white," I toss back, knowing it'll upset her delicate Southern heart.

"What?" She practically screeches. "You can't wear black to a wedding! It's not done. It's not allowed!"

I sigh, a smile playing on my lips. "I'd love to talk more, but I have to go. Lots to do before the big day. Can't wait to see Daddy . . . and you . . . in three days."

"Maren, I'm not done speaking with you."

"Sorry, I'll call tomorrow to talk to him. Give him my love," I say and then flip my phone to airplane mode. My new goal is to make a plan that will piss Satan's sister off without ruining the wedding or upsetting my dad.

"She's a peach," Devney says after a few seconds.

"A Georgia one," I say with disdain. "Ugh! I hate her. She's going to find a way to ruin this."

Devney sighs. "Look, my mother is . . . difficult too. I get it. Remember that this is for you, Oliver, and your dad. That's why you threw together a wedding in less than a month."

I lean against the hood of the car, grateful my best friend is here. "I'm crazy."

"We know this."

"But there's nothing I won't do for my dad."

Devney looks at me, pursing her lips. "You know, I get it. I do. But, like, aren't you excited to marry your man who no one has met yet?"

"I am," I say quickly. "Oliver is a nice guy. He's smart and really good at his job."

"Definitely marriage material," she says.

"Shut up!"

We both laugh and then get in the car. "I just hear you talk a lot about your dad and the wedding, but I want to make sure you're doing this for the right reasons, that's all."

I sigh, gripping the wheel. I don't know exactly how I feel. I like him. I mean, we've had fun the last few months, and when he asked me, I wanted to say yes.

At least fifty-two percent of me did, which meant I should because of the two percent tipping point.

So, yeah, when asked I said yes.

Now that we're coming up on the big day there's no way I'm going to second-guess myself.

"I think I could really love Oliver. He's so nice and caring. I mean, we don't know each other all that well and everything has moved at lightning speed, but that's sort of my life."

"Is it? You? The careful planner who doesn't do anything without a million outcomes mapped out. Please, I'm not buying that. You still can't say you love him and can't wait to spend the rest of your life with this man. Your glowing accolade is that he's nice."

She's not wrong, which is frustrating, but she isn't completely right either. Oliver and I really do like each other. So, considering that I don't know what love is anyway, maybe this is it. I know I want to be with him. I know that he makes me smile—when he's home. I am really good at being his analyst when he's on missions, and that's a very special chemistry.

When he's out and can't see, I'm his eyes. I work hard to make sure he and the team are always safe and up to date on whatever information I have. That is a trust like no other. If we are able to rely on each other in critical situations, then surely, we'll be able to do that in our marriage.

"Not all of us have these grand feelings like you and Sean."

Devney's lips purse. "That's how it *should* be, Maren. Your dad being there is important, of course, but the wedding is about you and Oliver."

"It is about us."

"Is it, or is it about your dad?"

I shake my head, not willing to let her sway me. "I'm marrying Oliver. I weighed the risks, and if things had kept on the path they were on, we would have likely been married in a few years anyway. So, we're just speeding it up in service of others. Just because it's not perfect doesn't mean it's wrong."

Devney's eyes soften. "I'm not saying it's wrong. I'm the last person who can say that getting married quickly or any of that is bad."

"But you knew with Sean right away."

"No, I didn't," she clarifies. "It took me almost being engaged to Oliver Parkerson to figure it out. Sean was always elusive to me. He was my best friend for . . . ever. He wasn't the guy I was supposed to marry. We got drunk and kissed while I was dating someone else. I also know what I'm saying because I was living that life. I convinced myself that what I had with other men was good enough, but it wasn't." Devney reaches across the seat and takes my hand. "I know how you feel about marriage."

"It's forever."

She nods. "Then make sure you're forever-ing yourself with the right guy."

Even if I didn't think Oliver was the right guy, there's no way I'm backing out at this point. All my dad wants before he dies is to walk me down the aisle. I won't take that from him.

"I know what you're saying, and I love you for it."

Devney laughs. "But you're still doing it."

"I am."

She nods. "Then, there you have it."

I mean, I know what I want, and I've already considered all the possibilities. I want this. I could love him. I could at least see myself loving him, which is more than I have had with anyone else.

These are good odds.

I think . . .

MAREN

"I'm so glad you came down early with me," I tell Devney as we are entering the town of Willow Creek Valley.

"Me too. It gave me a break from the kids and forces Sean to play Mr. Mom for a bit."

Devney's husband is a major league baseball player. He's amazing but on the road a lot, so they go back and forth between Florida and Sugarloaf whenever they can to maximize time together. I understand how hard it is to do the long-distance thing since Oliver travels a lot too.

It's hard, but it's what we do for the people we love.

"When will he get here?" I ask.

"Tomorrow. He and the kids are flying to Charlotte and renting a car."

"Two kids on the plane by himself?" I ask. "Brave man."

She laughs. "Please, the nanny is coming too. She is usually off for the summer, but we asked her to come on the trip so he and I can enjoy the wedding."

I nod once. "Makes sense."

We pull up to the house they rented, thinking it would be better to have their own place than be right under her ex's feet. She said she talked to Oliver the other day, just to ease some of the awkwardness, but . . . I can't imagine anything will completely relieve it.

Oliver Parkerson and Devney were supposed to be the real thing. I truly thought they'd end up together, but seeing her with Sean is otherworldly. They love in a way that I've never seen before.

Devney and I get out and unload the bags, putting the favors and table charts over to the side.

Once that's done, we each grab a bottle of water.

"Do you want to head to the resort now?" Devney asks.

"Sure, do you mind driving? I'm beat."

We make our way back into the car and use the directions that Oliver sent this morning since the resort isn't on a map yet.

It's about a thirty-minute ride and about halfway there, I dig out my phone. "I need to call my dad and check in."

I grab my phone and dial his number. He answers, his voice is raspy. "Hello."

"Hi, Daddy."

"Hey, did you get there?"

"I did. Were you sleeping?"

He groans a little. "No, just had a bad night."

"Are you okay?"

"Never . . . better. I get to see you soon."

I smile, wishing he were here already so I could see him. "I'm really excited to see you. It's been too long." Six months of Linda finding one reason or another to keep me away. She has nothing this time to use as an excuse.

"Are you there yet?"

"We are. We're heading to the resort now."

"Good. I'm glad you made it," he says before yawning. "I can't wait to meet Oliver."

Nerves hit me a little. "I can't either."

"I'm going to rest. Have fun with Devney."

"I will. I love you, Daddy."

"Love you, Princess."

We hang up, and my phone rings almost immediately afterward. I answer it, thinking he forgot to say something.

"You okay, Daddy?"

"Maren, hey. It's me."

I blink a few times and smile. It's not my dad, it's my fiancé. "Oliver, hey! You're back in range."

"Yeah, I got back yesterday."

"Oh. I didn't hear from you or know you were back."

Devney peeks at me. I hit the mute button and tell her, "He got back yesterday and didn't call."

Even though I left him two voice messages. But . . . . whatever.

I unmute the phone.

"Yeah, I was going to call, but I didn't know what to say," he explains and then exhales deeply. "I just . . . I'm not really sure there is a way to say it."

The hesitancy in his voice causes my heart to pound and my mouth to go dry. "Say what?"

"Look, I have a lot of shit going on at work and . . . I don't know, Mare, it's like, we got engaged really fast and are getting married even faster."

"You know why."

"I know, and that's not . . . I mean, I was away the last week and we didn't even try to reach out to each other. Isn't that strange?"

My lips part as my mind goes in circles. What the hell do I say to that? "We've never been that way."

"And yet, all the other guys do. They call or send a message. You and I don't, not unless it's mission related."

"I'm not understanding what you're upset about. Do you want me to sit at home and cry when you're gone? You didn't text me or call me while you were gone either. I didn't know this was an issue."

Devney pulls the car over to the side of the road and waits.

"No, that's the thing. I don't think about it either.

23

Neither of us does. When I'm gone, do you miss me? Do you even want to see me? Do I want to see you?"

It feels as though I've been punched in the chest. "We're getting married in a few days."

Oliver sighs, and I squeeze my eyes closed, knowing I didn't answer his question.

"Which is why I'm calling. I don't think it's the right time. I think we should wait and see how this goes."

"*You* asked *me*," I remind him with a very high-pitched yell. "You got down on your knee and asked me to marry you! I didn't do that! You said you wanted to do it quickly, to give my dad what he wanted. Now you want to wait?"

"After hearing about your dying father's last wish. Of course, I did."

"I never pushed you to propose, Oliver! I was sharing what he said!"

I never said I wanted to get married, just that I hated I wouldn't be able to give my father what he always wanted.

Oliver didn't hesitate. He asked me, and I thought . . . I thought it was the right thing. I looked at all the possibilities, and I was . . . stupid. I'm so stupid.

"I'm just sharing how I feel with you. I don't think this is right. We need more time. We can push the wedding back."

I shake my head, unable to process this. He can't do this to me. Not now. Not when my dad is dying and he says this is all he has. What the hell am I going to do now? This is a fucking nightmare. I can't do this. My heart is racing and I am freaking out.

"We don't have time, Oliver."

"Why not?"

"Because he's *dying*. He doesn't have months or years. We have to do this now. We can't back out. You have to marry me."

Oliver sighs. "So, are you upset that I'm not ready to marry you now or that you won't be able to make your dad happy?"

I pause, and my gut clenches because this was his idea and my father is literally dying. This is all he wants and now he's taking that away. "I'm upset because you decided to say this now! Two weeks before the wedding—over the fucking phone! You can't do this." I calm myself, working through the way to deal with this. "Just come here, okay? Just get here like you were supposed to, and we'll work it out. You and I . . . we care about each other, and this is important. You just have cold feet."

"I wish this were a case of cold feet."

"It is. Just grab socks and come to North Carolina so we can warm them. Please, Oliver, don't do this." The pleading in my voice is sad, even to me.

Devney gasps, her hands over her lips. "No!"

I nod as tears fall down my cheeks.

"You don't love me, Maren."

"I . . . I will. I know I will. I already feel it. I know that this is right. I'm begging you, just come here so we can figure it out together."

"You can't even say you love me. How is that not a concern for you? It's just been too short a time. We haven't even met each other's family or friends. It's like we live in this bubble, and now we're going to get married? It doesn't feel weird to you?"

"You can't do this to me. Not now. Daddy was sent home on hospice, and . . . I can't tell him that you're backing out. I can't." The last word comes out as a sob.

I just . . . I want to give my daddy what he wants.

Jesus. He's right.

He clears his throat. "I don't want to marry you *now*. Maybe in a few years, but . . ."

"But not now," I finish.

"No. Not now."

I nod once. "I wish you would've told me this weeks ago."

"I wanted my feelings to change. I thought they would."

25

"I don't know what to say at this point," I confess.

Devney takes my hand in hers. My friend, here to help collect the pieces.

"I didn't want to hurt you, Maren. I really didn't. I do have feelings for you, but we're doing this for the wrong reasons, and I think you know it too."

The saddest part is that I do know that, even if I don't want to actively admit it. My heart is more torn up over my father being disappointed than about what Oliver is telling me.

I don't know how I'm going to break his heart.

"So, I guess I'm supposed to go there now and cancel everything? I'm just supposed to be the one to pick up all the pieces you've broken?"

"I've already told my family, and they agree that we rushed into this."

"Fuck you, Oliver. You told your family before you told me. You talk about not wanting to hurt me, but you do this over the phone. You say you care about me, but you clearly don't or you wouldn't have waited this long. Then you tell me that maybe it will happen in a few years? Are you kidding me? I can never forgive you for this."

At least he doesn't sound happy about it. "Breaking your heart isn't easy."

"It sure seems easy to me. And don't worry, my heart isn't broken, it'll be my father's."

"And that's the answer, Mare. You're not even sad about calling off the wedding. If that doesn't tell you something . . ."

"I don't have anything left to say to you."

"I wish things were different. I wish you were devastated over this ending, but neither of us are, are we?"

"No, I guess not."

"I'm sorry. I really am. I hope you spend this weekend with your family and you and your father have some time together. I think that's what you need most."

I huff, not really caring what he thinks anymore. "Goodbye, Oliver."

I hang up the phone and look at Devney. She leans over the center console and pulls me into a hug. "It'll be okay, honey. I'll help you handle everything. We'll figure it out."

I shake my head, wiping the tears from my cheeks. "I can't believe this."

"I can't either. Are you okay?"

I huff and rub my temples. "No. I don't know. He's partially right. I don't love him, not the way that you love Sean. Not in the way that should have me wailing and sobbing because he called off the wedding. Instead, I'm so mad and hurt because it's going to hurt others, most of all my dad."

She rubs my arm. "I'm sorry. I hate this for you. I know that it would have meant a lot for you to give your dad that memory. You may not realize it yet, Mare, but you wanted that too."

I look out the window and breathe through my nose. "I do. I wanted him to walk me down the aisle too. I wanted to have that memory to hold on to." I wipe away the tear that falls. I was so focused on giving it to my dad that I failed to see I wanted it for myself too. "What the hell do I do now?" I ask, turning back to her. "I have family and friends flying in. I mean . . . I'm going to look ridiculous—more so than when I told them I was marrying a guy none of them had actually met."

"Well, I did think you were a bit crazy when you told me," Devney says with a laugh. "But if you were happy, who was I to say something. I'm totally supportive."

My head falls back against the headrest. "You kind of are, and I love you for it. Switch seats with me. I need to drive."

"Okay . . . why?"

"I think best when I'm driving. My mind works better in motion."

We swap seats, and I pull away from the shoulder of the road. We have about ten more minutes before we reach the resort. I have exactly that much time to decide if I want to call everyone and tell them the wedding is canceled or if I let them all come and force them into a weekend gathering. We can make it a last party for my dad. Linda will lose her mind, but who cares about her? My mind goes in circles as the possibilities cause different outcomes.

"Are you going to tell your dad now?"

"No. If I do, they won't come and then I may not get to see him before he . . . ."

"Right, because Linda doesn't let anyone at the house. What about the rest of your family?"

"I don't know. If I tell them, they won't come either. What if this is their only chance to see him where Linda had no damn excuse."

Devney sighs. "Okay, so . . . we don't tell them anything yet. We'll let them show up and then . . . surprise. No groom. You don't think they'll be upset if they find out he dumped you before the wedding?"

I focus on the road, taking the turns and letting my mind roam a bit for options. "Maybe. I don't know."

"Okay. Well, I'm here. I've got your back, and we'll get through this. We can keep this all on the downlow, and when they get here, I'll help you explain it. It's better to have the weekend with your dad than to cancel."

"Yeah," I say with defeat. "All he wants is to walk me down the aisle. I know it sounds crazy, but he says it's the only reason he's fighting to hold on. It's probably best that Oliver did it before we were all together, otherwise my father may have tried to kill him."

She laughs. "Well, too bad we can't just conjure up another Oliver for you to marry. Your dad never met him, so it wouldn't be like he would know the difference."

As I take the next turn, the craziest idea hits me.

What if I did have an Oliver I could conjure up?

"What's the face for?" Devney asks.

"What face?"

"The one that says you're about to do something stupid."

Not stupid. Completely and utterly insane.

"I have an idea."

Devney shifts in her seat. "I was worried you did. What is it?"

"Well, there's an Oliver right here, and . . . he's a friend who would help if I asked."

Her mouth drops. "Oh no. No way. You can't ask Oliver Parkerson to marry you. That's . . . that's crazy!"

"Is it, though? You just said we need an Oliver."

"Maren! That is not what I meant, and you know it!"

"Well, I can't tell my dying father that I don't have a groom and the one thing he wants is gone now too. I can't do it, Dev. I have to try something . . . anything . . . to give him this. He's going to die, and—"

I can't. That's all I keep thinking. I literally can't say it. I can't tell him that he can't walk me down the aisle or give me away. There's not a chance I can get the words past my lips.

I would rather lie to him and give him what he's always wanted than let him down. I have to at least try. If Oliver won't do it, then I'll have to break my father's heart and pray it doesn't kill him.

Dramatic? Maybe. Out of options? Yes.

"This is crazy," Devney says as we approach the resort where we are set to meet Oliver Parkerson and his family.

"It's desperation."

"You know this is insane, right?"

I sigh, pulling my blonde hair to the side. "I know."

"You're my ride or die bestie so I'll be right here and I'll do what I can."

I nod. "That's all I ask."

We turn into the drive and pass the sign for the Fire Resort.

Devney tilts her head. "I thought it was Fire*fly* Resort."

"Maybe the rest will be going up later?" I hedge my bet.

"Later? Why would it go up after they open? They are open, right?"

"Umm, not really. He booked the wedding as a favor to me. The resort doesn't open for a few more weeks. I guess we're a test run."

"God, the hits keep coming." Devney laughs in earnest now.

"You're who told me he was opening this place and I should call him about a venue," I remind her.

Devney raises one brow. "You cannot give me credit for this insanity. This is all on you."

"Heard." It changes nothing.

"You do remember I dated him, right?"

"Yes, but I'm not asking him to really marry me."

Her brows raise before she huffs. "I'm not saying that. I'm saying that Oliver might be a good guy, but he isn't going to agree to this. I just don't want you to get your hopes up and end up hurt when he says no."

"I can't be any more hurt than I am now. I remember him being great and always rescuing girls who needed it," I reply.

"True, but . . . this is just . . ."

"Crazy. Yes, I know."

"He'll never do it. He's not good at lying and none of this makes sense anyway. How are you going to explain this to the people who have met the original Oliver?"

The only people I invited who know the original Oliver are my bosses, and that's an easy fix. There's no risk of anyone finding out unless someone opens their mouth. We will make our plan and stick to it and everything will be okay.

It can all work out perfectly, providing I can appeal to Oliver Parkerson's knight-in-shining-armor side.

"It'll be easy. His name is Oliver. Neither he nor my ex has ever met my family. So, all he'll have to do is pretend to be in love with me, and we'll fake the entire thing."

Devney laughs once. "And what? You pretend to marry him and then tell everyone it was a lie?"

"I'll worry about that later." I need a bit of time to work that part out.

She snorts. "Sure. Don't you think that'll upset your dad more if he finds out the wedding was a big sham instead of just telling him that the real Oliver called it off?" she counters. "You aren't thinking right. What is your plan? You just walk up to him and say, 'Hey, Oliver, it's been about ten years, but I need you to fake marry me?'"

"Do you have a better plan?"

Devney scratches the back of her head. "You turn around, pick up your morals you left on the road somewhere, and we tell your dad when he gets here."

"That's plan B."

She groans. "Of course not. Look, I haven't seen Oliver in years. I have no idea if he's dating someone or married himself. You're assuming a lot of things here, so just . . . prepare yourself in case this doesn't work out. Okay?"

We pull up to a beautiful building. It has a rustic, yet elegant style that suggests this building has always been here even though it's clearly new. It has oak-color siding with a mahogany-colored roof. The porch wraps around the entire thing, and the sunlight reflecting off the lake makes it look majestical.

I exit the car and head toward the three people standing outside the main entrance. One man draws my undivided attention.

Oliver Parkerson.

He was always handsome with dark brown hair, scruff on his face, and toned muscles, but now he's freaking hot.

31

Now he's grown into every feature, filled out in every spot that a man should be, and I want to run to him and kiss him.

I mentally slap myself. This is Devney's ex, and I lost my fiancé fewer than twenty minutes ago. I should be devastated, not thinking about shoving my tongue down Oliver's throat.

No, this is a mission that has to be successful.

I walk toward him.

When I get to him, my hands start to shake. While I know why I'm asking this of him, it's not easy.

I smile, hoping to hide my nerves. "Hey, Ollie, it's good to see you."

He shifts his body to the right. "Yeah. Hey, Maren."

He looks just as uncomfortable as I feel. God, it has to be hard seeing Devney for the first time since they broke up. Maybe he still loves her.

Shit. I miscalculated.

Well, if he does, it doesn't change the fact that I have to ask him if he'll do this for me. I need him to help me make my father's last wishes come true and trust that we'll get everything fixed after.

"It's been a long time."

I'm stalling. I'm really not sure how to say this.

"It has. How are you?"

Here's my opening. Not wanting to wait another second, I decide to say it all now. "Well, not so good. I . . . I have a problem, and I think you're the only one who can help me."

He blinks. "Me?"

I nod.

"How can I help?"

I bite my lower lip before saying, "I need you to marry me."

There I said it. Now to pray he agrees.

five

OLIVER

I 'm clearly losing my damn mind. "You what?" I ask.

"I need you to pretend to marry me. It doesn't have to be official, but, well, I have no groom, and I need a groom to get married," Maren sputters.

"I'm confused." I'm lucky I can get these two words out. Between her being a walking wet dream and her asking me to marry her, my brain is fried.

Oh, and then there's Devney, who I haven't seen in years, standing thirty feet away. Yeah, totally not firing on all cylinders.

Maren smiles, and my heart trips over itself. I shut down the idea of feeling anything for this woman because there's no way in hell I'm going there. I'm done with women and their bullshit.

But, God, she's something else.

"My fiancé, Oliver, decided that marrying me wasn't really what he wanted to do as of now . . . or ever."

"You're here to cancel the wedding?" I ask, knowing full well she asked me to pretend to marry her.

"That would probably be the easier thing, but you see, my father is dying. He's been sick for a really long time, and about six months ago, the cancer came back. He was fighting—Lord only knows why because I would have given up a long time ago—until a few days ago when the doctors told him the treatment wasn't working. He's . . . there's nothing else they can do other than let him die without pain. He told me all he wants is to have the memory of walking me down the aisle, and now . . . he won't."

The desire to agree rises high. "I'm sorry to hear that."

She nods and then fidgets a little. "Thank you. He means the world to me, and when he said he feels like leaving me without someone to love me and care for me was destroying him, it destroyed me. I can't do that, Ollie. I can't . . . I can't let him . . . I need to give him this peace before . . . before . . ." She traps her bottom lip between her teeth, but I can still see it tremble.

I step back because this beautiful creature might just get me to agree, and that is absolute lunacy. "I'm sorry about your dad." I pause, searching for an easy way to let her down. "I don't know what more to say."

"Tell me you'll help me. It won't be real," she rushes to say. "We'll go through the entire thing as though it is, but . . . I wouldn't ask you to really marry me. It's just . . . well, I need to do this for him."

My head is spinning, and thank the heavens above my sister finally joins us.

"You must be Maren." Stella's voice holds a hint of amusement. If she knew what Maren had just asked me, she wouldn't be so happy.

"I am."

"I'm Stella, Oliver's twin, and that is my brother, Josh."

Josh waves.

"It's great to meet you."

"Likewise. We're really happy to help you with the wedding. I know you have been dealing with Oliver, but I'd like to make sure that this goes off as smoothly as possible. Therefore, I'll step in for the final coordination parts. Flowers, cake, final dinner menu, and seating chart. All the fun stuff."

Maren smiles. "I really appreciate that, but I'm not sure there will be a wedding." Her pleading eyes turn back to me as my sister's gaze burns a hole in my cheek.

Stella cuts her gaze to Josh.

"My fiancé—well, I guess ex-fiancé now—called it off." Maren launches into the lengthy speech about her father, recounting everything she said to me. Hearing it again isn't any easier. I wish I cared about my father so much that I'd beg someone I haven't seen in ten-plus years to fake marry me just to make him happy.

Stella, the bleeding heart under all that steel, wipes at her eyes. Great. Not the reaction I expected.

"Oh, Ollie, you have to!" Stella says quickly, her hand going to my shoulder. "You have to do this for her. Can you imagine? Her father needs this."

"You want me to marry her?"

Maren steps back in. "Fake. We won't be married. We'll do all the things we need to make this look real, but it won't be legal or anything. We won't be married, we'll just have a wedding."

"I'm not going to do that."

"I know I'm asking a lot, but . . ."

Yeah, no shit she is. "I can't marry you."

"Fake."

She bites that lower lip again, and I want to slide my thumb against her skin, tug her lip free, and then kiss it.

Yeah, this is so not going to work.

"Believe me, I wish there were another way. I am sort of desperate and haven't thought every part of this through, but I know this is the right thing."

"I don't think you've thought any of this through," I say.

"She's thinking with her heart," my sister defends.

Maren smiles, and the sun shines brighter. What is with this girl? What is with my reaction to this girl? "I know this is a big ask, and if you say no, I'll understand. I just can't help but think of him being so sad. This trip is all he has to look forward to. My stepmother keeps him couped up, making him go to a million appointments and making more excuses as to why his family can't come visit. He's exhausted. He's been fighting this cancer for almost fifteen years, and . . ." Tears fill those beautiful green eyes. "I want to give him something happy."

"I don't think lying to him would make him happy."

"I think it's better than disappointing him."

I run my hand through my hair. "I know you're desperate, but I'm not the right answer here."

I look to Devney, feelings that I'd buried coming just a little closer to the surface, and I hear all of it whisper again.

Nice.

A great guy, but not the guy.

I like you, but I love someone else.

I wish it were different.

How many times does a man need to be the last option? Not only is this entire thing insane but also it is wrong on so many levels. Maren is upset, rightfully so, but someone has to be rational here. Apparently, it's going to be me.

I step to her. "I think that, in about an hour, you're going to see that this was a bad idea. I can't pretend to marry you. I have no desire to fake marry anyone." Stella's fingers dig into my elbow, but I continue. "Maybe your family can use this time as a reunion, but marrying you—pretend or otherwise—isn't the right idea."

A tear falls down her cheek, and she brushes it away. "You're probably right. I . . . well, I'm . . . it was stupid."

"Don't say that. Ollie is—" Stella stops talking when she sees my face. "He's probably right, which isn't something that happens often."

Maren attempts a smile, but her eyes are still filled with tears. "It's fine. I'm going to go back to Devney's rental and try to figure out what to do. I'm sorry there won't be a wedding."

Stella speaks quickly. "Don't say that. Let's meet tomorrow and discuss a plan."

"I wish there were more I could do," I say, feeling like I'm two feet tall. She looks so goddamn broken. I hate it when girls look like that.

She shrugs. "Me too, but I understand."

Maren walks back to the car and settles into the passenger seat. Devney gives me a small wave, and I lift my head. As soon as they turn down the drive, my sister glares at me and slaps me in the arm.

"You are a jerk."

"Maybe so, but at least I'm not fake engaged right now."

I turn, not wanting to hear her tirade that I'm sure is coming.

"She needs you."

"She needs a therapist." I stop, facing her quickly. "Wait, you actually want me to pretend to marry her? You think it's a good idea to lie to everyone?" I bite back the asshole remark about how lying comes naturally to her, but that would be mean.

"I wanted you to at least not make her cry!"

I shake my head, going back inside where I'm not surrounded by crazy women.

I grab the folder that's sitting on the front desk, and Stella rips it out of my hands. "What is your issue?"

Stella huffs. "You. What exactly is your brilliant plan now, Oliver? Do you see all the work being done? It cost a fortune to speed up construction for the second wedding *you* booked. A wedding that is now going to be canceled. Do you know how much we are going to lose now that this event isn't going to happen?" I have the good sense to look sorry even if I'm not sorry at all. "Your going along with Maren's suggestion would have saved us thousands of dollars and cost you nothing but a few days of your time."

"I get that, but . . . are you kidding me, Stella? You want me to just lie to everyone? Say vows to someone who doesn't love me?"

"Oh, it's called acting. You can manage it for a few days."

Little does she know I'm a pro at it.

"I get that you don't understand the issue, but normal people don't fake marry people. This isn't like asking someone to go to prom."

She covers her face with her hands for a second. "No, it's not normal, and I do understand your feelings on vows and promises. We all love you for it, but we love money too. I love this resort, and the fact that I am eating rice and beans for the third day because we pulled all the money out of savings proves it. Sacrifice your morals for a few days so that woman can give her dad what she needs and you don't have to deal with your other siblings."

"I'll come up with something. I always do."

She doesn't look impressed. "What about *all* the people who are going to cancel once she calls this off? We already lost half our bookings from the groom's side. How are you going to come up with the additional funds we owe to get this done on your timeline?"

"I'll sell my body for sex."

"But not for a fake wedding? Idiot."

I scoff. "Not for a week of lies."

Stella looks to the ceiling and then sighs heavily. "I love you, Oliver, but I'm going to have to kill you."

"Wouldn't be the first time you've threatened it."

"Why won't you do this?"

"Why the hell do you think I should?" Of all my siblings, she is the one I thought would be against this. Well, maybe Grayson too. He hates lying more than anyone.

"Because she needs you." Stella takes both my hands in hers. "She needs you to help her because she loves her dad and doesn't want him to be sad. The pain in her voice broke my freaking heart, and I know it broke yours too."

"I don't have a heart to break," I say, wishing she would drop this. I don't want to think about Maren's eyes and the sadness in them. I don't want to replay the words and desperation laced in every syllable.

Stella releases my hands. "You're ridiculous. I don't get why you won't at least entertain it."

"Because it's crazy, Stella! Pretend to be her fiancé? Fool her family and put on a fake wedding? What happens after when she has to tell everyone it was a lie or that she's getting a divorce? It's seriously the most insane shit I've ever heard."

"I mean, yeah, it's a bit crazy, I'll agree to that, but it's also really sweet. You can help her. It's not like you're really going to be married and you need to do it so I don't kill you."

It just feels fucked up. I have cloaked myself in lies before. I allowed myself to believe relationships were real, convinced myself, and I don't want to go down that road.

But that's not this. I guess. It's all lies, and we know it is.

Then I remember the pain in her voice.

I wanted to help her.

"I know that look," Stella says.

"What look?"

"The one you use when you don't want me to see into your bruised soul. You may fool everyone else, Ollie, but you suck at fooling me."

"You suck at not being annoying."

She grins. "There it is. The way you deflect with humor. I think something happened that scared you when you saw her and that is why you won't do it."

"No, I won't do it because only an absolutely unhinged person pretends to marry someone for the sake of her dying father."

"How about for the sake of their business?" she counters.

That's one part of this that I can't avoid. If they cancel, we are in some serious trouble. Losing four rooms is bad, but losing the whole wedding event will be a huge issue. It's the money we needed to push the production schedule up.

"I—"

"Just listen to me," Stella says with her hand up. "You may not understand her reasons, but they're valid to a woman. She needs her friend to be her hero, Oliver. You can be that for her. It won't be like you can't just walk away at the end of it. You pretend for a bit, give her father the closure he needs, and at the same time, you save the resort from being crushed by financial ruin before we start." She lifts onto her toes and kisses my cheek. "I love you and know you'll do the right thing."

Then she leaves, taking what is left of my self-respect with her.

six

MAREN

"Oh, honey, stop crying, you're going to burst a blood vessel," Devney says as she rubs my back.

"I am just so stupid. I don't know what the hell I was thinking. Not only am I going to crush my father but also I embarrassed myself so badly."

She keeps handing me tissues and rubbing circles on my back. "It'll work out, Mare. I know it's hard, but I'm sure it'll be okay."

It doesn't feel that okay. It feels a lot like devastation. I know that it's probably not all that bad, but I just keep thinking of how disappointed my father is going to be.

I wish, more than anything, I could give him this one happy moment before he dies.

I flop back, feeling worn out and exhausted. "I guess it will be, but I'm not going to tell anyone yet. I don't want to give Linda a reason not to come up."

She nods. "I think that's a good idea. It gives you guys a chance to spend time together."

"Yeah, and most of his siblings will be here. None of us have really had a chance to see each other that much." I sigh. "I feel so broken, Dev. I feel like I can't keep it together and nothing makes sense."

Devney's smile is sad. "You've had a lot happen in the last few hours. Your fiancé called off the wedding and then the whole Oliver thing, so give yourself a day to just breathe. Tomorrow is a new day, and we'll come up with a plan to make the visit special."

My world is crumbling, and there's nothing anyone can do that will make this better. I am so angry at my . . . ex for doing this to me. I mean, I get not marrying me if he doesn't really want to, but he should've had a damn clue about it before now. Then I'm angry at myself because I had the clues and I ignored them, which is unlike me. I just wanted to give my father what he wanted.

I wanted to let him have his moment before I lost the chance to.

"I'm going to clean myself up," I say to Devney.

She pulls me in for a hug. "Okay, I'm going out front to call Sean."

"What are you going to say?"

She shrugs. "I guess there's no point in him coming. I hate to have him fly down with Austin and Cassandra if he doesn't have to."

Yeah, she's right. "Makes sense."

"Go do what you need to, and once I get off the phone, I'll order some junk food and wait out here for you with a bottle of wine."

Thank God for my best friend. "You're the best."

She grins. "I know. Scoot . . . go."

I head into the bathroom, and when I see my face in the mirror, I actually recoil. Lord I'm a mess, and not a hot one. I splash some water on my face, and when that doesn't help, I dunk my face in a few times, hoping for it to do something helpful. I just end up looking like a drowned rat.

Great.

I sit on the toilet, since I'm already feeling down in the dumps. Did I really want Oliver to say yes? Would I be relieved if he hadn't pointed out that I was being a nutjob? I don't know. I really thought it was the best option to try to salvage the situation.

Then the guilt hits. As much as I want to see my father, having him drive all the way up here only to be disappointed, seems so selfish and wrong. Maybe it's best I tell Linda, listen to her bullshit, and let them stay home.

I don't know what to do. I always know. My gut is what has saved lives more times than the intel has. It's what I've always relied on to get me where I am today, and it's broken.

I'm broken.

A knock on the door causes me to jump. "Coming," I say to Devney, forcing myself up out of my self-pity.

When I open the door, it's not Devney standing there. No, it's a very put together Oliver Parkerson.

He stares at me, and his lips quirk to the side. "You still want to get fake hitched?" he asks, and all I can do is blink at him.

"What?"

"I asked . . . if you still need me to be your pretend fiancé."

"I heard you, but . . ."

Oliver leans against the doorjamb. "I said no because I really couldn't wrap my head around it, and to some extent, I still can't. But after you left, I felt really shitty for saying no." He steps inside. "I think it's fucking insane, but if you need me, I'll do it. I'll pretend so that your dad won't be crushed."

My heart begins to pound, and I don't know what to say. For the first time since the breakup happened, I feel hope. I let out a huge squeal and bounce into his arms. Oliver laughs as he catches me and falls back against the wall.

"Jesus. I take it you want to do this?"

I lean back, staring at my friend. "You have no idea how much this means to me. I know it's crazy and is a lot to ask, but yes I absolutely still want to do this. I will never be able to repay you, Oliver. Never."

"You're really sure? You want to lie to everyone you know?"

I bite my lower lip but nod. "It's not ideal, but it isn't as if I concocted this whole thing from the start. I'm just subbing out the man to make my father rest easier."

He raises one brow. "And if he figures it out?"

"I think we'll be okay. He's not well and . . . we don't have that long to lie."

I go into a little detail about how this will work. Being that my father has never met Oliver one-point-oh, there's no chance of him finding out unless we tell him. We just have to sell him on the fact that we love each other, which should be easy enough. Oliver is a great guy, and Devney has sung his praises about being an amazing person.

"I hope not because I really don't want that on my conscience."

"I think it'll be fine. I'll start coming up with a very in-depth plan. The only other small thing is that . . . well, my aunt gave me her beach house in Myrtle Beach for my—our honeymoon. I have to go or she'll think something is up. Well, we have to go. It's important that I stay there for at least one night, but we have it for five days. And you can have it after that one night."

Oliver sighs deeply. "We'll figure all that out. I'm not sure taking off before the opening is a good idea, but we can do at least one night."

I hate to look a gift horse in the mouth and all, but something about this is bothering me slightly. I open my mouth, hesitate, and then decide to ask anyway. "Why are you doing this, Ollie? I know you said you felt bad, but . . . is there something more?"

"I don't know what it's like to love one of my parents so much I'd be willing to ask someone I haven't seen in almost a decade to pretend to marry me. I figure that must be pretty special and rare." He smiles, and I do as well. "Also, you booked the whole resort and we spent a lot of money to

44

get it ready in time. Therefore, my family threatened to kill me and bury my body somewhere in the woods. Considering my brother-in-law is a wilderness guide, it seemed like a high probability that I would never be found."

At that, I burst out laughing. "Well, either way, I appreciate it."

"You say that now, but you're stuck with me through this."

I extend my hand to him. "We're in this together, right?"

He shakes my hand. "God help us both."

Oliver's sister wasted little time telling the rest of his family, and two hours after he showed up at Dev's rental house, I'm sitting at his brother Grayson's house with the entire clan going over what should happen next.

"How exactly is this going to work?" Grayson asks, tucking his daughter into some swing thing.

I clear my throat. "Well, my family has never met Oliver one-point-oh, and the only thing they really know about him is that he works with me in Virginia Beach."

"I clearly don't do that," Oliver says.

"I know, but I think it's easy enough to explain. I can say that you are still with the company, but you also help with your family business. The only person who will give us any pushback is Linda, but I've gotten good at managing her."

"You don't think your dad will be suspicious?" Josh, his oldest brother, asks.

I shrug one shoulder. "He might, but I don't know that he fully absorbs everything all the time. Sometimes we'll have a conversation about something, but the next time we speak, he has no recollection of it. It's horrible, but it just may save us a lot of questions."

Oliver shakes his head. "I can't believe I agreed to this. I think your dad is going to figure it out quickly."

Josh turns to him. "Then you better get busy selling it to everyone, including yourself, that you're in love with her because we have to pay the chef, kitchen staff, wait staff"— he lifts his hand when Oliver goes to interject something— "which we wouldn't have hired for this weekend if you hadn't booked the wedding. The plus side is that this family could use a bit of time together, and a wedding is a good reason to do that. We'll stay in the vacant rooms and get a firsthand view of the staff."

Stella speaks next. "And the more you act like this is crazy, the sooner someone will figure it out. So, you should stop."

Oliver looks to Stella's husband. "We truly have no money? You didn't squirrel some of it away?"

He grins. "Nope."

I know that look. I grab Oliver's hand. "I know this isn't ideal, but . . ."

"I know," Oliver says. "It's not just about that. I agreed to this to help you too, so I'm going to do what I can to help you pull this off. Now, what about your colleagues who are coming?" he asks me, his voice softening.

"My work friends will be there, but they're all really . . . good . . . at pretending."

"What does that mean?"

Yeah, this part is going to be super fun. As much as I'd like to get into it, I can't with his family here, so I kind of dance around the answer. "I work for a security firm, and we are good at adapting to different scenarios that may arise."

He blinks. "That's vague."

"Yes, and as my fiancé, you would know that since you work there too. It's fine. We'll get the story straight. As for everyone else I invited, the only people coming from our mutual past are Devney and Sean."

"Great, my ex-almost-fiancé and her new husband she left me for."

I cringe. I knew that them seeing each other was going to be really strange, but now, he'll have to be around them constantly. She's the maid of honor and he's the groom. It won't just be in passing. I feel terrible. "Is this going to be weird and horrible?"

Stella laughs and then turns her head.

Oliver groans a little. "Yes. No. I don't know. Devney and I were fine two hours ago, so I'm sure it won't be a big deal."

Even though he says it, I can hear the turmoil in his voice. I read the way his body tenses and how he shifts just the smallest amount. He may not love Devney, but the circumstances of their breakup still suck.

She cared for him, and I know that was difficult for them both.

Just one more thing for me to feel guilty about.

"I'm sorry."

"I'm over it, Maren. I really am."

There's a cough from somewhere in the room, so I drop it. "Okay. I'm glad."

"Me too. Honestly, the biggest hurdle is that I have a lot of stuff I need to do at the resort while also playing groom."

"No worries about that," Grayson offers. "Since you're now part of the bridal package, all the work things will be handled by Stella. All you need to do is be the doting fiancé and get a tux."

All of Oliver's siblings start to laugh.

"Fuck off."

Grayson chuckles and turns to me. "Your dad arrives in what, two days?"

"Yeah," I answer.

"That means you have forty-eight hours to figure out how to convince him that you're madly in love with her, can't keep your eyes off her, and that he should let you have the thing he loves most in this world. As a dad of girls, I can tell you that you're not good enough."

"I'm aware of that." Oliver's voice is so low I almost missed it, but then his voice grows to a normal level. "I'm not worried about her dad. Dads love me. Everyone loves me."

"I don't always," Stella adds on.

"Liar."

She rolls her eyes. "Fine, you're lovable, but that's not what we're talking about, and you know it."

He turns to me. "Will you be able to find me irresistible?"

The flutters in my stomach tell me everything. "I can manage it."

"It's because of my stellar looks and winning personality."

I laugh, and it's so big and heartfelt and real that I might cry. "Yes, because of all that."

"See," Oliver says while looking around. "She can't resist me. Now, let's talk about how we're going to get the resort ready."

They launch into business talk, and I spend time forming the rest of my plans to make this actually work.

seven

MAREN

I open my suitcase and take out all the documents I need for today. Oliver is coming over to pick me up so we can head to the municipal building. He asked why we needed a marriage license when we weren't really getting married, and I had to explain to him just how horrid Linda was. She would want to see it, and if we didn't cough it up, she would throw a fit.

When I step into the living room, I find Sean playing a video game with Austin while Cassie is napping.

Sean looks up and pauses the game. "I think Devney and I should talk to Oliver today before all the lies and deceit really kick into gear."

I huff. "It's one white lie."

"No." He chuckles. "It's a white gown and a big-ass lie."

He glances to Devney, who looks up from whatever she's reading. "It's probably a good idea. I haven't really gotten to talk to him since we got here because you pretty much stunned him stupid when you proposed."

Sean chuckles. "You said he was enamored, not stunned."

I glance at Sean. "What does that mean?"

"She mentioned he had a deer-in-the-headlights look

when he saw you," he explains. "She said he couldn't stop staring and that he might have been drooling."

I snap my gaze to her. "He did not. He was confused."

Devney shrugs. "I was watching."

"He was looking at you."

She lifts one shoulder and then returns to her book. "I didn't see it that way."

I'm not sure what they're talking about. I was watching Oliver too. He was uncomfortable the whole time. He only stared at me when I told him I needed him to be the groom.

A car pulls into the driveway, and all I can think about is how wrong Devney is.

However, I can't change any of this.

There's a knock on the door and the three of us stand. I release a heavy sigh and open it. "Hey."

Oliver smiles. "Hi."

There's a small flutter in my stomach when he steps closer, but I tamp it down, unsure of what it is about. "Do you . . . want to come in?"

He shifts his weight and then nods. "Of course. I'd like to see everyone and say hi."

I wonder if he honestly feels that way or if he's doing it to appear unfazed by seeing Devney and Sean together.

As soon as I step aside, Sean moves forward. "Oliver, it's good to see you." He extends his hand, and Oliver takes it.

"You too, man. I saw your last game in the playoffs. Such a fucking bad call."

Sean shrugs. "It was a tough blow, but we'll get them next year."

Devney comes toward us. "Ollie." Her smile is warm as she reaches to give him a hug.

I wait to see if he stiffens or pulls away, but it's almost natural. He doesn't look uncomfortable or regretful. He releases her and steps back, looking toward the living room. "I heard you guys had a baby?"

Sean smiles as though he can't help himself when he

thinks of his daughter. "We did. She's a few months old, and . . ."

"Sean, guess what?" Austin barrels into the room and then looks up. "Oliver!"

"Austin, my man, look at you!" Oliver squats down and pulls him into his arms. "You're so big."

Austin looks overjoyed, and my heart swells. My father always said you can tell a lot about a person by the way kids react to them. It's clear that Austin has a deep affection for Oliver.

The two of them chat about baseball, and Sean rubs the top of Austin's hair. "He's really remarkable," Sean explains.

"I remember going to his games and thinking how talented he was," Ollie says with a smile. "It's really great seeing you guys. I'm honestly happy that everything worked out for you all. Truly. I know people say that when they're in this situation, but I mean it."

Devney wraps her arm around Sean and leans into him. "You have no idea how much that means to me. I hated that I hurt you. It wasn't easy. I promise you that."

"I know," Oliver says easily. "I think things worked out exactly how they were meant to."

Sean laughs. "You mean with you getting talked into marrying Maren?"

I roll my eyes. "We're not actually getting married. I'm just doing what I can for my dad."

"You don't think this is a good plan either?" Oliver asks Sean.

"Hell no I don't. As a father, I would be devastated if I found out my daughter lied about getting married. Don't get me wrong, I understand why Maren wants to give her dad this, but I worry it'll all backfire."

I worry the same, but I have plans. Plans and contingencies, which means I'll be able to get through this successfully.

Or I'll die trying.

"All right," I say. "While I'd love to sit and talk about

how this is going to fail and disappoint everyone, Oliver and I have things we need to do." I turn to Devney. "You're going to handle the room stuff and finalize the itinerary today, right?"

She nods. "I'll take care of everything on my list."

Oliver furrows his brows. "What room stuff?"

"We have welcome bags for everyone, and Stella and Devney are going to update all the names on the programs so they match the new plan."

"And the itinerary?" he asks.

"Well, we have to do things to keep people occupied for a week. Stella is who helped me come up with it yesterday, but we have to reprint everything."

He runs his hand through his hair. "I just . . . I have stuff to do at the resort. I'm not sure how I'm going to split all my time."

"I'll help," I offer. "I'm really good at planning."

He smiles. "I see that."

He has no idea . . .

~

"You're getting married?" the little old lady behind the counter at the registrar's office asks.

"I am, Mrs. Garner," Oliver replies smoothly as he places his hand on my back.

"Oh! This is just wonderful! I have to tell Marivett, she'll be just floored. Delia didn't tell us you were getting married when we were over visiting with her and Josh the other day. Heavens me, I am just beside myself. Who would've believed this? Another Parkerson tying the knot so quickly. And you, my sweet, wonderful Oliver, you're nothing like that wastrel of a father you have. Thank God for that. You're a fine young man, just like your brothers and Stella of course. Why, if I were younger, I would be chasing you around this town."

52

Oliver shakes his head. "You wouldn't have had to chase me far. I might have even let you catch me. Now, about the license?"

Mrs. Garner ignores him. "And you're just a vision. What's your name, sweetheart? And how did you meet our Oliver? He's so dreamy it's no wonder you're in love with him."

"I'm Maren, and we went to college together." At least that isn't a lie.

"Oh, and you realized that you were in love from the start?" She clutches her hand to her chest. "I'm sure you saw him from across the room and just knew. Like magic. I think love is like that. You see someone and *boom* . . . it happens. That's how it was for me, you see. I met my husband in first grade. He was a stupid boy because they all are at that age. When we got out of school, he went to work for his daddy and I went away to college. When I came back, we saw each other and were married a week later. Your story must be so romantic. Nothing like those two girls beforehand who broke your heart."

"Something like that," Oliver says under his breath. "Would you be able to get us the forms, Mrs. Garner? I have to take Maren to a few other places today."

"Yes. Of course. I'll need you both to fill this out and then we'll issue the certificate today."

"Thanks," he says. When she walks away, he turns to me. "This is going to be an issue."

"What?"

"In about ten minutes, the entire town will know about our upcoming wedding. I'm going to have to explain to everyone what happened when you never return to town." He runs his hands through his hair. "I didn't even consider this. Shit."

It's a good thing I have already thought of this issue. "You just need to blame me and tell everyone that I'm a

53

horrible girl who broke your heart. They will see how you're the victim."

He shakes his head and gets to work with his portion of the form. "It doesn't work that way for the Parkerson men."

"Why?"

"My father is a piece of shit. He's known around here for being a cheater, manipulator, and jackass. People here will assume I'm at fault no matter what I tell them because of him."

Oliver finishes and hands it to me. I take it, filling out all the appropriate boxes, still a little shellshocked we are doing this.

"She seemed to love you," I note absently, pondering over his statement about his father.

"Not sure that will stop the gossip. It won't really matter that I'm nothing like him or that I'm the easygoing Parkerson who laughs at everything."

"I remember that about you," I say softly.

I never really thought about why he did that. Why he always seemed to make himself the center of the laugh. Maybe it was because he was trying so hard not to be so serious.

"Yeah, well, nothing about this will be funny when the town sees our marriage fails and I look like the man I loathe."

"I'm sorry, Ollie." And I really am. I hate putting him through this. I scrawl my signature at the bottom and turn to him. "I want you to know that no matter what gossip is spread, you are a hero to me. You're kind and helping a friend when you didn't have to. I know you have reasons to do this as well and while it's not completely selfless, you have the best intentions."

Before Oliver can comment, Mrs. Garner is back. "Are you done with the form, honey?"

Oliver hands the filled out form to her. "Here you go."

She takes it with a smile, looking at me. "You are so

54

beautiful. It's no wonder Oliver couldn't help but fall in love with you."

I smile. "Thank you. It's me who is the lucky one though."

He chuckles. "Clearly, we know that's not true. Mrs. Garner has known me since I was in diapers and is well aware of my failings."

She makes a dismissive noise. "You are nothing close to a failure, Oliver Parkerson. You were always my favorite."

He leans in. "Don't tell anyone this, but you were mine too."

She blushes a little. "You and your silver tongue."

Oliver winks. Literally winks at the woman. "Remember, it's our secret."

"Sign this before I fill in that I'm the bride," she jokes.

Oliver moves his hand up my back. "If I wasn't in love with Maren, I might just take you up on that."

The blush that paints her face is adorable. "You watch this one, sweetheart. He's one of a kind and you're a lucky woman to have a chance with him."

I grin. "I'm a lucky girl."

"Yes, you sure are. Now, you'll have to come by the house tomorrow and pick up something for you both."

Oliver tilts his head. "For us? How could you have something for us?"

She pats his hand. "You don't worry about that. I already have Marivett working her busy little hands."

He groans. "Already?"

"Already what?" Mrs. Garner asks.

"You told her?"

She shakes her head. "Well, I had to get to work on a wedding present." She gasps. "Oh! When is the wedding? I do hope it's a big one."

I step in quickly. "No, it's just immediate family. We want it really small. My father is in cancer treatments, so we can't expose him to too many people."

55

Her eyes go soft as she takes my hand in hers. "You poor thing. The Lord took my Vincent just ten years ago. It was so hard to watch him go. Is he responding to the treatments?"

I shake my head. "No, the doctors say it won't be long now."

Moisture builds in my eyes, and I look away. Oliver wraps his arm around my waist, pulling me to him as emotions start to become too much. I sink into his embrace, letting his strength keep me up.

You'd think I would have come to terms with this. He's been sick for so long, suffering and trying to live for whatever reason. Years ago, I thought I had accepted that my father wouldn't live to see me married or meet my children. Now, I'm faced with the reality of it, and it's so much harder than I thought.

Oliver clears his throat and rubs my back. "Thank you for everything, Mrs. Garner."

"Of course. I'm sorry to make you cry, sweet girl. Come by tomorrow, don't forget."

I wipe at my tears and push a smile onto my lips. "We'll be there."

As we exit the courthouse, Oliver chuckles. "You have no idea what you just agreed to."

Maybe not. "How about we go grab lunch and you can tell me what I'm in for."

"Food is always a yes."

I grin. Such a guy.

eight

OLIVER

We got the license taken care of and picked out wedding rings that will be ready in a few days.

Of course, I looked like a total asshole because I never bought her an engagement ring since we aren't really engaged, but try explaining that to Mrs. Villafane's son. I really hoped to have lunch out of town, since we'd seen enough people for the day, but my sister demanded to meet with Maren, so we're here at Jennie's.

"Thank you for today," Maren says as we sit.

"It's not a problem."

She tucks her hair behind her ears. "I wouldn't say that. You did get a lecture on women and diamonds."

"Don't remind me."

"I could always use the one I had—"

"No." It might be easier, but we both already agreed it was better not to. She took it off and plans to give it back once she's back in Virginia Beach.

"I agree, but I don't want people to say anything."

"Will your family?"

Maren shakes her head. "No, I don't think so. They know I'm not really traditional, so it won't come as a surprise. They know we rushed everything, so we can just say we plan to get one later."

That'll work for me. "Then we'll just go forward not using your ex's ring."

She nods once. "Perfect. So, Oliver Parkerson, silver-tongued charmer that you are, tell me what you've been up to for the last ten years."

I lean back in my seat. "You know up until I left Sugarloaf, right?"

"I do."

I figured Devney told her everything, and I would rather not rehash being dumped. "After we ended things, I went to Wyoming to open a new inn for my father. It was . . . a damn mess. While I was there, my family kind of went crazy. Dad was cheating on Mom—as always—and we were all sick of cleaning up his messes."

"I'm sorry you had to deal with that."

I plaster on my smile and shrug. "Could've been worse. I could've been Grayson and had my dad sleep with my ex— who is Amelia's biological mother." Her eyes widen. "Yeah, he's a winner, and that is reason number 794849 that I will never get married. My blood is tainted."

"I very much doubt that. You can't be all that bad, you're fake marrying me to make someone you never met happy."

"*Oh*, buckle up for the stories . . ."

Talking to her is easy, and I fill her in on all the drama my father created. She needs to know why we left the company we built with our dad and went out on our own. She listens, dipping a fry into the ketchup and swirling it around.

Once I finish, she sits back. "Wow."

"Yeah."

"But, wow in a good way, Oliver. You could have stayed under your dad's thumb because . . . why not? You were making great money and you liked the job. But you took a chance and did something amazing. No matter what, you have this really special family who came together. I wish I had that."

No, she doesn't. She has no idea what she's wishing for. Nothing I've done in my life has been heroic or great. I deal with one shitstorm after another, and the cycle never ends.

"So, tell me about your supersecret job," I suggest.

She reaches down and grabs a folder. "Okay, so I work for Cole Security Forces and in order for me to disclose anything beyond that, you have to sign this."

I take the folder from her and read over the single document inside. "You need me to sign an NDA?"

"Yes."

"Because what you're about to tell me is supersecret spy stuff?"

Maren jerks her head at the paper. "Go ahead and sign."

Now I'm really intrigued. I grab the pen and scrawl my name on the line. "Signed."

"Okay. I work as an analyst for a clandestine division of Cole Security Forces, and a large part of my job is acting as a liaison between my team and various alphabet agencies in the government."

"But the truth is . . . ." I prod.

"The truth is a lie. Do you understand?"

Not even a little, but the word clandestine is screaming at me.

"I do . . . not. Are you a spy?"

"We frown upon that word."

She's kidding, right? "Wait, you really are?"

"No, I'm not. I work for them. I'm not in the field."

My mind is coming up with all kinds of shit thanks to all the spy movies I've watched. She's like . . . fucking cool.

"Considering you work for a security firm, I'm going to assume what you do is dangerous."

She nods.

"Maren, if you want me to be on the same page as you, you need to tell me a bit more. We're supposed to work at the same company and be getting married. I get you can't tell me everything, but I'm lost here."

"I know, and I know you signed the NDA, but there are very few people who really know what I do—or did. I don't know how much to say when everything inside of me says not to speak at all. Even Oliver and I didn't talk about work and I am his analyst. It's like my job and I aren't the same. They're separate parts of me. My dad is the only person I've ever disclosed anything to, which was limited, but he loved it. He had dreams of being a field agent, like Oliver is."

"No shit," I say with a little awe.

"Yup."

"I'm fucking badass."

She rolls her eyes. "You are, but not for that reason. My ex, *Oliver*, does a lot of covert missions. I'm part of the support team. My job is analytics and risk assessment, so I help outline the team's tasks and troubleshoot all the possible failure points." She pauses and runs her finger along the rim of her glass. "Basically, I find the best series of actions to get our guys in and out safely. Then I find every alternate situation they might run into and find them a way out of it. My goal is to get the team in and out with the least amount of risk or injury."

I blink a few times. "Injury?"

"Sometimes it's inevitable."

"Okay. And you said you work with other agencies?"

"Yes, we do."

I'm impressed. Not going to lie. I want to ask a million questions, and I fully plan to, but she really doesn't look like she wants me to ask which agencies, so I set that question aside for now. "What do you tell people who ask what you do?"

"I do admin work for a security team. All very boring."

"Sounds like it's anything but boring."

Maren giggles. "Really, not many people ask anything beyond that. My aunts and uncles know very little. Daddy knows a lot more since he sort of lives vicariously through me. Of course, I withhold a lot of the info to keep the team safe, but he doesn't mind. Still, he will think you work with me, so he's going to want to talk shop with you. There's really no avoiding it." She chews on her lower lip, drawing my whole focus to that single action. "I'll be with you almost all the time, so I can handle it if he does, but if he gets you alone . . ."

"I'll need to be able to divert?"

"Which isn't going to be easy. It's what he loves, so you're going to have to answer without actually answering."

"I see," I say with a smirk. "I get to make up stories, and you'll have to go along with it?"

Maren's eyes widen. "Uh, well, you probably should not do that."

"Probably."

"Oliver," she says with a little warning in her tone. "You have to stick to the story."

"The one that you wrote."

"Yes, because it's the best option."

I lean back in my chair, rubbing my chin like a villain. "We shall see if I do that."

She tosses the napkin at me.

"I'm kidding. Look, I'll go along with this and do my best for you and for your dad."

She smiles softly, tucking her long blonde hair behind her ear. "Thanks. You are really just . . . you are an amazing man."

So amazing that I'm still single and have been dumped by two women I wanted to marry. Yeah, I'm totally fucking great.

"Well, good thing that I was here when you needed me."

"It is, but that doesn't change the fact that I'm clearly out of my mind."

61

I take her hand, squeezing. "Maybe you are, but you're following your heart."

"If you ask anyone who works with me, I don't have a heart."

"Anyone who has ever met you knows that's not true. If you didn't, I wouldn't be sitting here with you."

Heartless people don't fake weddings for their dying fathers. Just a fact.

"Well, it's all for him."

I can see she's uncomfortable so I change the topic back to safer grounds. "Tell me about your childhood, the things your fiancé should know."

"You remember my mom died when I was little?"

I nod. Her mother was killed by a drunk driver while she was on her way home from work. It was truly horrific and something that really shaped her life. Maren was always the designated driver and wasn't above stealing someone's keys to keep them from driving if they had been drinking.

"After that, he was my everything, my best friend. I was all he had left of her, so we clung to each other. We were a team, you know? Still, it was like I was so afraid to do something stupid or get hurt and break his heart that I wouldn't dare come close to taking risks. Then he married Linda, and I felt like I lost him." She squeezes my hand again, reminding me that her palm is pressed to mine, but when I move to pull away, she tightens her grip. "It was slow at first, but he changed. He was still overly protective and didn't want me out of his sight, but it felt like he never wanted Linda to think she was left out, does that make sense?"

"It does, but didn't you tell me he didn't want you to go to college so far away? That doesn't sound like a father who doesn't care."

"Oh, yeah, that was a huge fight. He begged me not to go."

I remember her struggling a lot with being away. "Why did you?"

Maren shrugs. "I needed to, otherwise I never would have figured out who I was outside of being his daughter. My leaving was what allowed him to be around *only* Linda."

The way she says her name is almost a sneer. "I take it you don't get along?"

"How'd you guess?"

"Oh, I don't know . . . just a hunch."

Maren grins. "She was wonderful in the beginning of the relationship. She never pushed me to think of her like a mother or overstepped. My father got sick shortly after they got married, and even then, she was so great. Dad would've died if it weren't for her. I'm sure of it."

I clear my throat. "Then what changed?"

"Time, I guess. He got better, and they seemed happy, so it took me a long time to notice that something was off. She controlled everything. What he ate, where he went, who he talked to, and how often they spoke. She became the gate-keeper of him."

"I'm sorry. That had to be really hard for you, to be cut off from your best friend."

I'm not sure I would have ever noticed if my father stopped calling me when I was in college or if I would have even cared. Even back then, I despised him.

She lifts her shoulders and then drops them on a sigh. "He's not the same, and I don't entirely blame him. I've changed too. Now, I play her games because, if I don't, I won't have access to him. She's already cut off my uncle Jim because he basically called her out on being controlling."

"How big is your family?"

She bites her lower lip. "Pretty big. My dad has five siblings. Aunt Eileen, who you'll love, is divorced. Aunt Marie, who is a pistol and is married to Arthur. He indulges her every whim. Uncle John, who is married to Gail. He's a dean at a college in New York. Then there's my uncle Jim, who refused to come if Satan's sister was invited because he didn't want to cause drama. Then my aunt Shannon is the baby, and she swore off men years ago. All of them together are amazing and loud and funny, and . . . well, I think my dad really needs them. It's been a few years since they've been together, which is another reason this wedding is so important. I want to see Daddy happy. I want to give him this wedding because I think it'll give him closure with his siblings he misses."

"And if this backfires and he ends up heartbroken?" I ask because I think she might be ignoring the fact that it's a real possibility. She's so focused on figuring out how to make her father happy that she isn't seeing how crushed he will be if he finds out his daughter lied to him.

"Then I'll figure it out, but . . ."

"But you still want to try."

Her big green eyes are wide and open, full of vulnerability and hope floating through them. "Do you think I'm horrible?"

"No."

After hearing how much this means to her, I don't know if I would've said no even if I didn't have the resort to think about. None of that seems to matter as I look at her.

Which is fucking stupid.

Maren is literally coming out of a failed engagement, lives hours from here, and isn't someone I have feelings for.

Yet.

I can't stop looking at her and wishing I could take all her pain away. I need to get my ridiculous hero complex under control. Lord knows it's done enough damage over the years. I don't need another reminder of how I'm good but not good enough.

Before I can think much of it, Fred, the permanent fixture at the diner, appears next to me. "I hear you're tying the knot."

Bill, his counterpart, stands next to him and answers. "You don't hear anything. *I* heard he's getting hitched."

Fred slaps his back. "It's the same thing, you dumb-dumb."

I offer a tight smile and release Maren's hand. "I see you spoke with Mrs. Garner."

Bill shakes his head. "Kristy knows too?"

"You didn't hear it from her?" I ask.

"No, I heard it from Jeremy. Came in here for his coffee and sandwich before his shift and said he heard it from Joey, the plumber, who heard it from Michael, who is working on the traffic light, who heard it from one of the Andrews sisters."

"I'm sorry I asked," I grumble under my breath.

"So, it's true?" Fred jumps in, looking over at Maren. "Please tell me it ain't you. You're much too pretty for this boy."

She clears her throat to cover a laugh, and I bristle. "What does that mean?"

They ignore me, staring at Maren with wide grins.

Maren returns their smile. "It's nice to meet you."

Bill sits beside her and practically purrs. "The pleasure is all ours. Believe me, we are the ones who are *very* happy to meet you."

Oh, Jesus. "You two get away from her," I warn and reach for her hand.

"You don't want to marry him." Fred jerks his head at me. "He's not all that bright."

"And has bad hair and no skill with the women," Bill says.

"You have no hair," I fire back at Bill.

"In my day—"

"Which is far gone," I finish.

Maren giggles, and I swear, her entire face lights up. She's so fucking beautiful that it hurts to look at her. They're right, she would be much too good for me if she were mine.

She just needs me to pretend to be hers, which is really proving to be far too easy.

65

"Now that you've all met, you should go back to your stools before someone takes them."

Bill waves dismissively. "They can have it if I can have her."

I roll my eyes. "She's taken."

"By whom?" he asks.

"Me, and you know it."

I wish I could say this was all for show or that I was protective of her out of some sense of obligation to our arrangement, but I'd be lying. A part of me—a part I'd like to pretend isn't really there—wishes it were true. Maybe it's because she's so fucking pretty. Maybe it's because it's clear she'll go to any length to give the people she loves what they need. Maybe it's because, when she looks at me with those big doe eyes, I want to fall to my knees in front of her.

Whatever the damn reason is, I need to remember that she doesn't want me that way. She is only doing this because of her father.

And this is fucking fake.

Maren leans into me. "I think I have a good guy right here."

Fred chuckles. "He's all right . . . I guess. Don't forget, though, not all that bright."

I shake my head, the old people in this town need a different hobby. "Don't you have some other person to harass?"

The door chime rings and Stella heads our way, making Bill and Fred tense. They may think they are tough and like to give everyone shit, but they're afraid of my sister. In all honesty, we all are.

"Hello, boys. I hope you're not bothering Oliver and Maren." Her brow raises as though she knows exactly what they were doing.

Fred's eyes turn soft. "Never, sweetheart. We were just meeting the newest member-to-be of Willow Creek Valley."

Shit. I didn't think about this. We haven't had much

time to talk about our story, the town people assume she'll move here.

Stella doesn't miss a beat. "That's very kind, but as much as we'd love to visit with you both, we have wedding plans to finalize."

And just like that, they leave. I really envy this woman sometimes. Stella sits and drops a binder onto the table. "Now that we've taken care of that, let's get to work on this wedding and ensure that no one will think that you two aren't in love."

MAREN

I'm not as sure this is such a good idea anymore. Today, Dad and Linda arrive, and when we planned this after Oliver one-point-oh proposed, it made perfect sense for them to get here before everyone else. I wanted to let my father spend some time with Oliver before the wedding, get to know him, see how much he adored his baby girl.

This . . . well, this is utter insanity. Last night, Oliver and I spent three hours going over each other's lives, friends, and family dynamics, and I still don't feel ready.

Hence why I'm pacing the lobby while Oliver sits in a chair watching. "You know, the flooring is new, and I don't have enough to replace it."

I stop moving and shake my head. "We're going to do this, right?"

"Yes."

"But, like, we're going to get away with this, right?"

My heart is racing, and I can't seem to stop fidgeting. There's too much at stake. These last few days have been fine because it was only a plan—an abstract concept I could pick apart and alter if I needed to. Now, it's about to stop being a plan and become reality.

I hate reality.

69

"Relax, Maren. We'll just . . . fake it till we make it."

"Yeah, we'll be fine. We just have to sell it and . . . lie."

He walks over to me, taking my shoulders in his strong hands. "We have a plan, and since you're a planner, it's probably a great one."

"It is."

"If you do say so yourself."

I smile at that. "If I do."

"So, we stick to it, and if one of us goes off the rails, the other will have to adapt."

"Are you planning a revolution?" I ask, somewhat as a joke.

"Well, I am a spy, after all. It's important to think on one's feet in my line of work."

I groan and let my head fall back. "We are so fucked."

Oliver shrugs. "Hey, you have your fun, I'll have mine. If I happen to tell a little embellishment regarding my last mission where I saved a Spanish princess, what's the harm?"

"For one, there is no Spanish princess . . ."

"All part of the lie, sweetheart."

"I've created a monster," I mutter. "You need to deflect, not embellish."

"Sit and relax. You're going to make yourself sick."

He leads me over to the couch and then settles next to me without dropping my hand. I lean in, resting my head on his shoulder, and inhale his musky cologne. Why does this man smell so good? I shift, wanting to erase the space between us, and feel like I'm losing my mind. This is Oliver, who isn't the man I thought I wanted to spend my life with just a few days ago, my friend who used to be in love with my best friend.

This web could not be more tangled if I tried.

We aren't a thing and I need to remember that.

I make the mistake of glancing toward his face as I try to make sense of this. Oliver's blue eyes watch my green ones, and the connection has tingles racing up my spine. I lean back, breaking the spell as I tuck my hair behind my ear.

The stress is getting to me, and I'm keyed up about seeing my dad again. Not knowing what to expect has always made me anxious, unbalanced, so my reacting that way to Oliver is nothing more than my subconscious reaching for something familiar. A friend.

I decide that, whatever it is, my best course of action is to use it to help sell the lie. I'll just have to make sure I don't buy my own snake oil.

Oliver laughs. "I don't know how the hell I get myself in these things. I swear I'm like a magnet for the most insane situations. Seriously, though, I'm going to slip up on the job part, so please make sure you don't leave us alone together."

I smile. "Just be vague or circumvent the questions and you'll be okay."

"Got it. I'll keep things brief, keep my answers short, and if I get in serious trouble, I'll fake choking or something."

I giggle. "My co-workers will play along. They're really good at making up elaborate bullshit stories."

"Seems like it's an occupational thing."

I shrug. "Sort of."

"Oliver!" one of his brother's calls from the front of the resort. "Your fake father-in-law-to-be is pulling in the drive."

Nerves hit me like a ton of bricks, slamming the air from my chest. "Remember, I haven't seen him in about six months. You and I have been together for three months, and you're hopelessly in love with me."

We get to our feet. "Right."

"Okay. We'll be good. We can do this," I say because it has to be true.

I smooth down my dress, close my eyes, and inhale. I am a goddamn badass who is going to make the only man in the world I've ever really loved happy. He's going to get to walk me down the aisle and give me away.

71

I start to walk toward the front door, but Oliver's hand wraps around my wrist. "Wait."

I turn. "What?"

Please don't say you can't do this and are backing out.

"Before we go out there, lie to everyone you know, and try to convince your father that we've been together for three months. I have to do something."

My mind starts to turn, thinking what he could mean. I stare into his beautiful eyes, blinking a few times. Then he lifts his hand to cup my cheek. His thumb strokes my skin, and my heartbeat turns erratic for a totally different reason. We stand in the lobby, our breaths mingling as the energy around us changes.

"Oliver," I say softly, not thinking of anyone or anything but him. It's strange and a little unnerving how much I want him to kiss me. How much the thought of it excites me.

I shouldn't want to be kissed by him. He's my friend, and we're pretending. Only, I don't see any artifice in the way he's looking at me. It's pure lust and desire, and I am here for it.

His lips turn into a sly grin as my attention drops to them. "One time before we have to do it in front of others."

I nod, wanting it way more than I should.

And then, slowly, he presses his lips to mine, and I forget this is all fake as I get lost in the best kiss of my life.

ten

OLIVER

I never should have kissed her.

Not because it isn't amazing or a lack of chemistry but because we sure as fuck don't. All I want to do is haul her to me and kiss her for hours, make her leave my freaking mind for good.

Her hands grip my face, holding me to her as I tangle my fingers in her hair. Our tongues push against each other's, and I swallow her breathy moans. Jesus Lord, there is no way I'm going to survive this.

I never want this to stop. If this is fake, then she's winning an award.

However, her father is waiting and I'm expected to walk outside to meet him for the first time.

How am I supposed to do that now that I've tasted the mint on her tongue, felt the heat of her breath? And am going to have to deflate my, er, semi.

Maren's eyes are glossy as we struggle to catch our breath. "Wow," she says, her fingers pressing against her lips.

I put on my normal, everything-is-sunshine-and-nothing-bothers-me façade in case that was her faking it. "And that wasn't even me trying."

She lets out a breathy laugh. "Thank God for that, I guess."

Josh yells out again. "Dude!"

"We're coming!"

I extend my arm to Maren, doing everything I can not to shove her against the wall and kiss her again. "My love."

Her hand tucks into the crook of my elbow, and she sighs deeply. "Here goes nothing."

We walk out toward the front entrance, passing the cleaning crew, who are wiping things down to get rid of all the construction dust. Our floors were delivered late last night, and by tomorrow, the contractors should be done with the installation in the entire resort. Stella has planned out which rooms will be done at certain times, and we're to stick to the parts of the resort that have been completed. Right now, they're finishing the guest room her parents will be staying in. If all goes well, that'll be done within the hour.

The passenger door opens, and Maren rushes forward to help her father out. At one time, he was a tall man, probably stockier too. The man before me is frail with almost leathered skin, but his eyes, they're kind and full of unshed tears.

He and his daughter embrace, and then she wipes the tears on his cheeks. "Daddy," she says before holding him tight to her again. "I've missed you so much."

He laughs a little but doesn't release her. A woman exits the driver's side and walks over. "That's enough now, Patrick. You have to let her breathe."

This must be Linda.

Maren steps back, the joy that was in her gaze dimming at her stepmother's interference. She doesn't say anything to her, though, she just guides her father toward me. "Daddy, I'd like you to meet someone."

"Mr. McVee." I extend my hand to him. "I'm Oliver."

He smiles, shuffling his feet forward. His voice is barely

there, but I hear each word. "Thank you. Thank you for loving my girl." He doesn't shake my hand, instead, he pulls me into a hug. I hear a gasp and what sounds like a soft sob from Maren. He pats my back twice and then pulls back, looking at me with a smile. "I am so happy to meet you, son. You're a good man and smart to see the treasure she is."

I'm a fucking liar, but I force myself to remember why we're doing this.

He's clearly overjoyed, and this might just bring him the peace his daughter is hoping for. It doesn't really sit well that it's all bullshit though.

"I don't think anyone can look at her and not see how special she is. I'm just lucky she thinks I'm worthy," I say with an easygoing grin. Thank God for the years I spent perfecting this persona.

Maren takes my hand again. "This is Linda, my dad's wife."

I shake with my free hand. "Nice to meet you."

"Yes, likewise. It was a very long drive, do you happen to know if there's a place my husband can rest? He's very sick and requires a lot of breaks. It's also time for another breathing treatment."

"Of course, Linda," Maren says with ease, but her grip tightens just a bit, portraying her true emotions. "We'll take you into the lobby."

"We'd prefer to just check in to our room."

I glance at my watch, knowing we need at least another forty minutes before I can put them in the room.

I give her my most charming smile, the one that all the ladies seem to love. "Mrs. McVee, I'd love to show you there, but first, allow me to give you a short tour. I'm sure that you all will love Melia Lake, the views from the back deck are stunning and we can have some food and drinks out there. With you all just getting here, I'd like to have some time to talk and take in the fresh air."

Linda blinks a few times and then shakes her head. "Oh, but . . . I . . ."

Patrick speaks before anyone else can. "I'd like that. Some fresh air would be nice."

"But you need your medications."

He nods. "And I can take them on the deck."

"No other guests are at the resort yet," I explain. "So, we'll have complete privacy other than my siblings, who are still working to get everything ready for when all the guests get here."

"Your siblings?" Linda asks.

"Yes, my family owns this resort."

Her eyes widen. "You didn't say that, Maren."

Maren tilts her head toward me, resting it on my shoulder. "It's why it was so important to have the wedding here. Oliver and I wanted something that brings both our families together."

Her father smiles widely, and we all walk toward the back.

"Wow, this is amazing," Linda says as she takes in the view of the lake.

It really is. My siblings and I have done a damn good job here. With our architect and design team, we were all able to use the land to help in every way. I'm proud of this place and all the work we put into it.

Now, we just need it not to tank.

"We're going to expand that dock area in a few years, but we want to keep it in line with the rest of the resort. Down that trail"—I point to the one on the left—"my brother-in-law, Jack, has a cabin where he does all kinds of wilderness retreats and excursions. Families can take overnight trips or daytime hikes."

Maren's father nods. "And what about that area?" he rasps as he points to another cabin that was not a planned addition.

"That's a children's area. My niece thought there should

be a place for little kids to go when they don't want to be with their parents anymore. My brother, who can't seem to tell the kid no, thought it was a great idea. The inside of it is amazing and should be experienced, but I'll leave it at that so I don't ruin your experience of seeing it for the first time. We also have a teen area on the property."

"So, you help your family and also work full-time with Maren as well?" he asks.

Maren steps in. "Oliver is more of a silent partner in the resort. He's just helping while they're starting up."

"You said he was just on a mission," Linda adds.

"Yes, he was."

Linda turns to me. "How are you going to split your time?"

"I won't. I'll work there and come here when I'm need-ed," I explain. "We're not concerned."

Patrick begins to cough, and as Linda starts to fuss with him, he waves her away and takes a seat at the table.

She glares at Maren. "Get your father some water. It's in my bag."

Linda continues to make comments under her breath as Maren hands the bottle to her father. "I knew we shouldn't have come up here. You don't take your health seriously enough. We should've stayed home where you could get proper care. Now I have to make do with whatever is here."

Patrick grabs her hands, holding them against his chest. "I want to be here."

The two of them stare at each other, and finally, her shoulders fall. "I know."

He nods. "I'm fine."

Maren sits beside him. "I'm sorry, Daddy."

He turns to her quickly. "It's the nature of my sickness, Princess. I'd be coughing here or in Georgia. I'd rather be here with you and Oliver. I already told Linda that I want the rest of my days to be filled with the people who matter."

I hope I know that kind of love one day.

My phone pings with a message from Stella, letting us know their room is ready. I lean over, pressing my lips to Maren's ear, inhaling the floral scent of her shampoo. "Be the hero and get them to their room."

Her hand moves to my cheek. "It's done?"

I smile, rubbing my nose against hers, wanting to kiss her so much I ache. "Yes."

She leans back, and the loss of her steals the breath from my lungs.

"Daddy, why don't we get you up to your room. You and Linda can rest, and when you feel up to it, we'll go for a walk or whatever you want." Her voice shakes a little at the end.

"Good. We'll let your father rest before we push him again," Linda says, getting to her feet. "Since this entire weekend will most likely do him in."

Maren's hands tremble slightly, and I grab them in mine. "We'll make sure he takes it easy," I assure her.

After a lot of underhanded comments from Linda, we finally get them settled, and I am again amazed by the brilliance that is Stella. The room looks as if it were done weeks ago. There isn't any dust or hint that this was a construction zone just a few hours ago. Linda gets Patrick settled on the sofa that sits close to the window, and we promise to come back in an hour.

Once we're out in the hallway, Maren leans against the wall. "We did it."

I nod. "We did."

She pushes off, coming to stand in front of me. Lifting up on her toes, she presses her lips to mine in a brief-but-searing kiss. "Thank you."

Her one hand rests on my chest, right above my heart. "It's nothing."

"It's something to me."

The way she's looking at me makes me feel like I'm twelve feet tall.

What worries me is that she might mean something to me by the end of this, and that would be really bad.

I'm sitting in the lobby, waiting for Patrick to make his way down. He asked me to meet him here—without Maren.

She owes me so damn big for this.

Josh plops down beside me.

"How are things going?" I ask.

"Hectic, but thank God for Stella and her schedule."

I nod once. "She's a pain in the ass, but she's great at getting things done. Odette really stepped up too."

"Seriously, she saved our asses by contracting all these crews for a fraction of what we would have paid without her help."

My siblings hate me. Well, they love me, but they're none too happy. If we hadn't had this wedding booked, then the weather delays for construction wouldn't have been that big of a deal. But I did book it, and it left us scrambling to get the resort ready. It's a small part of why I am not fighting everyone about this wedding. I owe them. I know it. They know it. So, it's happening.

"How is Delia?" I ask, moving onto lighter topics.

"Still refusing to marry me," Josh muses, resting his head on the wall.

"You can marry Maren."

"I think you've got that one covered."

"This is what I get for being a nice guy," I muse.

"Can't argue with you there. However, you can say no, Ollie. No one would do this other than you. You know that, right?"

My brothers like to talk a big game, but if Delia or Jessica asked either of them to fake marry them to make their parent happy, they would've done the same shit. Jessica has always had a hold on Grayson. Fuck, he bought a huge

79

piece of land because they shared a kiss or some shit there. And Josh? He moved into Delia's house, pretending it was to keep her safe from the kid who was breaking into cars. They're so quick to paint me one way while failing to see their own crap.

"You know you're full of shit, right?" I toss back.

"How?"

"Because if this were Delia, you'd do anything."

"So, you're in love with your fiancée?" Josh asks without missing a beat.

I roll my eyes. "That's not even possible."

"That's my point. Yeah, I'd do it for Deals because I love her. I love her more than any man can love another woman. What's your reason?"

I don't love Maren. She's a friend who needs help and also happens to be really fucking hot and a great kisser. That part's a nice bonus. Yeah, I'm attracted to her, which any man would be. That doesn't mean anything.

It's lust. Pure and simple lust.

My desire to help her comes from my being a good fucking human. I may not understand it, but it matters to her.

Plus, it's not like I'm ever going to actually marry anyone. I have zero desire to go through this bullshit in real life, so I might as well do it for pretend. However, I'm not telling that to my brother, who used to think love is a lie we feed ourselves to now thinking everything is awesome.

"Oh, I don't know. Our psychotic sister threatened my life by offering me as a midnight snack to the monster she thinks lives in the woods."

"I think it was more murder, but the end goal would be the same."

"I'm so glad you're able to remember her threats so easily. I can't keep up."

Josh smirks. "Usually I can't between her and Delia, I'm

80

usually fearful of my life. However, Stella isn't the real reason and we both know it. So, what gives?"

I fight back another quip and tell him a small part of the truth. "Because she asked me to do something for someone she loves. Plus, I get to be the hero of the family."

He shrugs with a chuckle. "I'm sure it doesn't hurt that she's pretty."

"She's more than that."

"Oh?" Josh asks with a smirk. "Do I detect feelings?"

"Don't be a fucking idiot—if that's possible."

"You know, I remember you and Alex giving me loads of shit when it came to Delia," Josh reminds me. "You were spouting off about feelings and when something's right. I'm not saying that it's fate or whatever, but it's something."

My brother is making zero sense. "What's something?"

"The way you look at her."

I don't look at her in any way. "I look at her the same way I look at you."

At that, my brother lets out a loud laugh. "If you say so."

A headache is starting to brew. I move my fingers to my temple and start to massage it. "I can't get into this."

Josh slaps me on the back and then gets up. "I'm just saying that you're the only one of us who wanted to be married and live the family life. You thought you'd marry that girl in high school. Then you wanted to marry Devney. Now, you're getting everything you asked for, so maybe it's everything you want too."

"My God, Delia has made you soft. Where's my brother who was all . . . fuck love? Bring that guy back. At least he still had his balls."

"And there is the Oliver I know"—Josh tosses back— "always ready to cast shit off as a joke when it feels a bit too real."

I flip him off, and he returns the sentiment before walking away.

81

Everything I want. What the hell does he know about what I want? I want a girl who fucking loves me. Loves me like Jess loves Gray or Delia loves him. That's what matters. That's the real thing. I've been searching for that.

"You look lost, son," Patrick says in a raspy voice as he comes to a stop in front of me.

"Not lost, just . . . siblings."

He chuckles low. "I have five of those, I know your pain. May I sit?"

"Of course." I move over, allowing him more room.

As he takes the place Josh vacated, he lets out a long sigh. "It's hard to get around some days," Patrick admits. "Other days, I can't get around at all, but thankfully, that's not today."

I nod, not sure what to say.

"I'm sure you're wondering why I asked to speak with you."

"Not really. I figured we would have one of these talks," I say with a grin.

"Yes, I guess that's true. Fathers and their daughters. A child is a wonderful gift a man can receive. Of course, when my wife was pregnant with Maren, I wished for a boy. Not sure why, but it was more of what I thought should happen. When we had her, I realized how nothing happens that shouldn't." He grins and pats my leg. "She's the best thing in this world, and knowing that you'll be here to care for her when I'm gone, well, it's everything to me."

Shit. I may have been expecting this conversation, but I wasn't expecting the emotions that came with it. I clear my throat and look away.

Patrick continues. "I'm dying, and that's a hard thing—mostly because I see the fear and sadness in the people I love. I hear Linda cry when she thinks I'm asleep, and Maren, well, she's good at hiding things, but I can see it in her eyes. I don't think there's anything that girl wouldn't do for me."

82

He has no freaking idea. "I think you're right about that."

"I want to tell you, man-to-man, that I will never be able to express how much this means to me. All of what you're doing, it's . . ."

"What?" I ask for clarification.

"The sense of peace it gives me to know that she'll have you by her side, that you'll be there to hold her together when she falls apart, is something I can't explain. I've held on for so long out of fear that those I love would need me, but Maren has you now."

If I hadn't been going to hell before, I would be now. "Patrick," I say, hoping the rest of what I want to say will suddenly come to me, but truly, I'm at a loss.

"I'll be able to rest easy knowing she's not alone, but I need you to promise me something."

No, no, no. I am not promising the McVee family anything else. I'm already in enough freaking hot water. I need to find a way back into the big guy's good graces.

He continues on as though my silence is acceptance. "Promise me that, even when things are hard, you'll always remember how special she is."

Okay, that I can do. "I promise."

"Good. And that you'll always be there, even when I can't be."

I stay silent, feeling like the worst human being ever. Patrick rises, his hand resting on my shoulder as a tear falls down his cheek. "You're exactly the kind of man I wished she'd find."

And I'm the worst person who ever lived.

eleven

MAREN

My entire family has arrived. My aunts, uncles, two cousins, the Parkersons have settled into their rooms, and both groups have gathered down at the lake for an informal meet and greet.

Well, it was supposed to be informal. I'm not sure Stella knows what that word means. There's a full bar and servers, handing out champagne and hors d'oeuvres. Everyone is smiling, laughing, and getting along wonderfully.

Oliver comes up beside me, his hand settling on the small of my back. "Everyone is having a good time," he says against my ear.

"I know, make it stop."

He chuckles. "You want them to hate it?"

I press my hand to his chest, leaning in as though we're talking about something that has embarrassed me. "No, but this is almost too easy."

Oliver kisses my forehead. "Relax, let everyone have fun."

I sigh, smiling up at him. "What about you? Are you having fun?"

"I'm not even sure what's happening anymore."

"Same," I admit. "It's like our families have been friends

for a lifetime, and I was an idiot for spending so much time worrying about them getting along."

I thought that it would be awkward, but it hasn't been. Everyone hugged, my aunts gushed over how handsome Oliver was, and my uncles wanted to talk about the land.

Oliver and I fall silent, too lost in watching each other, until there's a slight tapping on glasses.

We turn to look around, and my eyes land on his brothers, who are all grinning.

"Kiss her, Oliver," Grayson says first.

Then Josh steps forward, lifting his glass. "To the happy couple."

Oliver grumbles under his breath, but his smile doesn't falter. He pulls me to his chest and then kisses me softly.

Josh laughs. "Kiss her like you mean it!"

He mutters again, and this time, I catch something about brothers and death before he plants one on me again. This kiss isn't soft like the one before. He kisses me hard, and before I know it, I'm kissing him back.

My fingers grip his shirt, holding him tight until the laughter has us breaking apart.

I blink a few times, unsure of what the hell came over me, and Oliver steps back. "Good enough for you, brother?"

Josh grins. "Improvement for sure." He raises his glass again. "As the best man, I'd like to say a few words."

"No," Oliver says quickly.

"It's tradition," Josh says smoothly, and his girlfriend, Delia, gives me an apologetic look. "My brother is the best person I know. He's giving, willing to do anything for a friend in need, and always putting the people he loves first. It's a gift, really, one that neither I nor my other siblings possess. Oliver truly is the best of us. Maren, it's been an honor getting to know you, and we welcome you to the family."

Everyone raises their glass and takes a sip as Josh makes his way over to us.

"I behaved."

"Kind of," Oliver says, draining the rest of his glass. "Also, who made you best man?"

"What, you were going to pick Grayson?"

"I was going to pick Stella since she has bigger balls than you. Or maybe Jack since I like him the most right now."

"Since it's not real, it doesn't matter." Josh shrugs as Delia wraps her arms around his middle.

"I'm so sorry for that. I made him promise to behave, but we all know that's like trying to control a tornado," Delia says as she looks up at him. "All things considered, it could've been worse."

"It will be," Josh promises. "The actual speech will be much more fun."

She sighs. "This is the first time we've let him around adults since Everett was born, he's a bit rusty."

"Honestly, I'm not surprised. If someone in my family decides to do a speech, they'll be doing the same. My aunts and uncles are all smartasses who would thrive on chaos," I explain.

When I was little, my family was always up to mischief, usually my father was the object of their torment. It didn't matter that he was the oldest of them, he was the easiest target. Daddy loved his hair and would spend hours making sure it was always in the right place, he agonized over his clothes, and it's still a constant joke. Vanity will be my father's ultimate downfall.

"Good, then we'll find out everything we can about you so we can embarrass you tomorrow at the rehearsal."

Linda and my father approach, and Oliver takes my hand, squeezing just a little.

"Maren, dear, your father is getting tired, and I need to set up his medication. How much longer will this be?"

I look to my father, who rolls his eyes, saying, "I'm fine, Linda."

"You are not fine. You are sick and need to take care of

yourself. Maren doesn't understand what it's like for you. She doesn't come around often enough to see your daily struggles," Linda argues. "I'm the one who manages everything, and believe me, I know when you're overdoing it and need rest."

He closes his eyes but nods. "You're right."

I want to scream. To throw my hands up and tell him to be a man, take a stand, not to let her control this, but I've learned that it doesn't help. "I would be happy to get you situated somewhere so you don't have to leave, Daddy. I really would like for you to stay and spend time with the family."

He looks to me. "I would too. Maybe once I take my medications . . ."

"And a nap," Linda adds on.

"And a nap, I'll come back down."

Aunt Eileen stops next to my dad. "Are you heading up to bed, Pat?"

"Yes, I'm tired. Linda is making sure I don't overdo it before the big day."

She looks to Linda and makes a sound through her nose. "I see." I share a glance with my aunt because we both know the truth—Linda is done. "Well, it's too bad you can't tough it out a bit longer. We were going to sit in those chairs by the lake, but I understand that Linda might think it would be too hard for you to relax in all this fresh air. She often has you guys leaving early when she gets tired too."

Linda bristles. "I'm not saying it's too hard to sit. I'm saying your brother is ill and needs to rest."

"Then let him rest by the shoreline. We'll make sure he doesn't get up," she suggests. "He also hasn't gotten to see his daughter and siblings in quite some time, which means he can push a little if he thinks he's up to it. Since we all know the nature of his illness, we also know that time is fleeting. So, if my brother thinks he can manage, he should get the choice. Do you think you can manage it, Pat?"

Dad looks to Linda.

There is nothing she hates more than being questioned or talked into a corner. "If that's what Patrick wants, then fine. But I know my husband, and he is ready to lie down."

My father smiles. "I'd like to stay, sweetheart. The fresh air is good for me, and we can rest in the chairs. Will you come sit with us?" Daddy asks Oliver and me.

"Of course," Oliver says before I can. We walk down there, Oliver helping my father down the pathway.

"This is very dangerous for you," Linda says as she slips a little, but Oliver steadies her. "If I knew I might break my neck to spend some time with your sisters, I would've protested more. This is incredibly dangerous for you. If you fall, then what?"

"The crew has plans to build steps so this isn't quite so steep, but we had to focus on the indoors first," Oliver explains.

"Don't worry," Dad says with a wave of his arm. "I'm being careful."

We reach the bottom and get Daddy settled, and Aunt Marie comes down with a pillow and blanket. "Here, this way Pat can rest and be comfortable."

They fuss over him, and he rolls his eyes. "Enough. I'm fine."

I kiss his cheek. "Everyone just loves you."

We all sit around, telling stories of when I was little, and Oliver laughs as my family regales him with stories of my childhood that no one should know. How I got sick after my uncles took me on the spinning cups ride at the beach. How I cried after my first kiss because I thought he was trying to do something to hurt me with his tongue. And, of course, how I got locked in the store refrigerator when I was seven and playing hide and seek.

The Parkersons make their way over to us and start with their own stories. I end up perched on Oliver's leg, and his

89

hand moves up and down my back as if it's the most natural thing in the world. It feels like it is too.

It's as though this man is exactly the man I've always wanted. As though, a few days ago, I didn't have an engagement called off.

This makes no sense. How can I not be completely wrecked over losing one-point-oh? I should be curled in a ball, sobbing about my lost love, but I've barely thought about him.

I haven't wished it were his lips kissing me or his hand in mine. If that isn't a sign that I never should've agreed to marry him, then I don't know what is.

But this Oliver . . . he's different.

He's kind and funny and open and adorable. He has gone out of his way to make me comfortable and befriend my family.

I think I might be going insane because a part of me wonders if maybe there's something here.

I look down at him, and he smiles. "What?"

"Nothing," I say quickly, my hair falling over my face.

Oliver doesn't let me get away with it, he pushes it back, forcing me to look at him. "Are you okay?"

I don't feel okay. I feel lost and out of control, but I won't say that aloud. Instead, I nod and focus on my emotions.

I like this. I like being with him, and none of this is supposed to be real. I don't want to like him, at least not as more than a friend. Only, when he looks at me like this, I forget it's a ruse.

I forget that I'm supposed to be acting.

The tapping of the glasses happens again, and I'm not sure if I'm happy that I'm going to kiss him again or upset because I wanted to kiss him without the clanging.

Oliver's hand slides to the back of my head, pulling me to him. Our lips touch, and I want to cry when my father says, "This is all I ever wanted for her."

twelve

MAREN

"Y ou seem nervous," Devney says as she helps me move my wedding dress into my new room.

"I am."

Every member of my family has told me how lucky I am to have Oliver. He's always smiling, laughing, or making jokes, and appears as though he's in love with me. Even Linda seems smitten with him—at least she is when she's not pointing out something else that's hard for her. Oliver handles her like a pro, though, easing her worries and finding a way to make her smile.

The worst part is how much I find myself wanting to be near him.

"Why? You've done it. You get married tomorrow and give your dad everything you've been trying for."

"I know!" I say as I sit on the bed. "That's the issue. I did it!"

"I'm not following."

I stare at my best friend, wondering how she's confused. "I didn't think we would pull it off. But we did. And it's been great. And he keeps kissing me."

Devney smiles. "I see."

"Do you? Do you see? I'm a lying horrible girl who keeps kissing this guy who makes my toes curl."

Her jaw falls slack. "He makes . . . your toes curl?"

"And that makes me a horrible human. He's your ex."

"Yes, but I'm married—happily."

I groan. "And I like him. I can't like him."

"Yes, it's always best not to like the man you're about to stand up in front of God and marry."

"*Fake*. Fake and it's my boss, not God. Please don't ever say that around Mark or he'll start thinking he's a prophet or something."

She laughs and takes my hand. "Listen, all of this is good. Oliver is a great guy and . . . well, it's a little weird, but not bad that you like him. You guys don't even look like it's acting, which says something."

"Yes, it says I can't do this."

"Maren, you have to get it together. You're doing this. You have to."

"No, I can't."

"So, you're going to what? Go out there and tell everyone the truth now? That's your big plan?"

I flop back, my head bouncing on the mattress. "I have no plan. I have no plans because I'm a bad planner."

"I love you, but you're nuts."

"Yes. Add that to the list. I'm a liar. Nuts. A hussy who likes kissing your ex. Which also makes me a bad friend. I'm going to hell."

"You're not going to hell. Well, we all probably are, but not because of this."

I sit up quickly, causing her to jump. "And what about what I'm doing to Oliver. Huh? What about the pain I'm inflicting because of my selfish need to make others happy?"

"Oliver didn't look like he was suffering too much. Look, he's a good guy, and there's nothing he wouldn't do for a friend. And while I know this isn't what he thought he'd be doing this weekend, he's doing it to make you happy. Just don't hurt him, Mare. If Oliver didn't want to help, he wouldn't."

"I know and the last thing I want is to hurt him."

Devney broke Oliver's heart. He loved her and was ready to propose to her before she called off their relationship to be with her now-husband. I know how hard it was for her, still is. She loved Oliver, but he wasn't the right guy and they ended things as amicably as two people can. Still, I know he's a good guy. I'm watching it all play out.

I sink back onto the bed and drop my head into my hands. "What the hell am I supposed to do?"

"You do what you set out to do. You go out there and make your father happy. Then you deal with it all."

"I don't want to."

There's a knock at the door, and Devney heads over to open it. "Hey, Ollie."

"Hey, is Maren . . ." He looks in, seeing me lying on the bed. "Is she okay?"

I lift my hand. "Just . . . regretting my life choices."

He snorts. "What the hell does that mean?"

I look at him from the side. "Just let me lie here and live in my shame."

Devney huffs. "I've tried to talk sense into her, but she's spiraling." She pats his chest. "I wish you luck and call me if you need reinforcements."

"Traitor!" I yell as she walks out.

Oliver closes the door and comes to stand beside my bed. "As much as I wish we could just stay in here and pretend the world doesn't exist, we have to go since we're the main event. Are you almost ready for dinner?"

I close my eyes and groan. "No."

I feel the mattress depress as he sits. "No?"

Opening just one eye, I peek at him. "I'm having guilt and shame and regret for what we're doing."

"I would think it's normal to feel that. Your family is really great, and lying to them isn't easy."

93

I push up onto my elbows. "No, it's not. My family just seems so happy about all this."

"But, I mean, isn't that what we want?"

"Yes, and it's an issue."

He lies down beside me. "All right then. It's an issue, but there's not a chance in hell I'm backing away now. You pulled me into this, and we're going until the bitter end."

"What if I told my dad?"

"And what? How does that end well?"

"It doesn't."

He shifts to his side. "Look at me. You are doing this for the right reasons. Okay? You wanted to give a dying man his wish. More than that, though, this is something you deserve to give to yourself. You will get into your wedding dress, have your hair done, and allow a man who loves you to have a moment he dreamed of. After he dies . . ." He pauses and brushes his finger along my cheek. "You will still have that memory. It doesn't matter who the guy at the end of the altar is, it's about a father and a daughter."

I get to my feet. "I don't deserve your friendship."

He follows me, but pulls me to look at him. "What makes you think I deserve yours? Why are you really freaking out?"

I have no words. I can hear the steady thrum of my pulse and then, a tear falls as the truth slips from my lips. "I don't want to lose him. I'm not ready to lose my dad."

He tugs me into his arms as grief grabs ahold of me. I see the daily deterioration in him. I see how hard just breathing is. My daddy is dying right in front of me. Each day a little bit of the life he had dwindles away.

Oliver's arms are wrapped around me, keeping me from falling apart.

"I wish I could make him better," he says against my ear. "I wish I could do something."

I lift my eyes to his. "You can. You are, right now. As

94

much as you might not believe me, I didn't plan any of this."

"Any of what?" Oliver asks.

The only person I can be honest with is him. I didn't want to hurt anyone, but I also didn't think I could feel anything close to how I am right now.

"This. Us. The part of me that's . . . it's . . ."

It's a lot. It's everything and fake, but sometimes it feels so real. Like when he reaches for me or holds my hand, it's as though we really do want each other. Or right now, when he's comforting me.

"Not so hard pretending some moments."

"A lot of moments," Oliver clarifies.

That's what has me so twisted too. It's easy to pretend that I really care about him, that we feel right. When we are around everyone and I look for him only to find him looking for me, it feels right. And that is freaking crazy because he is Oliver—and not the one I was going to marry.

Still, I don't know how I could not feel this way. He agreed to my crazy plan and has been amazing through it.

Oliver's eyes meet mine, the energy around us shifts as if he is thinking about the same thing. My heart speeds up as his head dips lower.

"What moments, Maren?" he asks, his voice low and gravelly.

"Just some."

His hands move so he can splay his long fingers at the small of my back. His tall frame towers over me, and I lean in a smidge. He smells so good, like wood and leather with a hint of whiskey. My fingers itch to touch him, to slide up his chest so I can feel the muscles beneath his shirt.

"What about when I kiss you, are you faking it then?"

Oliver doesn't move, just stands there, looking into my eyes, and I shake my head slightly. "No. Are you?"

"No."

"If I asked you to kiss me now, would you be pretending?" I volley the question at him.

"Do you want me to kiss you?"

I do what I had been thinking before, moving my hands up along his chest, feeling his heartbeat beneath my fingertips. "This is crazy."

"I know."

"We're supposed to be . . ."

"Pretending," Oliver finishes before crushing his lips to mine.

We kiss, and oh God do we kiss. His warm mouth presses to mine before we both open to each other and our tongues meet. The heat of his body is against mine as we clutch at each other. I ache for him to touch me, to erase all the emotions that have been smothering me. When he's near, it's easier to breathe. It's as though his laughter and smile give me the ability to keep going.

"Oliver," I say softly before his tongue pushes back into my mouth.

He moans, pulling me tighter, and then we're moving. I feel my legs hit the bed before he guides me back and follows me down.

We kiss more, breathing each other in, and my hands are moving to the hem of his shirt, lifting it. I want to feel his skin against mine.

"God, you're so fucking beautiful," he says before resuming the kiss.

I feel beautiful with him.

His hands move against my side, sliding up higher, and I arch, wanting him to keep going. His mouth leaves mine to move down my throat. Just as he reaches the valley between my breasts, a loud banging on my door halts us.

"Maren! Your Heaven-sent Father has arrived," Mark Dixon, my boss, says from the other side of the door.

Oliver lifts his head, staring at me with questions. "Our reverend, my boss."

His head drops to my chest. "If that isn't a sign, I don't know what is."

"We'll be out in a second!" I call to Mark.

"Your boss is a minister?"

I turn back to Oliver and give him the lowdown, but the abridged version. "I wanted you to meet my bosses before the event since you're supposed to already know them," I explain. "I . . . forgot about that part since you know, he doesn't know that you're not the Oliver I was marrying a few days ago."

Oliver gets up, extending his hand to me. I rise, fixing my rumpled dress as Oliver turns his back to the door and straightens his own clothing. Once we're both presentable, I open the door, and Mark grins at me with one brow raised. "And what exactly were the bride and groom doing in here?"

"Zip it," I warn.

He laughs, elbowing Jackson. "I think we interrupted."

Jackson looks at my face. "I think so."

"Just get in here and don't be jerks, please. It's been a hard week, and I'd like you to meet Oliver."

They both chuckle. "I'm sure something is hard," Mark can't seem to help himself.

When they walk in, they come to a stop. "Umm, who is this?"

I clear my throat. "Jackson Cole, Mark Dixon, meet Oliver, my fiancé. Kind of."

The two of them glance at each other and then back to me. Jackson gets ahold of himself first. "I'm confused, where is Oliver?"

Glad they're so smart. "I have no idea. The last time I talked to him, he dumped me."

"When? Why?"

Jackson speaks next. "I'll kill him."

"Calm down. It's fine because . . ." *Because I'm falling for my new fake fiancé who is named Oliver.* ". . . it just is."

97

Mark's eyes narrow. "How is it fine? I never liked him. He has shifty eyes. Never trust a man with shifty eyes. That's what I always say."

"When the hell do you say that?" Jackson asks.

"All the time. Catherine is right, you don't listen."

I sigh heavily, gaining both men's attention. "Back to why you're both here. I would like you to meet my new fiancé."

"Wait, what? How in the span of two weeks did you get dumped and engaged again?"

"If you would let me speak, I can explain," I say with exasperation. Some days I love my bosses, today not so much.

I walk over to Oliver and grip his arm. "This is Oliver Parkerson. We have been friends since we were in college, and . . . well, he's helping me. Also, he's signed all the necessary paperwork for the company."

"Okay, but helping you how?" Jackson asks.

I sigh and then launch into the entire story. By the end, they both look gleefully amused by my antics.

"You just went out and found someone else to marry?" Mark asks with a brow raised. "I'm not sure if I'm impressed or worried."

"And you said you wouldn't be good in the field," Jackson says with a laugh. "You might just be as good as anyone else on our team."

"Charlie would be impressed," Mark says. "So, you want us to go along with this?"

I nod. "I need you to keep up the work part of it. Obviously, you'd know Oliver and he'd know you."

Jackson laughs. "Glad you were at least thinking there. Well, new Oliver, I'm Jackson and this is Mark. Let's get you caught up on us so you can survive this."

The three guys start to talk, and not even five minutes later, you'd think they were best friends. I'm convinced there isn't a person alive who wouldn't love Oliver. It's remarkable.

"Basically, when we start to talk about work things, you nod, smile, or laugh. It helps if you keep a beer in your hand in case you need to avoid answering a question," Jackson explains.

"No problem, I've been having to do this all week with family."

Mark shakes his head, letting out a sigh. "I want it to be on record that I think this is stupid."

"Yes, yes," I say with a groan. "Everyone does."

Oliver speaks up in my defense. "I thought it was stupid too until I met her father. I see it now, why Maren would want to do this for him. He's a great guy, and his time is fading away. I think this whole thing has given him peace."

Tears well in my eyes, and I step to him, needing to hug him, thank him, hold him because he's done something I can never repay. "You understand it?" I ask.

"I do."

"Hey, that's what you say tomorrow," Mark cuts in.

"Yeah, we'll save it for the vows tomorrow."

Oliver pulls me to his side and kisses my temple. "Tomorrow."

thirteen

OLIVER

"So, today is the big day," Grayson says with a grin.

"Shut up."

"You're really going to do this?"

I shake my head because, at this point, what else is there to say? Yes, I'm doing this. Why? Because I'm an idiot. Am I sure? No, I'm not fucking sure, but I said I would, so I'm going to. Over and over, my siblings have pestered me, asking the same shit. Except for Stella. No, my beautiful sister hasn't asked me anything, she just walked over to me, kissed my cheek, and then patted it.

I swear she does stuff like that just to drive me crazy.

"You know, I wish I could say I wouldn't," Gray muses as he kicks his heels onto the ottoman. "I think that, as much as we claim we would walk away, none of us would. Women are smart creatures."

I turn away, hoping it will stop him from talking, but of course, it doesn't.

"They know how to appeal to our hero complexes, and Lord knows you have the biggest one of all of us."

"Uh-huh," I say, pouring myself another glass of whiskey. At least whiskey doesn't talk, it just makes me feel good.

"You were always the first one to run to help Stella—or any girl, really. If they were hurt, you wanted to soothe them. If they cried, you dried their eyes. If they needed something, you'd find a way."

"You're making me sound like a pussy," I muse and then toss the drink back.

"You are that, but . . ."

I turn, huffing loudly. "Are you here to help or piss me off?"

"Which am I doing?"

"Take a guess."

Gray laughs. "Ease up, Ollie. I'm just saying that you're a good guy."

"No," I say, stopping whatever else he might be thinking. "I'm no better than Dad."

Grayson, the annoying dickhead he is, shakes his head. "You are not Dad."

"I'm fucking lying to everyone. I'm going to pretend to marry someone."

"For a good cause."

"And I am sure he thought all his lies were for a good reason."

Grayson tilts his head. "You really think that? You really think he gave a single fuck about anyone other than himself? I promise you, he didn't. He didn't protect us with his lies. He lied because he was too selfish to admit he was cheating on Mom. What is your gain in this? What do you get out of helping Maren? Where is your prize?"

I turn around again, going back to the bar area to pour another drink. I'm going to be wasted if I keep this up, but I can't seem to calm myself. My brother might be right that there's no real gain for me, but I'm still lying. Regardless of what I said to Maren, it feels a little different today.

"It doesn't matter."

"And what about Maren's prize? All she gains is making

102

a dying man happy. She doesn't get anything personal from it."

"So, lying is fine as long as you don't get anything out of it?"

Grayson runs his hands through his hair. "No, but if I were dying, and Melia was alone in the world, I would want to know that she was going to be okay. What she's giving Pat is a gift, and if you don't see that, then . . . I don't know."

I laugh because that was the same shit I told Maren yesterday.

I sit in the chair opposite of him, my drink in my hand, and I close my eyes. There's a sharp pain in my abdomen, and I take my punishment. "I really wish I knew how to say no."

Grayson leans forward. "Well, you don't, so best not to dwell on it because you and I both know you aren't going to call this off."

He's right. No matter how bad of an idea I think this is, I won't let her down. Why won't I let her down? Why do I care so much?

Is it because I like kissing her? Is it because, last night, I dreamed that all this was real? That I was watching the woman I love walk to me, ready to say the words I hoped someone would say. That's ridiculous.

I like her. I want her, but I don't love her.

I barely know her.

Yet, this morning, I wanted to call her and hear her voice. I wanted to curl up on the couch with her so we could talk about how we feel about what's about to go down.

Jesus. I need to get it together.

"I need to be alone," I tell my brother.

He sighs and gets up. I watch him walk to the bar area and grab the bottles. "I'll leave, but you need to stop drinking and get out of your head."

"Asshole."

Grayson leaves, and I'm alone without booze or

anything else but my thoughts. Before I can go down the rabbit hole of doom, someone knocks.

"Hi, Uncle Oliver," Amelia and Kinsley say when I open the door.

"Hi, girls."

"Are you excited?" Kinsley asks.

"Sure am."

These two have no idea this is all fake. Well, maybe Kinsley does. She's smart and devious like her mother.

"We came to keep you company while you wait to get married!" Amelia says with a huge grin. She rushes forward, wrapping her arms around my legs. "I'm so happy."

I'm glad someone is.

I'm not sure how much of these kids I can handle. "I don't think you guys need to stay."

My stomach roils, and I think I'm going to be sick. Maybe that last glass of whiskey wasn't such a great idea.

"But we have to," Amelia says as she releases me. "Daddy said we have to make you smile, and I always make you smile."

"You do," I tell her with sincerity. "But I am tired and just want to rest."

Kinsley clears her throat. "We were told we had to stay."

"In case I plan to run?"

She shrugs. "Unfortunately, you're considered a flight risk."

"You're too much like your mother," I say as I get a flashback of my sister at her age.

"I'll take that as a compliment."

She would.

The girls settle in, going on and on. Amelia talks a mile a minute, telling me about the new dance teacher she has and how much fun the class is now. "But I don't like putting my hair in a tight bun," she says.

"Uh-huh."

"It hurts sometimes because Mommy uses the clips I don't like."

"Sounds terrible," I say, not registering what she's saying.

I'm too absorbed with thinking of Maren and what she must be feeling. My thoughts go in circles, trying to wrap my mind around it all. Is she upset? Is she regretting it? Is she going to go through with it, or will I look like an idiot standing there with no bride?

My obligation to the resort is fulfilled. We successfully had our soft opening. The staff have been exceptional, and the issues we've found have been easily rectified. The fully booked rooms allowed us to push the project to the finish line. Also, Maren's aunt is a travel blogger and told Maren she couldn't wait to post about her stay.

All of this is good. I should be happy, but instead, I'm a wreck.

And I can't stop thinking about Maren.

A hand waves in front of my face. "Hello? Are you in there?"

"Yeah, sorry, I . . . ."

"You're freaking out. Are you going to bolt? I have a code word I'm supposed to use if so," Kinsley says, grabbing her phone.

"No, I'm not ready to bolt."

She shakes her head, watching me closely before typing on the phone.

"What's the code?" I ask.

"Chicken."

"No doubt it's what your mother picked?" I ask, and Kinsley smiles.

I hate my siblings some days.

I look down at her phone, and sure enough, the word is there. "Let me go talk to her for a second," she says while getting eye-to-eye with her younger cousin. "Come on, Melia. We need reinforcements. We'll be right back."

"I'm fine, Kins."

She shrugs. "I'd rather not be in trouble with the boss. She can get really scary."

"And who is the chicken now?"

"You."

"Just go so your mother doesn't freak out," I tell her with a chuckle.

She and Melia leave, and the room phone rings a few minutes later. I answer it with a very deep groan. "Hello, Stella. I'm not going to run. I'm just freaking fine—pissed off because our stupid older brother took my whiskey—but I'm not channeling my inner track star."

"That's great. Well, not about the whiskey though," a soft voice replies.

Maren.

"I thought . . ."

"That I was Stella?" she finishes.

"Yeah."

"I was having my own little freak out session before. Devney had to calm me down—again."

I sit on the bed, leaning on my knees. "Glad I'm not the only one."

"Look, I called because I wanted to tell you that it's okay if you don't want to do this. You've given me and my father a weekend that is something I'll cherish forever. While I know it won't be easy to back out, I would never hold it against you. If you could just let him walk me down, we can object or have someone else object. I know it's not giving him everything, but it's something. I bet I could convince Devney to cause a scene and tell everyone she's still in love with you. Sean wouldn't mind . . . much."

I huff. "No one would believe that."

She already had her chance to marry me and didn't take it.

"Maybe not," she agrees. "Whether or not you want to end it, I will always appreciate you for agreeing to any of it.

There would be no hard feelings, and I never should've asked you to do this in the first place."

The words I wanted to hear just a few minutes ago somehow feel wrong now. I know how her father feels and there is no way Maren wouldn't resent me if I took this away from them.

"Are you in your dress?" I ask, not sure why this matters more than anything.

"I am."

"Hair done?"

"Yes?" Maren says it as a question.

"Well, I'm in my tux, and everyone is already heading to the venue. It would be a shame to waste a perfectly good reception."

"Oliver," she says softly, "Even though the vows we'll speak aren't real, and even though we're just pretending, I imagine this is still hard."

I'm doing this to help a friend and to give a man who is dying something to hold on to. I'm not like my father. I'm not using anyone around me to gain something. The only risk is to myself, and well, I'm fucking used to that pain.

"I'm vowing to be there for you, Maren. Yes, I have strong feelings on marriage and divorce, but . . . it won't be legal, and it'll make your father happy."

It'll make you happy.

That is really the driving force on why I'm doing this.

"I just want to say that you, Oliver Parkerson, are one of the most incredible men I've ever known, and it's an honor to be your fake bride. I'll see you soon?"

"I'll see you soon."

She laughs softly. "I'll be the one in white."

I hang up and stare at the phone, wondering what the hell is wrong with me. She just gave me an out, and I couldn't take it.

"Quarter for your thoughts." Stella's voice is right beside me.

"It's supposed to be a penny."

She smiles. "Your thoughts are worth more."

Only she could make me laugh. "How did you get in here?"

She lifts the key card. "I'm an owner, and that means I have a master card. The girls said you were having a meltdown."

I shake my head. "More just . . . self-loathing."

"Yeah, I imagine you would feel that way. I know Grayson already talked to you, so I won't say the same shit he did. But I think what you're scared of is that you actually like Maren. You maybe have some sort of vision that she could be that girl for you, the one who would walk down the aisle toward you for real."

The denial is on the tip of my tongue, but I don't want to lie to my sister. "But it is all fake."

"It is, but when a man offers to do outlandish things to help a woman, sometimes he catches feelings along the way."

"Whatever."

"Just don't beat yourself up too much, Ollie," Stella says while reaching out her hand to help me up. "You're doing something kind, and kindness is always worth it. Plus, you guys are heading to a private beach house for five days so . . . who knows what'll happen then."

My eyes snap up because we're only supposed to be there for one day. "Did you say *five*?"

She nods. "I convinced her that you both deserved this vacation. You've had a hell of a few weeks and some rest and relaxation are what I think you both need."

Fuck my life and save me from my meddling sister.

fourteen

MAREN

Deep breaths.

I can do this.

It's fine. I'm fine. Everything will go just fine, and then, after the honeymoon, we'll come back and figure out how we announce our separation.

Yeah. All of this is great.

Perfect really.

Not a single thing . . .

"Oh, God," I say, starting to hyperventilate again.

Devney rubs my back. "Easy. You have a plan. Just stick to it."

I look up at her, the pillar of strength and unwavering friendship. "Right. Just stick to the plan."

She smiles, taking both of my arms and shaking me a little. "What's your reason?"

"My father."

"That's right. Remember that. All of this has been to make him happy, so be happy for him."

A tear falls down my cheek, and she curses before grabbing a tissue. "None of that," she says as she dabs it away. "This is a happy day, and you're stunning."

I nod. "There's that."

Kinsley and Amelia come rushing around the corner in their navy-blue dresses that Stella somehow found. I couldn't *not* have a junior bridesmaid and flower girl.

"You look like a princess!" Amelia beams. "I want to have a dress just like yours!"

"Someday, I'm sure you will."

Kinsley smiles just as wide as her cousin. "Are you just as nervous as Uncle Oliver?"

"I'm trying to stay calm," I say with a bit of a shake in my voice.

"Don't worry," she says with ease. "You both will do great, and it's clear you like each other a lot."

My heart falters for a second, and guilt threatens to overwhelm me. I hate that his nieces are going to be hurt by this. I turn to Devney, who grabs my shoulders again. "In and out, Mare. In and out. You have to breathe." She turns to the girls. "Why don't you guys go find the flowers that we put away."

They walk off, but Kinsley looks back before she rounds the corner.

"I'm not going to make it through this."

Dev focuses on me, eyes so intent that it's almost scary. "You are going to walk down that aisle for your father. All of this has been for him. Got it?"

"I got it."

She leads me through a few more deep breaths before I'm under control. She's right, this will be fine. I used to love drama club, so I just need to think of this as a play that I'm starring in. Oliver and I won't really be married, and we'll go on a vacation as friends.

Charlie, Mark's wife, peeks her head in the room. "Your dad is here."

It's time.

"Okay," I say a little breathlessly.

He enters, tears filling his green eyes as he comes to a stop in front of me. "My darling, you are so beautiful." The words come out as a whisper, and he nearly chokes on them. "Just like your mother."

My heart aches as the tear falls down his cheek. Very rarely does he mention my mother anymore. In the beginning, he spoke of her often, told me stories of their lives together and the joy of having me. But as the years went by, Linda got more and more upset when he brought up my mom. It was as though she worked hard to create a division in his life so there was a line between his life before her and his life now. His life, career, children, and first wife were no longer relevant. Only she is. So, to see him emotional as he remembers her touches me deeply.

"Daddy," I say, fighting back my own tears.

"She would've loved seeing you like this." He takes a step back, admiring my gown.

It has a sweetheart neckline with a lace overlay that covers the length of the dress. The bodice is fitted, and the back is lined with buttons. It's stunning, and I felt beautiful in it the moment I tried it on.

The planning of my wedding seemed like kismet from the day one-point-oh proposed. Whatever I searched for, I found immediately. My dress was the second dress I picked up off the rack, and it was in my size with no alterations needed. The venue was booked so easily, and it didn't cost a fortune since Oliver owns the place. The date we picked worked for everyone's schedule.

I guess I should have known that something was going to go sideways. Nothing is ever that effortless.

"I wish she was here," I tell my father.

"Me too, Princess. But I believe your mother is looking down on you. She has always been guiding you, making sure you have loving people in your life."

I bite back a remark about how I wish it was the same for him. "I have you," I say instead.

"Yes, you do, Maren." He starts to cough, so I help him sit as he points to the bag he brought. His medicines. I go

111

through it, lifting options until he nods at the inhaler. He immediately breathes it in and then the coughing slows.

"Daddy?"

"It's . . . getting harder to do this." The confession rocks me.

"What can I do?"

He shakes his head. "Nothing anymore. We just have to . . ." He coughs a few times. "Love. Because I don't have long."

I am not ready to lose him. The selfish part of me wants him to keep fighting, to keep holding on because I'm not strong enough to handle the loss. I need him, and I love him.

I wouldn't be doing any of this if that weren't the case.

Then the part of me that holds all my compassion reminds me that he's in pain. Each day is a fight, a struggle that is sucking the life out of him.

"I wish . . ."

"I know," Daddy offers. "But you have a wonderful man to be here for you."

Not only am I about to start sobbing because of the fact that my father is dying but also because I'm a big fat liar.

He stands, and when he starts to weaken, I rise, catching his arm to steady him.

"Are you okay?" I ask.

"There is nothing that will keep me from doing this. It's my honor to walk with you today."

"The honor is all mine, Daddy."

He kisses my cheek and then tucks my hand in his arm.

Devney pops the door open right on time, a huge smile on her face. "You two ready? It's time."

As we stand in the line, ready to go into the ceremony, I feel so much all at once it's hard to contain. There is sadness because it's fake and this isn't really my wedding. Happiness that I am able to give my father this moment, which is something I hope brings him great peace. Disappointment that I don't actually have someone in my life like Oliver.

He's going to stand beside me and give my family something they desperately need, and I don't deserve someone as great as him.

The music begins, and his nieces go first, and then Oliver's sister follows. She was a late add because it really didn't make sense not to have Stella be a part of it when she's his twin. Devney looks back at me with a smile before going through the door, letting it close behind her.

The music shifts, and it's our turn.

The doors open, allowing me to see the inside for the first time. It's absolutely stunning. White chairs line the silk runner in front of me. Huge, blush-colored flowers cap every row with long strands of greenery sweeping along the floor. The guests are all standing, but they all fall to the background when my eyes find Oliver.

"Ready, Princess?" Daddy asks when I don't move.

I can't look away from Oliver, and I'm unsure of why I suddenly feel so incredibly vulnerable.

He gives me a wide grin and then winks.

I smile, unable to stop myself. "I'm ready."

Each step with my father holding my arm feels like a gift. I catalogue each step, every tightening of my hand on his arm, and commit it to memory. I glance up at my father who has tears streaming down his face and he smiles at me. That lift of his lips is all I needed to know I did the right thing.

I will never forget a single second of this walk with him.

All the dreams I had of being a little girl and getting married could never measure up to this.

We reach the end of the aisle way too soon. Oliver steps forward, his eyes a little glossy.

Daddy raises my veil and then kisses my cheek. "I love you so much."

"I love you more." My vision is blurry from all the unshed tears.

He turns to Oliver, placing my hand in his. "I give you the most valuable thing I have. I hope you know that."

"I do," Oliver says with a strength in his voice.

When my father steps back, Oliver and I release a sigh as we step up to where Mark stands.

"Dearly beloved," he begins, "I am your faithful servant of all things weddings, and it is my great honor to be here today where I am able to send my blessings to everyone."

"Oh, here we go," Jackson mutters from his seat behind us.

"Love is something we can all celebrate. It is all around us each day, and these two, well, these two are something else. I've had the privilege of getting to know them. Maren is a wonderful woman, a little extreme at times, but you know . . . women."

I glare at him, but he carries on, totally unfazed.

"Oliver is giving, loyal, and honorable. I know this because he's willing to do just about anything for those who matter to him."

I glance over at Ollie, who casts me a worried look. Mark is definitely not who I should've let lead this. My ex would have been less of a risk.

"The world is full of selfishness and greed, but when I look at this couple, I see the opposite. Here stand two people who are willing to give each other whatever they need, regardless of their own wants. Maren and Oliver, please face each other."

We do, and I'm so nervous that I'm trembling. Oliver smiles reassuringly and rubs the top of my hand. "It's okay," he whispers.

"Maren, repeat after me," Mark instructs.

I say each word, staring into Oliver's blue eyes and wishing this could be a fraction of the truth. That we would love, honor, and cherish each other.

Oliver repeats the same vows without any outward nerves, and I envy him.

I wish I didn't feel like I was about to fall apart.

We exchange rings, and then, before I know it, he's pulling me into his arms.

My wrists are behind his neck, and this kiss is like every one that I've shared with him . . . incredible.

Applause erupts behind us, and we break the kiss before laughing slightly.

"Thank you."

He leans closer. "If I only ever have one wedding, I'm glad it was this one."

We hug a few people because that's what you do when you pretend to marry someone and then we head out, both breathless and laughing as we wait for everyone to follow out behind us.

fifteen

OLIVER

My brothers are the first to congratulate us. It's surreal. This is supposed to be fake. All of it, and yet, it felt so damn real. The entire time, I just kept thinking about who else I could see myself with and there was no one.

Each time I tried to picture the girl at the altar with me, I saw Maren.

Even with Devney standing right behind her, which I thought would be insanely awkward, all I saw was Maren. All I felt was her.

I was grateful I was supposed to act that way and think I sold it.

Her father is the last person out, Linda holding onto his arm. He hugs me, thanking me again, and then he and Maren embrace.

This. This moment is why I did this. To see their relief and joy is worth it.

"Can we go to the back room to talk for a second?" he asks Maren and me.

Maren looks worried but says, "Sure, is everything okay?"

He nods and takes Linda's hand. "Of course." Mark

appears before we walk off, and Patrick smiles. "Oh, good. You need to come too."

"Go where?" Mark asks.

"We are going to the back room to discuss something. Do you have the license with you?"

Mark nods. "I have it right here, but I'm going to handle that later."

"No need for that, son. Linda and I would be honored to be their witnesses. Every part of this is so special to me."

Oh fucking hell. I blink a few times, and Maren speaks quickly.

"Oh, no, Daddy, that's okay. We'll sign it later. I'm sure Mark wants to see his wife."

Daddy looks to Mark. "You can't wait three minutes?"

Mark opens his mouth a few times. "I . . . can . . . but—"

"Good, we'll take care of it." He turns to me. "And then we can give you two your wedding gift."

Linda and Patrick head toward the back room, but Mark, Maren, and I stand frozen, not sure what the hell to do or how to get out of this. I can't sign that piece of paper. I can't actually be married to Maren.

Mark turns to us. "Now what?"

Maren shakes her head, her eyes wide with panic. "I don't know. I don't know what to do. Someone tell me what we do."

I close my eyes and sigh. "We go, sign the thing, and figure it out afterward. If Mark never files it, then it's not official, right?"

Mark shrugs. "Yeah, technically. I think . . ."

"You *think*?" Maren hisses. "What kind of ordained minister are you?"

He chuckles. "The kind who got certified online. Listen, I'm sure Oliver is right. We'll just sign it, and I'll shred it later. No worries."

Patrick stops and calls our names, and all three of us turn like prairie dogs. There's nothing we can do at this point other than see it through. I take Maren's hand in mine and squeeze. "Let's go."

"We can't."

I turn to Mark. "Go stall and give us a second?"

"I'm on it."

He walks ahead, leading Patrick and Linda into one of the offices down the hall.

"Come, let's go. It'll be fine."

Maren keeps her voice low. "This wasn't supposed to happen."

"I know."

"This is too much."

I stop a few feet away, taking both her hands in mine. "What options do we have?"

"I don't know."

Maren looks like she's about to have a full-on breakdown. "We just stood before our families and got married, so we've kind of gone too far to turn back now. In for a penny and all that."

"And if you actually end up legally married to me?"

"Then we get a divorce and it'll just be a funny story we tell down the line."

I'm actually hoping that if Mark doesn't file the thing it won't be legal, but if that isn't the case, then she and I will have the shortest marriage in history.

We enter the room, and Mark already has the marriage license on the table. "So, this is it. Oliver and Maren sign first and then the witnesses."

Maren walks over, holding the back of her dress off the floor. "Right. I'll sign here."

She takes the pen, signs, and then hands it to me.

This is something I will never tell my siblings. Let them think this never happened. I sign it quickly, before handing the pen to Patrick so he and Linda can sign too.

Mark grabs it. "And that's all. I'm going to find my wife, and I'll see you all at the reception."

After he leaves, Patrick turns to us, looking exhausted. "Your mother, Linda, and I have a gift for you," he says before pulling out an envelope and handing it to Maren.

"We don't need anything," she says, holding it.

"Maybe that's true, but I need to give it to you. Open it when you two are alone." He kisses her cheek.

"Let's get you seated at the table. You're worn out," Linda says as she helps him up.

"It's a . . . long day," he says with a smile.

She nods. "Yes, and you will need a week to recuperate."

They leave, and Maren leans back against the table. After a few minutes of us staring at each other, she sighs. "Well, it seems we might actually be married."

"It seems it. Maybe."

"Maybe."

Maren smiles. "I swear, if there is money in this envelope, it's yours."

"I don't need you to pay me. You've already given me a vacation, which I hear you're coming with me on."

She looks away, biting her lower lip. "It was Stella's idea. Until my father passes away, she thought we should keep up appearances as much as we can. Plus, since it's in South Carolina, I can be close in case . . ."

I nod. "In case . . ."

Maren steps toward me, her hands move to my shirt and she adjusts my collar. "You had a crease."

"Thanks for fixing it."

"What are wives for?"

I laugh once. "Now what?"

"Now," she says solemnly, "we go in there and we have a really fun party. Tomorrow, we go on vacation, and when we get back, we figure out if we're legally married and I start trying to figure out how I can ever actually repay you for this."

"Welcome to the club," Jack says, slapping me on the shoulder. "You're a married man now."

"Kind of," Grayson says with a smirk.

Maybe not as kind of as they think. "You're both assholes."

"We know."

"Good, as long as no one is confused."

Thank God that Josh is dancing with Delia and not here to harass me with them.

"Do you need the talk?" Grayson asks with complete seriousness.

"What talk?"

Jack laughs. "The one about protection and what happens on your wedding night."

Fuck these two. "You are one to talk about protection. Either of you." Gray and Jack knocked up their wives before marriage. At least I'm possibly legally married. Besides, I don't need to worry about that shit anyway because I have zero plans to sleep with her.

"This is true, but we're not virgins."

"I'm not either."

Grayson grips my shoulder. "It's okay, Ollie. Some men like to wait—at least, that's what we hear."

"You're both fucking stupid." I drop my voice to a whisper. "And I'm not married, so . . ."

"Maybe she'll blow you as a thank you," Jack suggests.

I'm going to blow my gasket if these two don't shut up. But then the image of Maren on her knees, my cock in her mouth with her blonde hair falling down her back, hits me, and I might blow something else.

Damn them.

I turn my head, knowing that this conversation isn't going to get any better, and see her. She's dancing with her uncle, smiling as though the world is perfect, and even though none of this is real, her smile is. The weight of the world that has rested on her shoulders seems to have lifted, and I can at least be happy for that.

"Look at her," I say to them. "Regardless of what you both think, I helped her give her father something that matters."

Jack clears his throat. "You did the right thing. No matter what the two of us are joking about."

"It sucks, though," Grayson adds.

"What does?"

"That it's not real. I pretty much gave up on love and marriage after Jess and Yvette. I was fine with it too. Honestly, women are a lot of work."

Jack nods. "Try being married to Stella." Gray and I give him an icy glare. "Oh, please. Let's remember that all you Parkerson brothers were praying for me when I asked for permission. Let's not pretend like everyone in this room doesn't know the woman I love is a lot of work."

"True, but we can say that because we're her brothers," I inform him.

"Exactly," Grayson says in support. "You're not allowed to."

"I'm married to her!"

"Your choice," I say without apologies.

Grayson nods. "Yup."

"You two are ridiculous."

"No one is denying that, but back to Oliver being pathetic."

I hate my brother. "I'm not pathetic."

"You kind of are," Jack agrees.

"Only because you're pretending as if this doesn't bother you," Grayson finishes his original statement about it sucking.

I am so done with this conversation. "You're the only thing bothering me."

Jack turns to Grayson. "You're not bothering me."

"You're not bothering me either." Gray smiles.

"The only person bothered by this is the one who is denying his true heart's dream."

I blink a few times, wondering what alternate world I'm in. "True heart's dream?" I ask slowly. "You've spent way too much time watching fairy tales with Amelia. Jesus."

"We'll get to that in a second, but he's right."

I let out a loud sigh, wishing there was some emergency at the resort that I was the only one capable of dealing with so I could leave. I catch Maren's eyes, and lift my hand, hoping she'll come rescue me from Dumb and Dumber. She smiles, sways from side to side, and sips her drink.

She is so goddamn beautiful.

Someone punches my arm, and my hand goes to the spot and starts to rub it. "Ouch, you fucker. What the hell was that for?"

"For staring at your fake wife and acting like you don't like her."

"I do like her," I clarify. "I never said I didn't. You two are the ones spouting shit about my heart and crap. I'm just here for the fun parts, okay. While you two are following your wives and kids around, trying to make them happy, I've already accomplished that, and now I get to enjoy a party and then spend time at the beach."

"And you'll see all the shit you won't have," Grayson says without any humor. "You're going to remember all the things you wanted, Oliver. Whether you believe it or not, it's not going to be so easy to walk away from it and go back to being alone. I guarantee it."

I will not let him in my fucking head. I am well aware that I'll be alone. I'm the only single one left other than Alex, but he's in Egypt, living his best life. I'm here with all the happily married idiots. There's nothing that I'm more aware of than the fact that I'm living at the resort because I have nothing else.

Even the RV I was staying in is gone.

No, now, I live in a small cabin on the property so I can always be on call.

I down the glass of whiskey in one gulp. "On that note, I'm going to do all the fun stuff I was talking about and dance with my fake wife."

Fuck reality, I'm going to enjoy the fantasy for today.

sixteen

MAREN

"Did you have fun today?" Oliver asks as we dance in front of our family and friends for our last dance.

"I did. Your sister did an amazing job."

"Spending other people's money is my sister's true calling in life." The clinking of glasses starts again. "Fucking Christ. I'm going to kill my brothers."

We lean in and kiss, my heart melting with how much I like this. How easy kissing him is, and a part of me aches because it'll be over once we leave the reception. We'll go on our vacation, hang out at the beach for five days, and then come back to our separate realities. When my father passes away, that'll be it. Oliver and I can go back to just being friends.

And that makes me sad.

Our song ends, and the DJ calls everyone to the floor before starting the next song. At least we won't be forced to kiss again. He holds me close, swaying in perfect rhythm. "What do we do about tonight?" I ask.

"What do you mean?"

"Well, we have to stay in the suite together."

Oliver smiles. "We do."

"I just . . . I don't know what . . . you . . ." Good grief, I sound ridiculous. We are thirty-one years old, not fifteen. We can sleep in the same room and not have it be a big deal.

It's just that I'm wearing this dress and my emotions are a bit too close to the surface.

"We'll be fine," Oliver assures me. "I'm sure we can manage."

"You're right. I think my brain is exhausted from over-thinking everything."

"I'm sure. Are you at least feeling relieved we pulled it off?"

"I am," I tell him honestly. "It's hard, though, because I'm happy that we did this but I'm also a bit sad because I know this might be the last memory I have with my dad before he dies. I'm incredibly grateful to you, Oliver. You have no idea. I had the most perfect wedding. Truly. This was everything I could've dreamed of, but . . ."

"But it was with the wrong guy." The way his voice cracks at the end causes me to jerk my head back.

"No. It's not that."

"I just mean that I was not supposed to be the Oliver standing here."

He's right that he wasn't supposed to be him, but that's not what I was thinking. He is the right Oliver. He is every-thing, and if I had gone through with the wedding that was planned, it wouldn't have been this perfect. Oliver Park-erson is warm and inviting. He welcomed my family, and while our being in love was all for show, the way he acted wasn't.

Had I actually married my ex-fiancé, nothing would've gone as smoothly. He is nice, yes, but he's not comforting. There's no way he would've fit in with my uncles the way Ollie did, and my stepmother would have eaten him alive.

"Maybe not, but I know I married the best Oliver today," I say softly.

Slowly, I raise my gaze to meet his, and the desire swim-ming in his eyes weakens my knees. He leans in, without anyone tapping on glass or analyzing our interactions, and presses his lips to mine.

It's soft, sweet, and tinted with something more.

This is crazy.

Absolutely insane because I shouldn't want him to keep kissing me, but God, I do.

He pulls back, rests his forehead to mine, and says, "I am in so much trouble," under his breath as the song ends.

Me too.

Me. Fucking. Too.

We break apart and start saying good night to everyone.

"This was definitely the most interesting wedding I've ever officiated," Mark says with a grin.

"Considering it's only your second, that doesn't say a lot," Charlie, his wife, says.

"True, but you know . . ."

"Please don't ever agree to do it for anyone else."

"I make no promises. I have to uphold the rules so I don't lose my spot in heaven."

Charlie rolls her eyes. "Please, we all know you're going to hell."

He grins. "That's life with you, my sweet."

"Right. You're in hell." She scoffs and then gives me a tight hug. "We are so going to talk about this when you get back."

"I know."

"Mark is right," she says, pulling back and smiling. "You would've made an excellent field agent."

I roll my eyes and snort. "Please, I don't do danger."

"And you don't think this was dangerous?"

"That's a different kind of danger."

She looks at Oliver and then back to me. "True, but it isn't any less risky, my friend." Then her gaze moves to her husband. "I know all too well how my story ended with a man I didn't love and had to fake it with."

So not going down that road.

Jackson and Catherine nudge their way closer, and Charlie whispers something in Oliver's ear that causes him to laugh.

"Congrats on the nuptials," Catherine says with a glimmer in her eyes. "I can't wait to hear how the honeymoon goes."

"Stop it," I warn.

"Have fun, Maren. Seriously, if you were my client, I would tell you to just embrace this for the time you can. Life is hard, and you are always in your head. Allow your heart to lead this one just a little, regardless of the possible fallout."

Coming from a publicist, I'm a little shocked at that advice.

Jackson nods. "It's amazing what might happen when you do that."

Catherine tilts her head. "Aww. You're being all sentimental, Muffin."

"Weddings always do it." My boss is a man who could snap anyone in this room in half. He's tall, strong, and trained to be deadly, but when he looks at his wife, he's goo.

It's cute.

"Thank you all for everything," I say, knowing they could've imploded everything and went out of their way not to.

"We're a team, and if you had told us before you came up with this plan, we would've done what we could."

I eye him, not sure what that means and not sure I want to, but smile because I think he means it in a sweet way.

After they move down, Devney and Sean come over with a sleeping Cassandra and Austin looking like he's ready to fall asleep standing up.

I know she has mixed feelings on all of this, but she stood by me without ever wavering. "The wedding was amazing, and I don't really know what to say other than I love you and hope this works out for you both."

"What does that mean?"

She shrugs. "Just that . . . well, I hope you both are happy."

"What we did made me happy."

"Right. For your dad."

I nod. "Of course."

Her eyes move to Oliver. "Of course."

"We have to get these two to bed," Sean says, trying to adjust Cassandra while also keeping Austin steady. "Congrats, you guys."

Oliver's family comes over, bidding us the same well wishes, but his brothers start to make inappropriate jokes, causing him to flip them off. I hug Jessica, Delia, and then Stella, thanking them again for all their help.

We take the time to thank everyone who came but save my father and Linda for last. While she's normally a nightmare, today she was actually kind. She didn't wear cream, thank God, and told me how proud she was. It's hard to hate her when she acts this way.

She gives Oliver a hug first. "You have made us all so happy. We worried when we hadn't met you before this, but you're a wonderful person, and we're so happy you found each other."

Oliver smiles. "I'm very lucky to know her, and it was a pleasure to meet you all and become part of the family."

She hooks her arm in my father's. "Patrick and I couldn't be more pleased to have you as our son now."

Dad nods, tears in his eyes. "Family is all that matters in this world."

"I agree," Oliver says, placing his hand on my back.

"You sure you have to leave early tomorrow?" I ask my father, not wanting this time to end.

Linda speaks. "We have a long trip, and your father needs to recover from this weekend. It's imperative we get him home."

As much as I'd like to argue, she's probably right. This

took a lot out of him. I just wish . . . I wish we could have more time. More laughter and hugs. I wish he could just stay here and we could just pause time so I would never have to lose him.

Oliver's hand moves up my back, rubbing along my shoulders. I turn to him, feeling his sympathy with each stroke of his hand. It's as if he's telling me that it's okay and he's here. With tears in my eyes, I nod and step toward my father.

"I love you, Daddy."

"I love you most, Princess. You and Oliver are perfect for each other, and I can't tell you how much this has meant to me. To see it with my own eyes, just . . . joy."

My chest grows tight because he saw what we wanted him to see. Oliver squeezes my shoulders. "Linda, my mother is over there and she mentioned needing to speak with you."

"She did?"

He nods. "I can't remember what it was about, but I know it was important."

"Oh. Of course."

He gives me a wink and then leads Linda towards his mother.

This man.

I know that couldn't be easy because Linda doesn't like to leave my dad and not be privy to the conversation.

However, I'm going to take advantage of this private time I get.

I help my father over to a seating area and take his hand in mine. "I'm sad," I admit.

"You shouldn't be sad on your wedding day," Dad says with a wheeze in his voice.

"I think all brides are a bit emotional."

"Happy tears, Maren." He brushes away my tears and then cups my cheek. "I want only happy tears."

How can I be happy when I know what's to come? "I

130

am happy, Daddy. Thank you so much for being here and dancing with me," I tell him.

"Even if it was more like swaying?"

I laugh a little through my tears. "You were never a good dancer."

"No," he agrees. "I didn't have moves." My father's hand settles on top of mine, and he closes his eyes for a moment. "I will never forget this day. The way you looked or the smile on your face, and even though my time is limited, this will carry me through."

I look at our entwined hands, tears falling again as I struggle to control my emotions. "I'm glad that we had this."

He lifts my chin with his free hand. "I'm glad you have him."

Oh, Daddy. I don't. I don't have him.

I want to tell him, but I keep my lips clamped. This is what's giving him the strength to let go. I have to remember that.

"I'm glad that you are my father. You taught me to be strong and fight for what matters."

He smiles a little. "Well, you're an incredible woman, and if I had any part in that, I am clearly a great father."

"You most definitely are."

My father looks over to where Linda and Eveline are chatting. "Walk me to Linda?"

"Sure."

Arm in arm, my father and I make our way to the lobby. He'll leave very early in the morning, and I pray I have the chance to visit him in Georgia at least one more time.

When we reach them, Linda is laughing at something. "You have a wonderful son. He's just the sweetest man," Linda says with her fake smile and deep accent.

"He is pretty wonderful. All my kids are."

Oliver's back is straight and I can sense the tension in him. Inviting his mother was a source of contention among

131

the Parkerson siblings, but he relented. I got to meet her for just a few minutes at the rehearsal before Oliver whisked me away from her.

I place my hand on his back and he relaxes just slightly.

Linda sees us approach and returns her attention to Eveline. "Trust me, you will love going on that cruise. It's the best trip we ever took. Even if we had to spend a week in the hospital—with no help—when we got back."

"Thank you so much for the suggestion," she says. Eveline rests her hand on my forearm. "You look absolutely breathtaking. I'm going to say goodbye to Stella and the boys. I'll see you in a few days, Oliver?"

He smiles at his mother. "I'll call when I get back."

"Good. Travel safe."

"Are you ready, darling?"

He nods. "I'm ready."

Linda walks over and kisses my cheek. "Be good, Maren. It would be nice if you both stop by when you're close to Georgia. I know it might be out of your way, but if you want to see your father before he dies, then—"

"We will do our best to get to you soon," Oliver says quickly, surprising us all.

Linda looks stunned. "Oh. That's a nice change. Good. It'll be great to see you both."

"Yeah, it really will," I say, falling a little more for this man who seems to truly care for me.

My father sighs heavily, exhaustion clear on his face. "Go rest, Daddy. I'll see you in the morning before you leave."

He kisses my cheek. "I will see you then."

And with that, Oliver wraps both arms around my waist, allowing me to lean against him as I watch my father walk away, praying I actually get the chance to visit him in Georgia.

seventeen

OLIVER

Maren and I make our way up to the honeymoon suite, which is the only room in the resort where my brothers and I let Stella have free rein and no budget. It's the first time I'm going to see it completed.

I swipe the key through the reader, open the door, and let Maren in first. I follow her, slowly taking in the room.

There are floor-to-ceiling windows, which offer the most stunning views of the lake and mountains, the floors are a light-colored oak that makes the entire space feel larger and brighter, and my and Maren's bags are already tucked off to the side for us.

"Holy shit," Maren says behind me, her eyes moving around. "This room is . . ."

"Amazing," I finish.

"More than that."

It really is.

Maren's aunt got to come up here late last night to take photos for her blog, and I really hope that article does this space justice. Otherwise, this is a very expensive room that no one will ever see.

"So, it's our wedding night," Maren says, turning and walking backward.

She's absolutely stunning. A few errant pieces of her blonde hair have fallen free of her updo. The bottom of her dress is looped around her wrist, and the one shoulder strap is falling down just slightly. Her smile is relaxed, and her eyes are bright.

I want so badly to pull her into my arms and kiss her again. Being able to do just that and not have to think twice about it has been the biggest benefit of today. Sure, we had to pretend to love each other, but half the time, it was just natural to be with her. To reach my hand out and touch her soft skin was a reflex instead of a calculated action.

I don't know when this became more real than pretend, but it has, and in a week, it will be over. She'll go back to her life, and I'll be here, alone again.

"It appears that way."

She laughs while shaking her head. "I don't have words for how today made me feel."

"Oh?"

I follow behind her as she makes her way deeper into the room. "It's like . . . a mix of weirdness and comfort. Does that make sense?"

"Not at all."

She giggles. "I didn't think it would. All night, I was just so conflicted. We are married, well, depends if Mark can figure that part out, but we never planned to be. But either way, there is no one else in the world I would rather be fake married to."

I raise my brow, moving even closer. "Why is that?"

A part of me doesn't want to know because I wasn't her first choice, but I can't resist asking.

She watches me, long lashes framing those gorgeous green eyes. "Because . . ."

I step again, watching her breath hitch because we are just a few inches apart. "Because?"

"Because you make me feel safe. I don't remember ever feeling that way before. I trusted you, and you didn't let me down. You stood beside me, even in all my craziness." She looks down, a faint blush painting her cheeks. "I liked it. I needed it."

I needed it too. I needed to be near her and to make her feel that way. All night, I sought her out, wanted to be sure she was all right. Even now, I want to protect her, keep her safe, hold her close.

I tilt her chin so she's looking at me. "I don't know what is happening between us. I can't figure out if this is real or just a product of what we created, but I know that I like being with you. I like kissing you, touching you, and talking to you. I'm not looking for anything. I gave up on love and relationships because they all end the same way, but I am glad I made you feel safe. It's what you deserve to feel."

She smiles softly and then lifts onto her toes. "I like kissing you too."

My arm moves around her back, and I pull her so her chest is to mine. "Then why don't I do it again?"

And then I do. Our lips press together, and she opens to me without hesitation. I slide my tongue into her mouth, loving the dance we create. She's playful, sensual, and sexy as hell. Her hands move up, tangling in my hair as she moans.

I could do this. I could strip her down and take her, make her feel so much more than just safe. I want to, but that would get emotionally messy, and I don't do messy.

When I pull back, her lips are swollen and her eyes are glazed over. "Why did you stop?"

Because I'm a fucking idiot.

"I just . . . in the spirit of this whole thing, I'm not looking for anything. I gave up on love and relationships because they all end the same way. I have this resort to worry about, and I don't know if either of us is thinking straight."

She takes a step back, swallowing but keeping a smile on her face. "Right. I didn't think that's what we were doing. I

135

know this was all fake for you—I mean us. And, well, you're probably right about not thinking straight. We both drank a lot and are probably just caught up in the whole thing, right?"

I nod. "Yeah. I . . ."

"I am so sorry I kissed you."

"Well, I kissed you first."

"Kind of. I mean, I leaned up onto my toes, which was when the kiss started."

I shake my head. "But I said I was going to kiss you."

"Which you did."

"Which I did."

Maren pulls her bottom lip between her teeth, and the urge to kiss her again rises.

Shit.

"It's fine," she says quickly.

It really is not fine, but I'm not going to argue.

"I'm glad."

"How about we get changed and watch a movie?" she suggests.

I don't really want to watch a movie, but it's really the only option we have.

"Sounds good."

We both head over to our bags, and she stops. "Wait!"

"What?"

"I almost forgot."

Maren heads to the other side of the room and starts going through the stack of envelopes. She pulls one out. "This. It's the one from my father, and he said to open it when we were alone."

"We're alone."

She nods. "I'm nervous."

"Why?"

"Because I know my dad, and he'll have gone overboard."

"Whatever it is, he wanted you to have it."

She sits on the couch, and I settle in next to her, taking her hand. "*Us.* He wanted me and my husband to have whatever it is."

"Open it," I encourage.

She pulls her hand away, carefully lifts the flap, and pulls out what looks like a document. I give her a second to read it, waiting for her to tell me what it is. But then her hand starts to tremble before a sob breaks free. I pull her to my chest. "Why are you crying?"

She hands me the paper, which turns out to be the deed to a lot of property in Virginia. Holy shit. He gave her land and a house.

"This . . . this w-was my m-mother's. It's her family's land that I thought went to my uncle."

I wipe her tears away. "Looks like it didn't, and now it's yours."

"He kept it. All this time. He kept it, and I don't know what to think."

I'm not sure I understand why she's so upset, but it's clear this means a lot to her. "Tell me," I encourage.

So, we sit in our wedding attire, and I listen to her tell me about her family's farm in Virginia. It was where her mother grew up and where she dreamed of raising her kids. When she died, she didn't have a will and the property went into probate, where her uncle argued it should be his. She thought he ended up with it because her father mentioned it and they stopped taking weekend trips out there.

"It's here though. He had it all this time, and . . . now it's mine."

"Maybe he saved it so you could raise your family there if you wanted."

Her head drops. "This is all too much."

I wrap my arm around her shoulders, and she leans into me. I hold her, not caring about anything other than giving her what she needs. I hate this part of myself, the one that wants to save her, help her, be there when I know it's all bullshit.

I am the friend, the guy who's good at offering support but is never more.

I've been nothing more than that over and over. I'm the best man, but not the best man for her.

I shove that aside because, no matter what role I play in this, I want to touch her. I'll take the selfish part that enjoys this and let it happen.

Maren lets out a long sigh and then smiles at me. "Thank you, Oliver."

"For?"

"Being so damn amazing. I couldn't have done any of this without you, and you are seriously the best."

The best is so often not good enough. "Well, I'm good at a lot of things."

"Like what?" she asks, the mood shifting.

"Oh, sweetheart, if you only knew."

A blush covers her face, and she looks away. "Men, you're all the same."

"We like to keep you women thinking that."

"Is that so?"

"Absolutely," I reply, getting to my feet. "Now, let's get out of this shit, get comfortable, and open the rest of our cards."

Maren takes my extended hand. "Sounds like a plan, Mr. Parkerson."

"Good thing you're so agreeable, Mrs. Fake-Parkerson."

She laughs and then heads over to her bags as I go to mine.

I grab my gym shorts and T-shirt, and when I turn around, Maren is tossing things out of her bag and muttering.

"You okay?" I ask.

She sighs heavily and continues her search. "No."

"Why is that?"

138

Tossing down the item in her hand, she straightens and glares at the mess. "Because someone repacked me."

"My sister and your maid of honor . . ."

"Yes, well, they didn't repack me the same stuff I packed."

"And that's a problem because?"

Maren grabs one of the items she tossed down. "Because *this* is what they repacked!" She holds up the very thin scrap of white silk.

My brows shoot up, and I grin. "Well, that was nice of them."

"Was it? Do you remember just about a minute ago when you were talking about all the things you don't want?" Maren's eyes narrow just a little. "When you reminded me that we shouldn't be doing any of the things that I really wanted to do?"

"Sure . . ."

"Well, good luck to the both of us then."

She lifts another item, and Jesus Christ, it's another see-through nightgown—if you can even call it that.

"You can't wear that."

"Oh? And what would you like me to wear then?"

"Anything else," I sputter. There's no way in hell I have enough self-control to be anywhere near her in that.

"There is nothing else. They packed three of these to sleep in. Apparently, your sister and my best friend think I don't need clothes."

Clothes. I heard that word. "Okay, what about shorts?"

She smiles without any humor. "Oh, they took care of that too. All I have are bathing suits and dresses. I'm going to kill them."

"We'll go shopping on our way to South Carolina tomorrow. For tonight, you can just wear something of mine."

My sister did not pack my bag, so I know I have clothes.

"Fine," Maren says with exasperation. "I'll do that."

I pull out a pair of basketball shorts and a T-shirt and hand them to her.

"Thanks."

While she's in the bathroom changing, I sink down on the chair. This is a disaster. I'm not sure how I'm supposed to endure this for five days. There is no way I'll be able to ignore this ache for her. Not to mention, she doesn't need me all over her. She was just dumped by the guy she was going to marry, which doesn't exactly scream ready to jump into bed with me.

I know from personal experience that almost marrying someone doesn't necessarily equal love. Hell, I watched the woman I loved date someone else immediately after we broke up.

I can't put myself in a situation that I know is going to crash and burn.

Been there. Done that. Own the T-shirt company.

Rubbing my hands over my face, I take a deep breath and stand. I'm a strong man who doesn't bend easily. I'll just plaster a smile on my face, get through the next few days, and then come back to the life I've designed.

I unbutton my shirt, and just as I'm about to remove it, the bathroom door opens to reveal Maren still in that dress.

"I need you."

I need you.

I need you to strip me down and make me scream for hours. Please, Oliver.

That's not what she says. No, she actually sighs and shrugs. "I can't undo my dress. Can you help me?"

Well, that's kind of like stripping her down. It actually *is* stripping her down, but the rest of that sentence hasn't been uttered . . . yet.

I clear my throat and walk over. She turns, pulling her hair over her shoulder, giving me a fantastic view of her back. She's so damn beautiful with her hair completely down so it cascades like blonde silk.

Once I'm behind her, she turns her head, peeking at me from the side. My fingers move to the button at the top. "You know, I am kind of glad this isn't really our wedding night," I say as I fumble with each one.

"Why is that?"

"Because if you were my bride, I would've torn your dress off you."

She shivers a little. "Really?"

"Absolutely," I say with a deepness in my voice that I hope covers the desire flooding my system.

I couldn't even last two minutes after that stupid pep talk I gave myself.

I focus on the buttons again and manage one more.

"Why is that?" Maren whispers.

Don't answer her, Oliver. Don't fucking do it.

"I would've needed you naked on the bed so badly that I wouldn't have cared that the dress was on the floor in pieces."

Maren's breath jumps as she turns, facing the mirror. "I'm sorry that this isn't your real wedding night."

"Me too."

She smiles a little as I undo the last button. "Thanks."

You are so not welcome.

"Of course," I say with an easy smile even though nothing feels easy inside me.

She steps back into the bathroom, closing the door behind her, and I get changed before falling into the chair that I'll be sleeping on.

How the hell did I get myself into this?

After what feels like an hour, Maren emerges, wearing my shorts, which are folded about four times and look like she knotted them or something. My shirt is huge on her, and while it should be completely unattractive, it's not. She's in my clothes. Naked under them.

"Thanks for letting me borrow this tonight." Her eyes

dart to the floor. "It's a bit big, but it's better than the nightie."

"Yes, better than that," I agree.

I would've died.

I still might.

She walks to the bed and slides under the covers while I shift on the chair. Maren lets out a giggle.

"What?"

"You look ridiculous."

"Thanks. Women often tell me that."

"I'm sure they don't."

I move again, sitting up a little because my ass keeps sliding down. This chair was not made for sleeping.

"You should know this now," I tell her. "You fake married a total loser when it comes to love."

Maren starts to braid her hair as she shrugs. "Can't be any worse than your fake wife, who got stood up before she made it to the altar and then literally begged you to pretend to marry her only to have you turn her down. Top that."

"I have one failed engagement and then one *almost* engagement where I didn't even get the ring on the second time. You . . ." I suck in a breath through my teeth. "You're behind the curve, my friend."

"Two? Wow. You really are a loser."

"See, you're welcome."

Maren shakes her head. "Come over here, Oliver. You can't sleep in that thing, and we are both adults. I'm sure we'll be fine in the bed."

I'm sure I will not, but there's not a chance in hell I'm going to get any sleep in this chair. Plus, I don't really want to look pathetic by refusing her.

"Fine, but you have to promise not to take advantage of me," I say with a brow raised.

Maren smirks, tying off her braid. "I vow not to take your innocence this night."

I toss the pillow at her, causing her to squeak, and then climb in.

We end up sitting side-by-side against the headboard, awkward and unsure of what to do next.

"Want to watch that movie?" I ask.

"Sure."

I glance around the room again, wondering why the hell there is no television in here. "Is there a damn television?" I ask as I toss my legs over the side.

"Didn't you design this place?"

"Stella had this room."

"It is the honeymoon suite. I guess she figured they'd be doing other things?" Maren says as she searches. "Ha! I found it!"

I glance at her, finding her holding up a remote as if it were a prize. "Okay, now we just need to find the television."

She climbs back into bed and pats the bed next to her. "Watch." Pointing the remote toward the opposite wall, she presses a button, and what I thought was a beautiful piece of framed artwork becomes a television.

"That is impressive." I move toward it, amazed because I never would have guessed it wasn't art. It's flush against the wall like a photograph and there is barely any backlight.

"I definitely need one of these," Maren says as she turns on *My Cousin Vinny*, which is already halfway over. "I love this movie."

"It's a classic."

She smiles. "Aunt Eileen can do her accent perfectly to match this movie. We used to watch it all the time and I would laugh as she'd recite it."

Maren sits up on her knees and says the lines word-for-word.

We both laugh, and her cheeks turn red when her attempt at an accent fails. "That was pitiful."

"I'd like to hear your New York accent." Maren smirks.

143

"Forget about it!" I give it my best, which is just shy of truly pitiful, and she falls back on the bed, laughing hysterically.

Maren fluffs the pillow and grins. "Who would've thought this would be how either of us would spend a wedding night?"

"Sure as fuck not me."

"Me either, but honestly, this is kind of perfect. It's like college again."

Except that I didn't want to strip her naked when we were in college. "In a way. While the movie and being with you is perfect, we're missing something."

"What?"

"Food." I grab the phone and call down to the staff to bring us up room service.

When I hang up, Maren is clutching her chest. "My hero."

"I do try." I puff out my chest.

"I am starving. It's so sad that we barely had five minutes to shove some food into our mouths."

I'd like to shove my tongue—or something else—in her mouth.

I mentally slap myself. "I agree. I know this was supposed to be a test run, and while I can say the staff was great, I have no idea about the food."

She purses her lips. "Hmm, you know, no one complained about anything, really."

"What do you mean?"

"Just the whole weekend. My family was so happy the whole time, and we ate all our meals here, so you *know* the food was good. If it wasn't, you guys would have heard about it, but no one bitched."

That's true. I was so caught up in all things wedding I didn't pay attention to everything around me.

"I feel like an ass for not doing my job."

Maren's hand settles on my arm. "You did so much

144

more than your job. You took care of everything. My point was a compliment, Oliver. Not only were you the most amazing fiancé but also you handled the resort smoothly."

I try not to let her words sink in. "I think my siblings did that."

"I think you had a much bigger role than you believe. This resort is going to be fantastic. I can feel it and see it."

"And what makes you so sure?" I ask.

"Because I believe in you."

Those words don't bounce off. They seep into my soul like a balm that I didn't know I needed. It covers the wounds, starting to heal the broken shit inside.

Damn her.

Before I can bristle about it, she's scooting closer. "What are you doing?" I ask.

"Just relax," Maren says softly.

Then she moves to her side so she's pressed against the length of my body. Her leg hooks with mine, her arm drapes over my stomach, and her head settles on my chest. "Maren . . ."

"It's cuddling, Ollie. I think we both deserve it after the day we've had."

My official protest comes in the form of me wrapping my arms around her, holding her tighter, and watching the movie. Yeah, after the day we had, I guess we do deserve it.

eighteen

MAREN

Yes. Yes. Yes.

I keep my eyes closed, wholly focused on the sensations that grip me. A hand that cups my breast, lips at my neck, and pleasure—so much pleasure everywhere.

My fingers slide into thick hair, holding his mouth against my skin.

A low groan fills my ears, and I grin.

This feels so good. His warm body against mine is perfect. I moan as his hot tongue glides down toward my chest.

"Don't stop," I whisper, tightening my fingers in his hair.

This is incredible, and I never want Oliver to stop.

Oliver. My husband.

My God.

My eyes fly open as I realize what the hell is happening.

"Oliver?" I ask with a squeak.

He lifts his head, eyes drowsy from sleep and desire. "You were saying my name," he says. "You were begging me."

"I was?" I ask, trying to recall anything. There is just a slight memory of . . . oh, the dream I had.

Oh boy.

He leans back more, watching me. "Did you . . . Shit. I swear you were."

"I did that. I was dreaming, and I guess . . . I'm—" I stop because the perfect excuse evades me. Mortified. Horny. Desperate. "Sorry."

"I'm not," he says quickly.

"You're not?"

"Not even a little. I would've kept going."

I watch him warily. "Even though we said we shouldn't."

"That was before I slept with you in my arms, and you rubbed your ass on me all night while moaning my name. I'm not *that* strong. I think it's clear we both want this."

My heart is pounding, and all the reasons for not crossing that line are gone. He has no idea how those words curl my toes, but there are so many possibilities where this ends very badly. There are plenty of ones where this goes well. Oliver and I can choose the path that has us both hot, sweaty, sated, and then divorced. No harm, no foul, no feelings.

I want him. He wants me. We are adults. So, let's get naked.

Fear of rejection keeps me from saying that aloud. I wait, each breath feeling like it takes a lifetime to leave my lungs.

Finally, I muster the courage and speak. "I know I do."

His hand lifts, pushing a strand of hair back from my cheek. "I want to make you feel good."

Oh, I want that too. "You have given me so much."

"I can give you more. Let me make you feel good, Maren."

"And what then?"

Oliver gives a devilish grin that I want to wipe off his face with my lips. "Then we go on our honeymoon and spend the whole time enjoying ourselves." He leans in, his mouth getting closer. "We lose ourselves before we have to come back to reality."

That sounds really fucking good and tempts me with a sense of something I haven't had in a while—hope.

"Reality sucks," I say breathlessly.

"Let's live in the fantasy for a while."

My hand moves to the back of his head, and I pull him so our lips just barely touch. "I can do that."

"Thank fucking God." Oliver moans the words before crushing his lips to mine.

The kisses we've shared over the last few days have been tame compared to this. Oliver and I are wild, no holding back as we each volley for control. He kisses me. I kiss him. Back and forth we go until I have no idea who is leading this anymore, and I don't care.

We are lips, tongues, and gasps, and that works just fine for me. He pushes me onto my back, his body covering mine as I tug up his shirt, wanting to feel his skin.

He pauses long enough to tear it off, and then my hands are back on him, needing to feel his skin. I slide my fingers along his spine, reveling in how each taut muscle pulses beneath me while he kisses my neck.

"I like you in my clothes."

"I'd like me out of your clothes."

Oliver rubs his nose down my neck. "I bet I'll like that too."

I'm wearing his shirt and shorts, and during the night, the knot I tied to hold the shorts up has loosened significantly. Just moving a little has them lowering. He sits up, removing my shirt.

"You have no idea how stunning you are," he says, and I blush under his gaze.

I know I'm pretty—not in a snobby way, but that's never been a complaint I've heard before. Even if I'd been totally oblivious to it before I pulled into this town, the way he had been looking at me all week would have convinced me he thought I was attractive.

However, the way he's staring at me now—full of heat and longing—causes my stomach to flip.

His sculpted chest and broad shoulders are everything I love in a man. Strength radiates from him, and I want to drown in it.

"Oliver," I say, moving back up to his face. "You are so damn hot."

How any woman could let this man walk away is beyond my understanding.

I push that thought away because he's here. He's mine now, and I have at least five days of fun in my future.

I trail my fingers down his chest and bite my lower lip.

"You're sure about this?" he asks, his hands going behind my back, pressing our bare chests together.

"I know I want you. I want this. I want to figure out whatever this is between us."

He rubs his thumb against my lower lip. "And then we walk away."

I make a soft moaning noise as I kiss his neck, unable to stop myself.

"Say the words, Maren."

I look into his deep blue eyes. "Then we walk away."

Oliver's smirk is cocky and sexy at the same time. "That's if you can walk when I'm done with you."

"Do your worst," I toss back.

"Challenge accepted."

I don't have time to draw a breath before he has me flat on the bed. I squirm, but he pulls me closer. His lips are on mine in another searing kiss before he moves down to my chest. His hands are everywhere, touching, kneading, squeezing, and caressing. It's sensory overload, but also heavenly.

His lips trail to my breast, where he kisses and licks around the tip before taking my nipple in his mouth. I cry out, hips bucking off the bed as he sucks greedily. His tongue moves back and forth, flicking it before I feel his teeth nip the delicate skin.

"Oh, God!" I cry out as his hand moves down my body before slipping under my borrowed shorts. When he finds no fabric underneath, he groans.

"Fuck, Maren. You're not wearing underwear?"

"I . . . I don't usually."

"So, you have none packed?"

I shrug a little. "Not really."

"Thank the Lord above."

He tears the shorts off my legs and throws them across the room.

I don't have so much as a moment to feel exposed before he's kissing me again, tasting his way down my stomach before going lower. "I've wanted to do this for days now."

"Days?" I ask.

"Weeks, if I'm being honest. Since I saw you again, I've wanted to touch you. Then there was that kiss. By yesterday, I thought I might go insane. There you stood in that white dress, so beautiful, smiling at me as if I were some goddamn hero."

I press my hand to his cheek. "You are my hero."

"No, I'm not."

"You have no idea how I feel about you."

Honestly, I have no idea how I feel. I'm conflicted because I shouldn't feel anything. I should be nursing a broken heart, not dreaming of Oliver's touch and mouth and what promises to be a very nice dick.

So, yeah, I don't know what this means because it's all crazy.

"Why don't you tell me." His voice is low and husky.

"I can't."

"Maybe you just need incentive." He moves lower, pushing my legs apart. "You talk and I'll lick. If you stop . . . well, I might stop as well."

"Oliver," I say, needing him so much. "Please."

151

"Please what, sweetheart?"

I turn my head to meet his gaze. "I need you."

"And I need to do this, so I suggest you start telling me how you feel."

I groan because this is not going to go my way. I mean, it is a little, but . . . I can't think and talk while he does . . . oh, God.

Oliver's hot tongue slides against my clit, and I grip the sheets.

"I want to taste you, Maren. I want to make you come on my tongue, so give us what we both want," he commands.

"I like you. I like how you make me feel," I say quickly while I have some of my wits.

He rewards me again with his mouth. Oliver moves back and forth over the bundle of nerves, sending heat all through my veins.

"You're selfless."

"Selfless?" he asks and then flicks me again. "I am clearly getting so much more than I bargained for."

"We both are," I say before a long moan falls from my lips. God, he's good at this.

As he licks, sucks, flicks, I keep talking. "You make me feel alive. You give me hope that there is more to love than I thought there was. I want you so much, and I don't know what to do," I admit, no longer sure if I'm speaking aloud. My orgasm is building so fast the words are a tumble of incoherence in my brain. "God, Oliver, what is happening? Why do I want you like this? Why do I need you?"

He doesn't stop, and each second that passes, I'm driven closer to the edge.

"I want you so much. I want this to keep going, and I want you . . . all of you."

My back lifts off the bed as it becomes too much. My orgasm rockets through me, causing me to call out his name and forcing him to hold my legs down so he doesn't have to stop.

After what feels like an eternity, the pulsing slows and he crawls up my body, turning my face to his. He reaches over, grabs a condom, and slides it on before returning to me. With his arms braced on either side of my head, his cock pushes toward my entrance. "This is going to complicate things."

I smile a little. "I think we've blurred all the lines already."

"I think so too." He pushes into me and freezes. "But this one . . ."

"This one—" I gasp, holding on to him.

"This one I'm going to erase."

For the next hour, we obliterate every line ever drawn, and I don't even care.

~

"That was . . ." Oliver says, staring up at the ceiling.

"Yeah."

It was so much. It was amazing and beautiful, and now I'm pretty sure I'm going to panic. We had sex. Oliver, my friend from college and my best friend's ex, and I just had sex.

Not weird. Nope. Not at all. We're consenting adults who just happen to have done the horizontal tango.

I need my notebook and time to jot down all my pros and cons. I have to think about what it means and why and where and . . . oh, here it comes—the freak out.

"Are you okay?" Oliver asks, turning onto his side to face me.

"I'm good."

"You're sure?"

I look him in the eyes and vow to fake being okay until I

can work through the options. "I will be. I just need to think."

"Isn't that the opposite of what helps?"

I shrug. "For most people, but I generally need to see something from all angles before making a choice. I don't usually rush into anything."

His brow lifts. "Really?"

Okay. I deserve that, but the last week and a half is nothing like my normal life.

"I am an analyst. The word alone should tell you what I do."

"I get that, but where in this did you think through asking me to marry you?"

"Well, while that was a bit rash, I promise I thought through the options, and it seemed like the best path to the desired outcome."

He grins. "I like this outcome so far."

"I do too."

"So, we're okay?"

I would love to say yes right away but can't. "Can you hand me that notepad?"

His brows crinkle, but he leans over, grabbing the small notepad and pen from his side table.

"Thank you," I say. "I need a second."

Oliver nods slowly. "I'll wait."

I think it through quickly, jotting things down in the order they enter my brain.

Feelings. That's definitely a concern. I feel more than I thought I would, more than I knew was possible. It's so strange and intense and fast that it scares me. However, I'm able to shut those emotions down. I've done it before, and I'll do it again.

Sex. That's a pro because what we just had was fantastic.

Marriage. We're married, and that's a pro and a con. Pro because it happened to make others happy. Con because we weren't supposed to actually *be* married.

Friendship. That one is tricky. We're friends, and I'd like to still be friends at the end of this. Not sure where this one falls. More of the outcome.

Honesty. Oliver and I were very clear about being nothing more than some amazing sex for five days, and at the end, we walk away as friends.

I put the paper down and smile at him. "We're okay. I think us being honest about our expectations made it easier."

He leans in, pressing his lips to my forehead before pulling me against him. "I'm thinking this is the kind of marriage every couple should have."

I laugh a little and lift my eyes to meet his. "How is that?"

"Two people who are friends, can talk about things, keep their hearts out of it, trust each other not to hurt the other, and have really fucking great sex."

I lay my head back down, thinking that it's exactly what I wrote on that paper. "We definitely have that."

At least, all but the heart part. That one, I think I've lost a little.

nineteen

MAREN

Oliver and I pried ourselves out of bed to say goodbye to my father and Linda before they headed out, then Ollie stayed downstairs to take care of some work things while I came back to the room to repack our bags for us.

There's a knock, and I smile, thinking Oliver must've left his key.

"Hey, did you . . ." I trail off when I see Devney waiting. "You're not Oliver."

"I definitely am not, but why do you look sad about that?"

"Nope, not sad at all. I just thought it was him."

"We're heading out in a few. Sean wants to get the kids home in time for them to get a good night's sleep before we return to life tomorrow."

I give her a big hug, loving that I had this time with her. "I'm going to miss you."

Devney smiles. "I'll miss you."

"Thank you for everything. I really can't repay you."

"Please, it's what best friends do. While I may not agree with your psychotic breakdown, I do understand it. Seeing your dad yesterday was really special, and I think it's something that you and him can cherish for the rest of your lives."

There's no denying that. Even when my father is gone from this earth, I'll be able to remember that walk we took, the love in his eyes, and the ease he felt believing I was married.

It's all a lie, but it's a good one as far as lies go.

"I know I'll never forget it. I have so much to fill you in on. But," I say, remembering the surprise I got last night. "I'll never forgive you for the repacking job you did."

She grins. "You're welcome."

"I wasn't thanking you."

"But you will later."

"Come in, I need to finish." I walk back into the room and head to my bag.

"Ahh, you're packing."

I purse my lips as I stare at her. "Yeah, about that. Seriously, I don't know why you thought I would need sexy lingerie for a honeymoon where we had no plans of anything."

Had being the word of the day here. Now I have plans. Lots of naked plans.

She's quiet as her eyes start to move around the room, taking in details as they jump from the bags to the bed.

The very rumpled bed with sheets that are barely hanging on and the pillows that have fallen to the floor. The gym shorts on the floor, and Oliver's shirt thrown over the lamp.

"Maren?"

Crap.

"Yes?"

Her eyes find mine, and she gasps. "Oh my God! You had sex with Oliver!"

"Will you be quiet?" I say quickly as I clamp my hand over her mouth. "The door is wide open."

She pulls it down. "You did?"

"Yes, but it's fine."

"Oh, this I have to hear." Devney walks over to the couch and hesitates before sitting. "Is this spot safe, or are there questionable body fluids on it?"

"You're ridiculous."

She shrugs, choosing not to sit. "I knew this would happen."

"You knew what?"

"That you'd have sex with him," she says while shaking her head. "I saw it the second you two were together in front of everyone. Oliver is not that good of a liar. You guys have feelings for each other, and last night . . . was inevitable."

She's insane. We are only feeding off the emotions we have been forced to fake.

"That's not true. But things have changed."

"How so?"

I sigh. "Well, we had the whole wedding, and afterward, my dad asked to go with us to sign the marriage license."

"No!" She covers her mouth with her hands.

"Yeah."

"Did you sign it?"

I nod. "What option did we have?"

"Okay, that's true. But . . . well, it's fine if you don't file it, right?"

"That's what we think, but Mark is going to look into it just to be sure."

"You know," Devney says, taking my hands in hers. "This is kind of brilliant. You signed the papers. Everyone thinks it's real and you love each other. If you can void the whole thing by conveniently forgetting to file the paperwork, then when you guys decide to"—she lifts her fingers in air quotes—"get divorced, you won't actually have to do anything. It can be a clean break."

I never even considered that. "You're right."

"I am, but that doesn't change the fact that you and Oliver had dirty sex on your wedding night."

159

Of all the conversations in the world I thought I'd ever have, this isn't one. Nothing about this weekend has gone to plan. Having the wedding, the groom, and then this morning has been a complete mind fuck, and I can't make sense of it yet.

Honestly, I don't really want to overthink this. I want to enjoy it.

"Maybe not, but we're both adults, and we're fully aware that it's nothing but sex."

"Oh. Sure. What you should say is that you've figured out a way to rationalize the feelings and dismiss them."

"I am not rationalizing anything."

She scoffs. "Please. You're the queen of it. It's what landed you in this situation to begin with, Mare. You were going to marry the other guy because of your dad, and you rationalized that it was worth it even though you didn't love your ex. Now, you have the feelings you didn't have—"

"I don't!"

"—for the other guy, and you're again, making excuses."

"Devney, listen to me," I say through gritted teeth. "I know what I'm doing."

"I don't think you do, and that's what has you so messed up. Honestly, when it comes to love, we're all stupid, irrational, and contradictory, just like you're being. You say you don't have feelings for him, but here you are, smiling like a fool."

"I have this under control."

I don't. We both know it. I have a million reasons I shouldn't go with him. I should head home, the office, my father's house, or anywhere but to Myrtle Beach with Oliver.

"I hope so. I know how amazing Oliver is. We didn't end things because he wasn't a great guy or treated me poorly. I actually don't know many people who are as good or as wonderful as that man. He let me go to give me the life I was too afraid to reach for, and I will always love and respect

160

him for that. Not a day goes by where Sean and I don't appreciate the gesture, and I really hate the idea that he might get hurt by this. He doesn't deserve it."

The last thing I want to do is hurt him.

"I would never hurt Oliver, not after everything he did for me."

"Then I wish you luck."

"For what?"

She grins. "For keeping yourself from falling in love with him." She taps me on the nose and then leaves the room.

We pull up to the house in South Carolina after the five-hour drive from Willow Creek Valley. Our trip was great. We laughed and talked about the funny moments over the week, discussed how to handle things until we figure out the status of our fake marriage, and enjoyed the drive. I loved passing through the small towns and feeling lighter than I have since this whole thing started.

The house is beautiful and sits on the beach just outside Myrtle Beach. It has nine bedrooms, a private pool, and a jacuzzi. Obviously, it's way more than we need, but it's free, so I'm not going to complain.

"Should I carry you over the threshold?" Oliver asks.

"If you want me to beat you with your own arms."

He laughs. "Let's go in."

I don't know why I've been standing at this door as though something will change if I go inside. The easy air of friendship we've had has been great, but when we walk through those doors, it's our honeymoon. It's sex and nothing to distract me from Oliver. I won't be able to hide behind friends and family.

"Maren?"

I turn, my back against the door. "I don't want this to stop."

"What?"

"The way we are now."

"Okay . . ."

He's looking at me like I'm crazy again, but I need to get this out.

"I need definitions."

"For words or something else?"

I drop my gaze to my feet as nerves assault me. "No. For us. I know we said things this morning, but I don't know . . . I need to know exactly what this is. What we are. What we feel. If I know that, then I can be prepared. I need that, Oliver."

He blinks a few times. "All right. Once again, you stun me."

"I'm good at that."

"Clearly."

I smile and let out a long sigh. "I told you that I like to know what's coming whenever I can, that's all."

"I get it—kind of."

I'm a headcase, but it's necessary here. I have to keep my feelings in check, and for that to happen, there needs to be lines drawn. "Okay, maybe we don't need a definition as much as we need boundaries. Parameters to work inside of. Like, we have sex once a day."

"I don't like that idea."

"You don't?"

"Hell no. I would like to carry you inside that house and already be halfway undressed with my hands all over you. So, no, I think sex once a day is a terrible rule."

My heartbeat spikes because I want what he just offered, but I shake my head to come back to myself. "It can't be a free-for-all."

"Why not?"

Why not? Hmm, I don't really have an answer for that. It just seemed sensible. "Because . . . we need to avoid getting caught up in it."

Oliver steps forward, and I have nowhere to retreat. "Maren, we had some fantastic sex, and I have been fighting a raging hard on all day with you in the car. I want you in every way as many times as you'll let me have you. If you want boundaries, we can find other ways, but I want you. I want you, and I am pretty sure you want me just as much."

My throat goes dry, and I nod, unable to deny it. I want him, which is why I was hoping we could have the rules. "I do, but . . ."

His body presses against mine, and my hand grips the doorknob behind me. "But?"

I lift up a little, no longer caring much about rules or boundaries and very much caring about Oliver's body touching mine. My fingers slide against the strands of his hair. "We can make the rules up later." I pull his mouth to mine and kiss him deeply.

Oliver pushes the door open so we stumble inside. Then he shoves me against the wall, pulling my shirt over my head. Our mouths find each other again as the frantic need builds faster.

We kiss, only stopping to remove an item of clothing for the other.

His hand hooks under my leg, lifting it as he shoves my skirt up. "No underwear?" he asks as his mouth finds my neck.

"I told you, I don't wear any."

"I'm going to enjoy this."

I very much think that's true for the both of us.

Smiling, I pull his mouth back to mine as he slips his finger into me. I moan when his thumb grazes my clit.

Oliver pushes me higher, not playing or teasing. It's frantic, hot, and I am desperate for him.

"Please," I beg.

"I can't . . ." he says, almost regretfully. "I can't fucking wait."

"Don't wait."

It doesn't matter that we're in the foyer, I need him so much. I want to lose myself in him—in us.

"Maren, I—"

I take his face in my hands, staring at him. "Take me, Oliver. Now."

He lifts me a little and then slams into me. My head falls back against the wall as he sets an unrelenting pace. He fucks me so hard that, before I can grab ahold of any semblance of restraint, the orgasm hits.

I scream his name, clawing at his back as he pumps deeper.

As I'm coming down from my high, he lets out a deep groan and follows me over the edge. He shudders a second before his legs give out and we sink to the floor with him still inside me.

"That was . . ."

"Reckless," I finish for him, feeling the stickiness between us.

He looks down, realizing the same thing that I just did. "Fuck! Shit! How the hell could I—"

"It's okay. I have an IUD, so we don't have to worry about that, and I'm clean. I get tested religiously."

"I'm clean too."

I sigh. "Good, then we have nothing to worry about."

"Let's get dressed and . . . see the house."

"Sounds like a plan."

Once we're cleaned up, we grab the bags we left by the door and go deeper into the house. The view from the living room is breathtaking. There are floor-to-ceiling windows that take up the entire back wall of the house, giving an almost uninterrupted view of the ocean.

"This is amazing," Oliver says, standing beside me.

"I love this house. She had it redone about two years ago so it was more in line with current trends. Even before she did that, this place was special. There's something so calming about the ocean. It's probably why I love where I live now."

"My family owned a beach house in North Carolina my whole life. I didn't spend a ton of time there. We went once a summer, but I've always felt more at home in the mountains."

Another thing we're opposites on. I tuck that little fact away for later when I try to remember why I shouldn't want more.

"I loved the resort, but I can't imagine not hearing the waves."

He shrugs. "I can't imagine not being in the forest. However, this, being here now, is really great."

I lean my head against his shoulder. "Why is that?"

"Because I've been killing myself with the resort. All of us have been going nonstop for months, trying to get things done. Since I'm the only one who isn't married with kids, I've had a heavier load to bear."

Almost everyone at Cole Security Forces is married with kids. Jackson and Mark have growing families and put a lot of emphasis on how important it is to balance. Natalie works from home a lot of the time when Liam is deployed or when she just needs to be there for her kids. Gretchen and Ben are on rotating shifts so one of them is always home with the kids, and there are no set hours, so everyone just does what works best for their situation. The only thing they ask is that we show up when we're needed.

It's great, and I fully support their priorities, but being single—it sucks. I'm always there. I work a lot, and sometimes it feels like the expectation for me to fill the gaps is greater because there is no one relying on me at home. I can be available to the company.

"It's hard when people think all you have is work, and that, because you're single, you should always be the one to sacrifice." I understand that sentiment all too well.

"They never say it is that way."

"But you still feel it."

He laughs once. "We're a pair, huh?"

"Overachievers with a high sense of responsibility?"

"That's one way to put it." He wraps his arm around me, pulling me against his side. "How about for the next five days we don't think about work or family or anything but having a good time?"

I look up into his blue eyes. "Do you think we can?"

"I think I can focus on much better things."

My stomach flutters at the lusty look in his eyes. "And where would you direct all that attention?"

He shifts me so I'm standing in front of him, looking up at his face. "You."

"Me?"

"You."

"Well, I think I can get on board with that."

twenty

OLIVER

I wake up to the blaring noise of my phone ringing. When I roll over, Maren isn't in the bed, which is odd, but I don't dwell on it when I see it's Alex calling and it's almost noon.

"Alex," I say with a huff.

"Married?"

"Egypt?"

My brother is a good guy, smart, funny, and not all that good-looking. He loved what he went to school for and absolutely hated our parents forcing him to work for our dad's inns.

After we walked away from the family company, he ended up taking a job offer that took him to Egypt. That means, we are down a Parkerson and Alex is out of the loop.

"Say what you want, I think my going to Egypt was a less surprising thing than you getting married."

"I'm assuming you know the whole story."

I sit up, rubbing my hands over my face.

"I know some of it. Josh was my source, so you know it's probably half bullshit. But I hear she's hot."

"Hey, that's my wife you're talking about."

167

Alex chuckles. "So, are you going to tell me everything or just let me make up my own version?"

"Your own version sounds fine."

"Ollie, stop being your normal joke-away-serious-things-guy idiot and tell me what the hell happened."

After throwing my legs over the side of the bed, I fill him in on how Maren and I came to be and how every stitch in our ridiculously sewn plan came undone. When I say it all aloud, I feel like a dumbass. This was destined to fail from the beginning.

"Sounds like we can blame Stella for this mess."

I nod, feeling vindicated. "Yes, yes we can. I said no, and she got all up in my feelings about doing the right thing. It is her fault."

"Agree."

"Now that we have that settled, I feel better."

"I'm sure you do." Alex snorts. "You shouldn't because, while you're cleaning up your mess of a life, she's happy with her husband."

"Still, I get to blame her, which we all know she hates."

"This is true. Do you like her?"

I jerk my head quickly. "Stella? Of course. She's our sister."

"You know I meant your wife."

I look toward the door, wondering where she is and if she can hear me. "I like her a lot. She's great, and . . . if we didn't do such a bang-up job fucking this up from the beginning, who knows . . ."

That's a lie. I know. I never would have allowed myself the possibility of a relationship. I really want no part in it. I'm happy alone. I'm safe alone. I don't have to worry or wonder if the girl I'm head over heels in love with wants to boink someone else. There's a lot of ease in that kind of living. I've had less stress, sex, and misery thanks to it.

Although, the sex part isn't exactly true anymore.

"Sorry to hear that, man. I didn't just call to bust your balls though," Alex says before he clears his throat.

"Oh? Did you finally decide to come home?"

"Nope. I am actually staying here. For good. I met someone, and . . . she's amazing. She's like, legit royalty. Her family isn't too happy she's falling in love with an American, but she's happy, so they're allowing it for now."

Jesus. Him too? "Dude, it's been like, a few months?"

"You married a girl after two weeks, let's not judge."

"You're getting married?"

"Not yet, but we will. She's the one, Oliver."

This is great, but I'm also sad. I hoped that Alex would go to Egypt, live his dream, realize it wasn't actually his dream, and come home. I know that makes me a selfish dick, but part of the excitement of opening the resort was us doing it together.

Regardless, my brother deserves to be happy and if that means Egypt, then so be it.

"Then hold on to her, Alex. With both hands."

"I plan to. I'm going to let everyone else know soon so I need you to keep this between us."

"Of course."

"Listen, I know it's early and you're on your honeymoon, so I'll let you go. Just . . . I talked to Delia yesterday, and she seems to think there's more to you and your new bride than you're admitting. Take your own advice and hold on if there's a chance it could work."

"Look at you, the world-traveling philosopher. Thanks for the call, we'll talk more when I get back."

"You got it."

I toss my phone to the nightstand and go to find the woman who should be in bed where I can do rude things to her. Today is the first day of our vacation. I refuse to call it a honeymoon because that would mean we're really married and I'm going to end up divorced. So, I'd rather not go there. This is a vacation. That's it.

I find Maren sitting out on the deck that overlooks the ocean with a book in her hand. She's so damn gorgeous. Even doing nothing.

"Hey," I say as I walk out by her.

She looks up, shoves the book behind her back, and smiles. "Hey, Sleepyhead. I was wondering if you were going to wake up anytime soon."

I grin. "Well, someone kept me up all night."

"And that someone isn't even sorry about that."

I take a step closer to her. "What are you reading?"

"Reading? I'm not reading anything."

I raise one brow. "You had a book."

"Oh, this? Yeah, it's nothing. Come on, we can walk the beach and then take the golf cart into town."

"Why are you being so elusive?"

"I'm not," she says a bit too quickly. Maren stands, holding the book behind her.

"Okay." It's clear she doesn't want me to see what she's reading. "I'm going to grab my shoes and we can head out."

"Great."

Maren turns, and I pounce on her, grabbing the book. "Hey!"

Being that she's a half foot shorter than I am, it isn't hard to keep it out of her reach while I read the title. *A Guide to Him Giving You What You Need in Bed Without Asking.*

I stare, reading it over again. "Do you . . ." I clear my throat. "Have complaints?"

I know for a fact that I am not selfish in bed. I make sure she's satisfied before I find my release.

Maren covers her face with her hands. "Ugh! This is like the worst few weeks of my life!" She drops her hands and looks at me. "Okay, so remember that I packed for my wedding and honeymoon *before* you ended up as the groom. So, I didn't get that book for you, I got it for the *other* Oliver. And, no, I have zero fucking complaints. Like, not even a blip of a complaint. I just didn't bring anything else to read, and well, I bought it, so I figured . . ."

I toss it over on the table and laugh. "So, you're reading it for fun?"

"It's very educational."

"And unnecessary."

"How so? Are you going to be my lifelong sex partner?"

I shrug. "We could always do that."

Maren huffs. "Stop it."

"I'm saying it's unnecessary because, if you want something—anything—you just have to ask me or tell me. Any guy who has the privilege of being with you should want to do the same thing—to give you joy and pleasure. If your ex didn't, well, it's a good thing you didn't marry him."

"Believe me, it was just one more thing I was worried about."

"Sex was that bad?"

"It wasn't bad," she defends. "It just was . . . boring. From the beginning, it was strange, and if I compare it at all to us, it's not even in the same universe."

"What you're saying is that I'm a sex god?"

She rolls her eyes. "With an ego the size of Texas."

"I didn't hear you say no."

"Fine, you're a sex god with impressive skills and a dick that is perfect. Happy now?"

"Yes," I answer with a grin. "Quite."

"Let's go before something else mortifying happens."

"Do you have more goodies in your bag?"

"Wouldn't you like to know?" Maren smirks.

Yes, I very much would.

My stomach rumbles, and she laughs. "Go get dressed and we'll get you fed."

"Food is good, but sex is better."

"Food is necessary and sex is later." She gives me a kiss on my cheek. "I'll see you in a few."

I get dressed and meet her downstairs. We head to the

golf cart. It's pretty cool that we can get around this little town on just that. We're outside of the main tourist area, but Maren says there's still a lot to do here, which works fine for me.

"Where to, wife?"

She grins. "Let's go to the right, there's a bar and I know the owners. They have the best drinks and appetizers anywhere."

"Your wish is my command."

When we pass other golf carts, the driver honks, so I honk back and offer a wave.

"Is that normal?"

"No," Maren says as the next person we pass does it.

"Okay, then what the hell is going on?"

"I have no idea."

I pull over, wondering if maybe something is wrong with the cart or it's some alert system I've never heard of. When I get around to the front, I see what it is.

"Your aunt must've been busy," I say, staring at the bumper.

"What? Why?" She comes out to stand beside me. "Oh dear God."

Yeah. Painted on the front is: Just Married.

"Congrats!" Another golf cart driver yells before the guy in the back calls out. "Kiss her!"

It's like being at the wedding again. However, kissing Maren isn't something I mind doing, so I pull her to me before dipping her back and planting my lips on hers.

When I pull her up, she's laughing. "You know, when you do that, it makes it look like we're really married."

"We might be."

That is something I should be furious about, but I can't seem to muster the energy to care. Maybe it's the sea air. Maybe it's because I'm having a shitload of fun. Maybe it's the girl in my arms, but I feel at ease.

Maren and I have no expectations, and whatever the hell

we're doing, it's not a chore. It's nice to be with her, and the sex is fucking fantastic—even without the help of a book.

"We'll get everything taken care of. I promise."

I try to come up with a response, but Maren's phone rings and her face goes pale. "It's Linda."

Please don't let this be the call. I don't want to see her cry and hurt.

She swipes the screen, and I take her hand in mine. "Hi," she says carefully.

A long breath leaves her lungs, and she smiles, looking at me. "Yes, Daddy, we're having fun. We are heading to Maggie's bar. Yes." She pauses. "I know. I'm glad you called. I wanted to ask you about the farm." Maren looks to me before shaking her head. "How? Why didn't you ever tell me?" Her eyes mist over before she pulls the phone down to relay information to me. "Apparently, he bought it a while back with the contingent that I could only get it once I was married."

Wow. "Seems there was more than one reason your dad wanted you to get married."

She nods and then goes back to the call. "I love you for this and I can never thank you enough. More importantly, Daddy, how are you feeling?"

They talk for a bit longer, and the relief I feel is immense. I really like her father. He's a good man who clearly loves his little girl. My father doesn't have a tenth of that much love for his kids.

"Sure, he's right here." Maren hands me the phone mouthing *sorry*.

I clear my throat. "Hi, Mr. McVee."

"None of that, son, we're family now."

"Of course. How was the trip home?"

"It was fine, Linda and I took our time, exploring as we drove. I just want to say how happy I am to have gained you as a son-in-law. It's clear how much you love Maren, and . . . well, Linda and I were beyond honored to grant you guys the deed to the farm. It has been in Maren's family for a very long time. I know you have your resort, and she has her job, but the farm has been well cared for, and I'm confident you two will enjoy it."

"I'm sure Maren truly appreciates it," I say, not wanting to elaborate.

"I'll let you two get back to your honeymoon. Have fun."

"We will, and we're both glad you're home and feeling well."

I hand the phone back to her so she can say goodbye before we climb back into the golf cart. "He sounds good."

"He does."

"What did he say to you?"

"That we'd enjoy the farm."

Maren looks at me, her lower lip clenched between her teeth. "Will you go there with me?"

"To the farm?"

I know that's what she means, but I'm stalling to think through this. Maren and I aren't a real couple. She doesn't love me or want to be with me. I was an available Oliver and a friend, nothing more. Yes, we're sort of married and having lots of sex, but I want to keep any emotions in a box so when she walks away, no one is hurt.

I need to avoid being fucking hurt again.

She tucks her hair behind her ear. "Yeah, I think it would be fun. You could see it, and we could maybe spend a day or two there. It's been forever, and . . ."

"I'll probably be really busy with the resort since we officially open fully in three weeks. I'm not sure about the time I have."

"Of course," she says quickly. "I wasn't thinking. I'm sorry."

I feel like a complete asshole. "It's fine, maybe we can do it before the resort opens."

She turns, her face lighting up before she throws herself

174

at me. "Really? Oh, Oliver, thank you! You are too amazing."

"It's nothing."

It's everything.

"There isn't a single thing about you or what has happened that is nothing. It means a lot that I'll get to go there with you."

Don't let that sink in. Don't let it become more.

"I'm happy that you feel that way."

Maren kisses my cheek. "Let's get lunch, and then"—her voice grows husky—"I can thank you in other ways."

I throw the golf cart into drive and head to the bar, looking forward to the "other ways" she has in mind.

~

"Are you all right?" Maren asks as she hands me a glass of ginger ale.

"I'm fine. I think it was the food."

She chuckles. "You barely ate."

I was incredibly impatient at lunch. I had maybe a bite or two of my food and three beers, but when we got back and I was ready for naked Maren time, my stomach revolted. I ended up taking a long nap and waking up around dinner time, feeling a hundred percent better. However, she's being a mother hen and won't let me off the couch until she's convinced I'm fine.

"I ate a little."

She hands me a cracker. "Not enough to soak up the beer. Now, just rest, and we'll find something else to do tonight."

"I'd like to be doing you."

"I would like that too, but . . ."

"But?"

"You're sick."

I roll my eyes. "I am not sick. I *got* sick, which isn't the same. I'm perfectly fine now."

I grab her, pulling her to my chest. "Oliver!"

"See, sick men can't do that."

"I think men who want sex can move mountains."

She's not wrong.

"How about we go relax in the hot tub?" Maren in a bathing suit—or even naked—would be a good evening.

"Are you sure your stomach is fine?" she asks.

"Maren, I'm a grown ass man. I got sick a few times, napped it off, and I'm good. It was probably food poisoning or something stupid."

"Okay. If you're fine, then we'll do that. I'll go turn it on while you get changed."

Since we're at the very end of the season, everything is quiet. It's almost like being on a private beach. I grab my bathing suit, opt against it, and wrap myself in a towel. As I'm heading down the stairs, Maren ducks into one of the five bathrooms.

"I'll meet you down there after I get changed."

"Okay. Feel free to come down naked," I offer.

When I get outside, I look around, making sure none of the neighbors can see this area. Since the house is on stilts, the hot tub is under the house and has a privacy wall on three sides. The only way someone could see us is if they were on the beach or standing on the dunes. This will be perfect.

I sink into the hot water, feeling the stress melt away, and leaning my head back, I close my eyes, and relax. It's been a crazy few months, and these last two weeks have been fucking insane. I never thought I would pretend to marry someone only to end up actually married to the girl who flipped my life around.

But here I am, falling for my wife even though I want no part of it.

I don't want to like her. I don't want to see how beautiful, smart, and loving she is, but then she does stuff like take care of me while I'm sick or go out of her way to make her father happy, and I can't help it.

There are no answers here. Maren and I won't be anything, and trying to think otherwise is foolish. I've done that before, and I will not go down that road again. So, I'll allow myself to lust after her, have as much sex as possible, and then go back to my simple life.

"Well, don't you look comfortable?" Maren's voice is beside me, her hand sliding against my arm.

Instantly, I'm hard.

This woman is going to be the death of me.

"I'm something, all right, but comfortable isn't the case any longer."

She presses to my side, the water barely covering her breasts. Yes, she's naked. "I'm sorry to hear that. What can I do to make it better?"

I love how playful she is.

"How about you come a little closer."

"Like this?"

She scoots a little closer, but her hand wraps around my cock.

"That is a good start."

"I agree." Her hand moves up and down slowly.

"I thought you were worried I was sick."

"I thought you said you were a grown man and were fine?"

I am more than fine. I'm on fire and need her more than ever. "I'm not sick."

"Good." Her voice is soft. "I want you, Oliver."

"I want you."

"However," she says coyly. "We're not having sex."

Well, that's not going to work for me. "And why not?"

"Because whether you're grown or not, you were sick, and as your wife, whether it's real or not, it's my job to care for you."

I grip her waist, hauling her on top of me so her legs straddle my hips. "I think it's also my job to do the same." I cup her breasts.

Maren's eyes flutter, and a soft moan escapes her lips as I rub my thumbs over her nipples. She shudders as her fingers wrap around my wrists.

"No, not this time." She shifts my arms so they are resting along the back of the tub. "Stay that way."

I'm not usually one who likes not to have control during sex, but the way she's looking at me—a little hesitant, a little hopeful—causes me to nod. I'll see where she wants this to go. All roads lead to happiness with the way she's licking her plump lips.

Maren grins. "Don't move."

"Or what?"

"Or I stop."

"I'll do my best," I promise. My fingers grip the sides so I have something to hold on to. I have a feeling this is going to be equal parts heaven and hell.

She leans in, pressing her lips to mine for a brief kiss. "Good, I plan to do mine." Her fingers wrap around my cock again as she pumps in a steady rhythm. "I want you to rest and let me do all the work."

"I won't move." She keeps going, pumping me harder, faster as her lips move down my neck. "I want to see you."

"See me?"

"Lift up so I can stare at your perfect breasts." Maren does as I ask, and I can't stop the small smile that forms because she gave me back the control of the situation without realizing it. I want to see if she'll give me more. "Let me kiss them."

Her eyes widen a little, and she sinks back down. "No."

"You said you wanted to take care of me, this is what I need."

"I don't think so."

I let go of the back of the tub, and her hand releases

178

instantly. "Maren . . ."

"Don't. Move."

As soon as I'm positioned again, she resumes jerking me off.

"I keep waiting for this yearning to stop, but the longer I'm around you, the more I want you," she confesses. "You make me feel beautiful, powerful, and cherished."

"You are those things," I say, and my grip tightens. This feels so fucking good. "You're more than that too."

"Kiss me," Maren commands.

I lean forward, wanting her mouth, wanting her, and we collide. I no longer hold the back of the tub, and I have her face in my grasp. I kiss her deeply, letting our tongues slide together as we both gasp. If all I'm allowed to do is this, then I'm going to make it the best kiss she's ever had. I play with her, retreating when she tries to go forward and over-powering her when she relents. I nip at her lip, pulling it between my teeth and then kissing it. Over and over, we do this dance, all while her hand pumps my cock.

"I need you," I tell her.

She moves her lips to my ear. "Sit up on the edge. I need something more."

"Sweetheart, not like this."

"Like what?"

"Where some asshole might be looking at you, seeing how fucking perfect you are, how beautiful you look without any clothes on."

While I know we have privacy, there's no way I want anyone else to watch this.

Maren stands, water sliding down her beautiful body. "No one will see." She moves over to the buttons and turns off the lights in the hot tub. It's completely dark as her finger slides down my chest. "Sit up on the ledge and let me suck your dick."

I do as she asks, and as she takes me deep in her throat, I decide that married life isn't bad at all.

twenty-one
MAREN

Tonight is our last night. First thing in the morning, we head back to Willow Creek Valley and then I drive back to Virginia Beach. It's been an amazing and much needed few days of relaxation. We've laughed, watched movies, had more sex than two humans probably should, and honestly, I'm insanely happy.

Oliver is . . . well, I like him. I like him a lot. I am falling so hard for him, and I don't know what to do about it.

I know the rules, and it's fine because I want the same thing he does—nothing. Only I want him and that's crazy.

Since keeping him isn't an option, I refuse to think about it and resolve myself to the plan I started with.

Denial of all feelings.

I smooth my hands over my black dress, shifting it into place. My hair falls in beach waves that brush the middle of my back, and my makeup looks soft but alluring. I look good, if I do say so myself.

I sit on the bed, slipping my heels on and buckling the clasp on the ankle. Stella and Devney may be assholes for the lack of sleeping attire, but they did a good job with these shoes.

I pick up my phone to send Devney a quick text.

Me: I'm still mad about the repack, but thanks for the heels.

Devney: That was Stella. I almost cried when I saw her shoe collection. There were literally hundreds of pairs all neatly aligned. It was magical. I'm jealous you two are the same size.

I laugh as I imagine Devney drooling over rows of shoes.

Me: Sounds fun.

Devney: It was. How are things with Oliver?

I know she's over him and he's over her, but it's . . . odd. I'm not sure what is off limits to talk about or if it's fair to Oliver. I'll stick to vague and friendly.

Me: We're having a great time. It was much needed for us both.

The three dots appear, dancing on my messages, but then stop. Then start. Then stop again before a text appears.

Devney: Is this . . . odd for you?

Me: Yes.

Devney: I am not upset. I want you to know that. Sean and I

talked a lot about this, and I'm truly happy for you both. I honestly wish you guys would give it a real shot.

I do too. I just won't allow myself to hope.

Me: We know what this is. It's only odd because we both have . . . you know.
Devney: Seen his penis?

I start laughing.

Me: That.
Devney: Well, at least it's a good one, and I'm not sending you apologies.
Me: Oh dear God. I'm going to dinner now. I'll be home tomorrow, so we can catch up then. I need to see if I have to murder my boss and find a divorce attorney or if I can tell Oliver we're all good.
Devney: Good luck and have fun tonight.

I put the phone in my purse and stand, feeling like a newborn calf that hasn't found its legs yet. I teeter and then right myself as I head downstairs.

Ollie is standing by the windows, looking out at the ocean that's invisible in the inky darkness. His broad shoulders, which carry everyone's burdens, are covered in a navy-blue suit. His dark brown hair is slicked back as if he ran his hands through it and it stayed. I lean against the wall, looking at him, wondering what my life is going to be like once I no longer see him like this.

Will we be friends?

Will we talk?

Will he come to my father's funeral? My mother's farm?

Do I need him?

He turns. His blue eyes go a little wide before he grins. "You look stunning."

"You do as well."

Oliver walks to me and brushes a piece of hair off my face. "Our first last date."

My heart flutters at the date part, but then I register he said last. I force a smile, hoping it appears real enough. "It is."

"Kind of crazy our first date was our wedding."

I laugh. "Well, maybe the rehearsal."

"That's true." Oliver looks away and then back to me. "I've had a great time with you. Not the sex, well, not *only* the sex. It's been more than I ever thought it could be. In another time . . . maybe we could've . . ."

Tell him, Maren. Tell him how you feel. Tell him it doesn't have to be the last date. Tell him you want to go on another date.

I don't tell him because what I hear next in my head is a reminder of another rejection that would come my way.

"I'm glad that we both feel the same," I say. "If we had felt this way in college, who knows, but now we have our lives and priorities."

His lips mash together, and he nods. "And, tomorrow, we'll return to them. But tonight, let's forget they exist."

I adjust his tie, mostly because I just can't look at him. I'm not strong enough to gaze into his eyes and keep this part of the lie. My heart is calling out to him when there's no chance for us.

We are only meant to be this.

"I like that plan."

"I hoped you would, being the planner you are."

184

I nod, not trusting my voice, and let him take my hand and lead me outside. Oliver opens my car door and then climbs in next to me.

"Where are we going?" I ask. He said he wanted to surprise me for our last night, and I was supposed to wear something formal.

"You'll see once we get there."

"You know I hate surprises."

Ollie laughs. "I figured since you love plans so much."

I've always hated them, since I was a kid. Maybe it's because every time I've been taken off guard, a tragedy happened. My mother dying, a colleague being shot, losing someone we'd been trailing and having it result in someone being hurt. It's never been a good thing.

Now I'm forced to sit and watch the scenery without making myself crazy with wonder.

"You're fidgeting," Oliver points out.

"I don't like being completely unaware of what I'm doing."

"Are you worried I might be taking you somewhere to kill you?"

I raise a brow. "Is that a possibility?"

"Depends."

"On?"

He grins. "On if you stop fidgeting and just trust me or not."

I lean my head back, looking at him. "Trust isn't something I usually give easily."

"I'm not all that great at it either."

He is better at it than he thinks.

"Could've fooled me. We had to trust everyone who knew the secret the last two weeks."

Oliver glances at me. "Those were my siblings. I would trust them with my life."

Which is maybe why I was able to as well. I shift again, looking out the window and spinning the wedding ring on my finger. My nerves are trifold. I have no idea where we're going, I don't know what I'm feeling, and I don't know how to plan for heartache.

This is the end. The last night before we walk away from what has been the best weeks of my life. I don't want that.

I want more.

I want it all.

I want *him*.

He takes my hand. "We're almost there. I promise, I want tonight to be fun and also special."

"Why?" I ask before I can stop myself.

"Why what?"

"What does it matter if it's special? Tonight is the end."

We're stopped at a red light so he turns to look at me. "The end doesn't mean it has to be bad. We're friends, Maren, we always will be. I like to think that, after all we've gone through, we can at least have a happy ending."

Tears start to prick at the back of my eyes, but I blink them away. This isn't a happy ending. This is horrible. This is not what I want, but it's what he wants.

He wants freedom, and I can't even be angry about it. It's not like we've been together for months, and he changed his mind. I will not make this man suffer any more than he already has.

"We've both been burned."

"Yes, we have," Oliver says, his hands tightening around the wheel a bit.

Oliver may always act like life is fun and grand, but I know what it's like to wear a smile when you're dying inside.

The first girl he loved broke his heart.

Devney destroyed it.

He's safeguarded himself against that kind of pain, and I can't blame him for it.

I reach out, placing my hand on his forearm. "I'm sorry that things didn't work out the way you hoped."

"Meaning?"

186

I let my hand drop. "You went through with marrying me when you deserved to have that experience with the woman you loved and wanted to spend your life with. And I'm sorry that any woman has ever hurt you."

"I'm not broken over it. Devney made the right choice."

"Doesn't mean it wasn't shitty for you."

He shrugs. "It was, but I'm fine. I have a good life, and she and I never would've been truly happy. Besides, I was meant to be on the market and up for sampling. Which you're welcome for." His voice is playful as he wiggles his brows.

I can't help but laugh a little. "You're right. I'm very glad I got to enjoy the goods."

"There's much more of that for tonight."

I roll my eyes. In the last five days, I've had more sex than I have most months. It's been fantastic, but I am not sure how much more my body can take. That doesn't mean I'm not going to find out.

When he pulls to a stop, it only takes me a second to realize that we're at the docks.

"You're going to dump my body in the ocean?" I ask.

"Hell no, I've watched enough murder mysteries to know how to get rid of the body much more efficiently."

"Good to know."

Oliver helps me out of the car, looping my hand on his arm. "Come on, our dinner awaits."

We walk down the pier and toward a yacht—or, at least, I would call it a yacht.

"Are we going on that?"

"We are."

He helps me across the gangway and onto the boat, where there is already a gentleman waiting for us. "Welcome, Mr. and Mrs. Parkerson."

I turn to Oliver, who smiles. "Well, it's kind of true."

"Yes, I guess it is."

"Did I say the names wrong?" the staff member asks.

"No, Michael, you didn't. This is my wife, Maren, and we're ready to head out if you are."

Michael nods. "Of course. I recommend you both go down to the living quarters until we get out a little deeper. The beginning part of the ride can be a little choppy this time of year. I'll be down shortly after to get your orders and have the chef start to prepare the meals."

"Thank you," Oliver says smoothly. He takes my arm, and we head to the door Michael indicated. "Watch your step."

"Ollie, what is this?"

"A boat . . ."

I huff. "I know it's a boat, but all this is too much."

"It's a wedding gift."

"Someone gave us a boat?" I ask with excitement.

He laughs. "No one gave us a boat, but we get to spend a few hours on it."

"Oh. Duh."

It's not a far stretch, we did get a house.

He takes me down the narrow steps into the living quarters. It's a lot bigger than I expected. There is a large couch against the back wall, a television opposite of it, and two chairs on each side. The room is gorgeous and painted in beige hues with four port hole windows along the left wall. You'd never imagine this was a boat. It looks almost like an apartment.

"There's a bathroom to the left and two bedrooms toward the front. There's another level below which is the staff's quarters and kitchen."

"Oliver . . ."

"I wanted us to do something nice that wasn't for show or for anyone else."

"This is a wedding gift from you?" I ask hesitantly.

"Yes, I called in a favor."

I smile so wide that my cheeks hurt and then launch myself into his arms.

"You are amazing! Amazing!"

"You've said so."

"I'm saying it again." I take his cheeks in my hands and kiss him.

He leans back, a grin on his lips. "What was that for?"

"Because this is so sweet. You're so sweet."

Because no one has ever done something like this for me.

He shifts his weight. "If this were real—if this were . . . different, I would do so much more."

If.

What a horrible word. If I were someone else. If I were better. If I were worth it. That one-syllable, two-letter word that could be filled with hope is, instead, my pain.

"You'll find someone, Oliver. One day, this woman is going to come into your life and she'll make you want to take chances again. She'll be worth putting your heart on the line for because she'll know how perfect, selfless, and wonderful you are."

He opens his mouth to say something, but then stops. We sway a little as the boat moves and he walks us over to the couch. After a minute of silence, he speaks. "I gave up on that dream a few years ago."

My heart is pounding so hard because I know I can't hold back. I don't just want sex with this man. I'm not saying we should be married, but I want to date him. I want to see if this chemistry and the way we are together can last.

I go through all the options in my head. The answers that may come from this, but I know if I don't take the risk, I'll regret it always.

"What if . . ."

"Don't," he says as his thumb grazes my cheek. "Not because I haven't wondered the same thing but because we both know that no matter what the answer to that question is, it won't matter."

"Ollie," I say pleadingly. "We don't know that."

He sighs, sitting back. "You're an analyst. You know

189

better than anyone how this could go, right?" I nod. "Then tell me what the most plausible outcome is?"

I don't want to answer him. I don't want the bitter truth to touch my tongue. The lie forms, a pretty illusion of what could be where we're happy, but I can't bring myself to say it. Because Oliver and my outcome is statistically bound to fail. We are destined for destruction, and I will not lie to this man, not even for just a little more time with him.

I wipe my cheeks. "We fall apart."

"Why?"

"Because of our jobs, mostly. I'll never leave my team and I'd never ask you to give up your resort."

Our fingers lace together. "You love the beach, I love the mountains. You want kids, and I won't ever let a child live like I did. Not to mention, we started this entire thing off on a lie."

The sad part is, he's not wrong.

"Sometimes it's just easy to forget all that."

"I know, but then I remember all the things we've said about what we want. I remember how it feels when you want something and it isn't yours to have. I've been second choice one too many times."

"Who says you're second choice now?" I ask.

Oliver shakes his head. "You were going to marry another man named Oliver, and I pretended to be him. You and I didn't start this because we wanted to date. We did it to give your father a chance to walk you down the aisle. I'm literally the last choice here. You chose the other guy, your dad, and then me."

"That's not true."

But it is.

"I have made a series of bad choices when it comes to love, Maren. I've deluded myself far too many times, thinking that if I just loved enough or tried a little harder it would be fine. It never is. The truth doesn't change just because two people wonder or wish."

"Isn't that the very definition of wishing? Wanting something you know is out of reach but desiring it anyway. Wishes come true, Oliver."

When I look at him, the statistical outcome stops mattering and all I see is a future I want more than my next breath. The two of us would grow old together and split our time between the resort and Virginia Beach.

As if it were always right in front of me, a new set of events unfold, a new map drawing carving a path through a hypothetical life. Mark and Jackson would allow me to work from home when I went to visit him. Neither of us would have to give up anything.

All we have to do is be brave enough to take the first step.

He rests his forehead on mine. "I can't risk it on a wish and I can't be anyone's second choice."

I lean back, cradling his face in my hands. I understand his hesitancy, but sometimes you have to take a leap, and I'm about to jump headfirst. I lean in, pressing my lips to his. "You're not and I was wrong about our outcome because it's not defined. We can make it work if it's what we both want and I want you. Take a chance . . . for us."

Oliver doesn't respond with words, instead, my back is against the plush couch, his body on mine and he's kissing me. There's a difference this time that I can't explain. It's as though he's giving in as well as saying goodbye.

I chase that away, kissing him back.

"You make me want things," Oliver confesses, looking down at me. "Things I swore I'd never want again."

"We can have them. We just have to try."

He closes his eyes, resting his forehead on mine. "We can try."

When he kisses me this time, I don't feel goodbye, I just feel hope.

twenty-two

OLIVER

"I'll see you soon," I promise Maren, lingering so I don't have to let her get into her car and drive away.

Time moved far too fast for me. We're back in Willow Creek Valley, but she's getting ready to head home, which will officially begin our attempt at a long-distance marriage.

The irony of this is amusing.

"I'll come back in two weeks. I have a mission this week I need to be in the area for and then we have a lull."

"All right."

"Can I call you tonight?" Her voice is full of embarrassment.

"You better."

"I'm going to miss you, Ollie."

I pull her to my chest, loving how easily she fits there. "I'll miss you, but thankfully, I'll have the memories of this morning to carry me through."

Her cheeks are painted a lovely shade of pink, and I imagine her naked, hands tied over her head, gripping the headboard as I ate her out. I fucked her so hard I pulled a muscle in my groin, but the memory will carry me through the weeks.

"Yes, well . . ." She steps closer, her finger touching the

hull of my throat. "Next time, I think maybe I should tie you up."

"You do?"

"Yup. Then I can torture you."

"Did you forget the hot tub?"

Maren smiles. "I'll never forget that."

I am a lucky man to have this woman. "Neither will I. Now, get your sexy ass back in that car and call me when you get home."

She leans in, kissing me again. "I will. Don't go marrying any other damsels in distress."

"I'll do my best."

Maren hesitates at the door to the car. "We're going to make this work, Oliver."

Her determination makes me believe it's possible. I'm not sure how, but she seems resolved.

"We'll figure it out," I say before kissing her forehead.

That's all we really can do. We'll try, and if it fails, then . . . I won't be shocked.

"I'll find out tomorrow what Mark did with the license."

"Yeah, that would be great."

He hasn't answered his phone the last few days, but Natalie told Maren that he's dealing with a situation and that she'd have answers for her when she returned. Whatever that means.

I have a gut feeling it means we're now legally married.

"I should go . . ."

I nod. "Yes, before it gets too late."

We kiss again, and the knot in my stomach grows. I don't want her to leave. I want to pull her into my arms, carry her to my bed, and make love to her again. I want Maren with me all the time. It's just not the reality we face.

She sighs and then gets in the car. We wave to each other one more time, and I watch her taillights fade away down the driveway.

I have no idea how much time passes before I feel a

hand grip my shoulder. "And how is the blushing groom and his new bride?" Grayson asks.

"Fuck off."

"Glad to hear the honeymoon was fun."

It was more than fun. It was perfect. However, I know how my asshat siblings are, and I'm not giving them anything they can torture me about.

"How's the resort?"

Gray sighs. "It's been fine. We had a few small issues, but we handled them. We have two rooms booked, but the guests won't be here for two more weeks. It isn't great, but it's something."

"It'll take a little time, we knew this." It's hard to open a new business and getting people to spend a night in a new establishment is harder. It doesn't help that Melia Lake isn't well-known on the map yet. The Firefly Resort is the first real lodging opening. Our hope is that more stores or restaurants follow our lead, and we can build the town up. After all, Willow Creek Valley was only popular after The Park Inn inspired the town to be eclectic.

"Yeah, but I hoped for a bit more for opening week. I guess we'll spend this time making sure those two families love it."

I shrug. "We built it, they will come."

He laughs at my botched quote from the movie we all loved. "I sure fucking hope so. Otherwise, my daughters are going to be in trouble when it comes to college."

We all risked a lot financially, and for Grayson, sometimes it feels like too much. "Do you regret it?"

"Not a single second. I worry, but that's par for the course."

"Yeah. I think this will all work out." I'm not just talking about the resort. I mean with Maren too.

Gray tilts his head. "All kidding aside, what happened with Maren?"

I look at my older brother, who has always been there

for me. He and I had a different relationship from what I had with my other siblings. Where Josh was the father figure, always bossing us around, Grayson was the brother who would hand me a beer and tell me not to say anything. He's who I talked to when things were bad and when our father fucked up, he came to my aid without hesitation.

He's been my best friend, and I know I can tell him, but I'm not sure what this is or how to explain it.

"I think I'm falling in love with her."

"You think?"

"It's too fucking soon. We didn't even decide to date until last night."

He grins, and we make our way toward the entrance. "I think it's funny that you think you have a choice of when it happens or how fast. You were falling in love with her before the wedding. All of us saw it. Also, I won the bet."

Great, another fucking bet. "What was it this time?"

"That you'd be in love with her before you got back."

"Who lost?"

"Josh."

Of course he did. "What did he bet?"

"That it would take her leaving for you to admit it."

"So, you all thought it was going to happen?"

He nods. "Yup. Even Alex, and he hasn't even seen you two together."

Alex can keep his stupid opinion to himself in Egypt. "He doesn't get a vote."

Gray laughs. "You tell him that. Anyway, Stella said it happened already and that she wasn't going to bet because she's not an infant."

"We don't deserve her," I say as the doors open.

"No, but we need her."

This is true. Stella comes around the check-in desk, rushing toward me. "Ollie!"

My sister pulls me in for a big hug, and I wince when she

196

hits my side. It doesn't hurt, but she slammed into it at just the right angle.

"Tell me everything. How is my sister-in-law? Is her dad doing okay?"

Since my siblings all know we signed the license, they have apparently claimed her.

"We don't know if we're actually legally married."

"Semantics. There was a wedding, vows, and you two had sex, so . . . sister-in-law status is acquired. How is Patrick doing?"

I give her the G-rated cliff notes of our trip and let her know that, as of this afternoon, Patrick was still holding in there.

She's planning to fly down to Georgia tomorrow if everything is okay at work.

"Are you going too?" Stella asks.

"No, I have to work."

"Right, but she needs you."

"So does the resort."

I'm not sure why she thinks I can just head off again.

Stella crosses her arms over her chest. "Oliver Parkerson, do you really think you're so needed here that you can't go? I mean, sure, you're important and all, but that doesn't mean some things don't trump work."

"Maren didn't ask me to go."

Gray laughs. "Dude . . . you know women."

"What does that mean?" My sister turns her fury on him. "*Women*?"

"It means that you all think we should have the power to read minds. How the hell is Oliver—or any man, for that matter—supposed to know what goes on in your heads? Half the time I don't even think *you* know what goes on in your head."

I nod in agreement, loving that Grayson is always so willing to stick his foot in his mouth.

"Excuse me?" Stella's head does that weird swirl that I swear only women can do.

"Don't act like you're confused. You know you do it too. I know you do because your husband has complained to me about it."

Oh, Gray, now you brought Jack into it. Bad move, brother.

"Jack has said this?" There's now a thick layer of frost around us.

Grayson, the idiot he is, starts to sputter as his error starts to become clear. "No. Yes. I mean, he hasn't said it so much as maybe agreed when I said it."

Stella slowly turns to look at me before going back to him. "I see. So, you were complaining about your own wife, who is a very lovely woman, I might add."

He throws his hands up. "Stop making this about you. I'm saying that if Maren wants Oliver to go with her, she should ask him to."

"Maybe she is afraid of being rejected."

I raise my hand. "I don't think so."

"Oh? And you're supposed to be the expert on women?" Great. The anger is back on me.

"I never said expert."

"Yes, because you don't have a vagina, therefore you can't be."

"Thank God for that or this conversation would be strange," I say under my breath.

Grayson chuckles and steps back. "Retract your claws, Stell. No one is saying they know better than you. Jesus, are you pregnant?"

She glares at him and then turns to me. "Look, Oliver, Maren is a woman who was dumped a few days before her wedding. She's in a state of trauma too. Her father is dying, her stepmother isn't an easy person to deal with, and she faked a relationship and fell for the guy. It's a lot, and I'm telling you now, she could be the strongest woman you know and she would still be vulnerable at the heart of it."

Then she turns to Grayson. "To answer your question, yes, I am pregnant. Jack doesn't know yet so keep your trap shut."

Gray and I smile. "Congratulations, Stella."

She softens a bit. "Thank you. It's taken a while, and it's still early. After losing a baby six months ago, I didn't have the heart to tell Jack yet."

I didn't know she lost a baby. She never said a word. "Stell—"

She lifts her hand. "It's fine. I'm happy, and so far, everything looks great. Just, I'm apparently a bit emotional and hormonal. Now, back to you . . . are you going to Georgia?"

As much as I'd like to keep talking about Stella, she'll never allow it. My sister loves nothing more than getting her way or her point across.

"She had a lot of chances to ask me, and she didn't." I take a step forward and breathe through my teeth.

"What is wrong with you?" Gray asks. "You're walking funny."

"I pulled a muscle."

"What? How?" Stella switches from annoyed to concerned so fast it's impressive.

I smirk, which causes my sister to make a gagging noise. "Gross."

"Jealous?" I toss back at her.

"That you pulled a muscle having sex? No."

"You should be," I say with a bit of male pride. "I clearly am doing it well."

Stella laughs. "That would be if she was walking funny, not you, dumbass."

"Whatever. I'm going to my office. I want to see if there are any leads for weddings we can book. The photographer called and let me know we should have images for the website by the end of the week."

"Good, that should help. Isn't Maren's aunt posting her article too?" Grayson asks.

"Yes, between that and the images on our website, we should be in good shape."

"We are. You? Not so much," Grayson points out as I hobble away.

It was worth it. So fucking worth it.

"Maybe you should go to the doctor . . ." Maren suggests over the phone.

"And say what? I had amazing sex with my wife and pulled something."

We've been married for less than a week, and she's already nagging. Okay, she isn't nagging so much as pushing because she's concerned. Still, I'm fine. It's swollen but nothing to be worried over.

"You can leave some of the details out, but I think you should at least go so you can walk."

"It doesn't hurt." Well, it doesn't hurt enough to tell her.

"Doesn't mean that you shouldn't have it checked out."

Maybe she has a point. "Will it make you happy?"

"Yes."

"Then who am I to deny you?" I say, grabbing my suit jacket off the back of the door.

"Are you unpacked?" she asks.

"For the most part."

She lets out a long sigh. "When I come back, I want to decorate your cabin if you'll let me."

"Come now," I suggest.

My place isn't anything to write home about, but it's far more comfortable than the RV I stayed in for over a year. The cabin is small but has everything I need, including running water and heat. That is a step up from the generator and thimble-sized hot water heater the RV had. As for decorations, I couldn't give two shits about them, but if it gets her here, I'm in.

"I wish I could. I need to get into the office and see if Mark is back yet."

"Still no answer?" I ask. It would be nice to know exactly what our status is so we aren't in the strange limbo anymore.

"No, but he'll be in today, and once I assess the team, what's going on, and whether we are legally married, I'll probably book my flight to Georgia."

"Any changes?"

Maren is quiet for a second. "No, but I assume he's gotten worse. I called Linda this morning, and she was in a mood. She said that if I cared, I would be there instead of waiting for him to be closer to death's door."

"Maren . . ."

"I know, I know," she says. "He wouldn't want me to just sit around, but she has a point. I need to go, and . . . well, I'll regret it if I don't."

She still hasn't said anything about wanting me there, but the thing is, I want to go. I care about her and want to help shoulder her burdens. We're trying to make this a real relationship, but we also need to keep up the charade about being married.

As her husband, I would go.

As her boyfriend, I want to go.

"What if I go with you?"

"What?" Her voice rises a few octaves.

"I can work remotely if I need to, but my siblings have everything in hand. I should be there with you . . . I *want* to be there with you."

She doesn't say anything. I can imagine her sitting there, calculating the words, creating a plan that has fifteen different contingencies before speaking.

"You want to go with me?"

"No, I want to *be there* with you. You shouldn't have to do this alone."

She sniffles. "If you're trying to get me to leave you, you're doing a shit job of convincing me you're not perfect."

"I'm not perfect."

Maren sighs deeply. "You might just be perfect for me."

And that's something that makes my heart pound. "Do you want me to go with you?"

"I want to be with you more than I want to be apart. So, yes, it would mean the world to me, and I think it would mean a lot to Daddy too."

"Then I'll see you in a few days."

That feels like a lifetime.

"One condition," Maren says before we disconnect.

"What?"

"You go to the doctor. We aren't going to be able to have sex if you can barely move."

"When you put it that way . . ." I say with a laugh. If I have to, I'll force myself to walk normally when I see her. Nothing is going to keep me from making love to her. Nothing.

twenty-three

MAREN

"So, how was the honeymoon?" Mark asks as he walks into my office.

"It was good. What's going on with the team?"

"You're going to give yourself an ulcer at this rate." He plops down in the chair across from me and gives me a rundown of what happened. Basically, the analyst who was helping out didn't jive well, leaving my guys exposed in ways I never would've allowed. She threw my plans out the window and went rogue.

She's no longer employed here.

"I should've been here."

"You were a little busy."

I shake my head, guilt hitting me in the chest. "They're my team."

"And they're all fine," Mark assures me. "Jackson and I had a long talk about this while we were out in the field. First, you're no longer having a set team."

"Mark!" I protest.

"Relax, Sharkbait, you don't run this company, we do."

I sometimes forget he is my boss and I still have to follow his rules. "I'm sorry."

"I know you're worked up, but we're doing it for a good

reason. We can't have everyone relying on just one person. What if I need you to head to California to handle something and your team goes out? Or what if Quinn is unable to go or Ben gets sick? This company is only as good as our weakest team, and that's all of us if we can't work as a unit. We want our people to be just as good as they always are, no matter who they are working with, and rotating everyone is the only way to do that. Plus, I don't know how you and the first Oliver are going to manage now that you married a different Oliver with, like, a day's notice."

He's right, and at some point, I'll need to talk to that Oliver and get this figured out.

"Is he here?"

"No, he's still out of the country."

So much for that idea. "Speaking of getting married, where is my signed marriage license?" I need to do some shredding.

I may be falling for Oliver, but we need to start things off right if we can. Meaning, not married and in the position to decide what we want going forward. If we try and fail, then at least the split will be as easy as possible for both of us.

"About that . . ."

Oh God. "You didn't." My head falls in my hands as I prepare for the worst.

"In my defense—"

"No, you are defenseless. You have no defense for filing it!"

"I didn't file it. Charlie did."

I blink a few times, jaw slack and can't speak.

"According to her, she thought you wanted her to file it. She said if you really hadn't wanted to be married, then you wouldn't have signed it."

"She knew!" I yell.

"I'm going to agree with you on that, but we know my devious wife likes to think she knows better than anyone.

Charlie said you're free to call her, and she'll give you some bullshit about mistakenly doing it, but the fact remains, it's been filed and you're legally married."

This is a problem. A big one.

Oliver doesn't want to be married—at least not like this.

"Mark, this is not okay."

"I'm sorry. I know that woman heard you and Oliver say not to file it, and I . . . I underestimated her and left it out. Really, I never thought she would do paperwork, she never does."

"I'll . . . find a way to fix this."

He gets to his feet. "I think Natalie knows a great divorce attorney."

"Yeah. Thanks. Listen, I need to take a week or two off again. I know the timing sucks, but my father . . ."

"Take whatever you need. We've got your back."

Mark winks and then walks out, closing the door behind him.

I lean back in my chair, letting out a heavy breath. This is not good.

The worst part is that now I have to figure out a new way to show him that he's not my second choice. I want to be with him. I want to build a life with him in whatever way we can. None of that is achievable unless I can first prove to him that, if I had the freedom to choose, I would choose him every time.

My phone rings, and it's Linda's number.

"Hi, Linda."

"Are you on your way yet?"

"Is he okay?"

"Yes," she says clipped. "He's doing the salsa now. No, he's not okay, Maren. He's exhausted after all the excitement from the wedding. He's having a hard time waking up to take his medication, and he is refusing to eat. I am beside myself, which you'd know if you were here. There are a lot of things I need to handle, and it would be wonderful if anyone from the McVee family decided to be here for Patrick."

Deep breaths, Maren. I can either lose it on her or I can remember that she's probably saying this from a place of fear and anger.

"I'm booking my flight today, and I'll be there. Oliver will probably come in tomorrow."

"You're both coming?"

"Yes."

She clears her throat. "That's . . . nice."

"We will help however we can so you can get a break. I'll call the family and see who else can come."

"We don't need a houseful of people," she bristles.

She wants help, but she only wants it if it's on her terms and never with us all in a group. However, this is about my dad. He loves his sisters and brothers. He loves his daughter, and for some reason, he loves her. So, for him, we are all going to be there and hold his hand. That's it.

"I'll arrange hotels and a rotation, but you'll have help around the clock, and we'll all be there for Daddy. In the end, I think what we all want is for him to feel loved and know that you also have support."

I hear her hiccup before she steels her voice. "Tomorrow."

"Tomorrow."

I hang up and then immediately call Natalie to ask for help.

twenty-four
OLIVER

I have small amounts of pain, nothing I can't handle, but this bulge isn't going down, and I woke up last night in a pool of sweat. If I hadn't already promised Maren I would go to the doctor, last night would have convinced me to get checked out. Also, I want to have sex again. The mistake I made was calling to make an appointment while Josh and I were out running errands. My choices were an immediate slot or having to wait a week. That is how I ended up sitting in a packed waiting room with Josh, who is the last person anyone wants around for embarrassing problems.

"So, you pulled a muscle during sex?"

"Can you maybe not say that loud enough that Mrs. Villafane hears?"

"She can't hear anything." He waves to her, and she waves back.

"You know they hear everything. Even the things no one actually says."

"Ehh, they're harmless."

"I don't remember you saying that a few months ago."

Josh waves to her again. "That was when she was meddling in my life."

207

"Right."

"Back to the issue, you were banging Maren and, what? You twisted wrong?"

"No, it wasn't like that. It just . . . happened. I don't know."

The weird thing is that I have minimal pain so maybe this is some overuse issue. Like, I haven't had all that much sex since Devney, so maybe my body is expelling a lot of backed up jizz. It could be a thing.

Mrs. Villafane smiles at me and then looks down at my waist. "My husband did that once too," she informs me.

So much for not hearing. I force a smile. "Good to know."

"We used to have a lot of sex back then. Wasn't much else to do. This town was even smaller fifty years ago, you know?"

Kill me now.

I glare at Josh. It's his fault I'm now stuck in this conversation. "I'm sure he was grateful for the lack of entertainment."

Mrs. Villafane moves to sit next to me. "I was quite good at role play to keep it fresh. It's important to do that in a marriage."

I sputter as my brother chokes on his laugh. "I hear Josh and Delia like to get kinky with handcuffs and things."

Her eyes widen, and she looks at him. "Joshua!"

"I don't!" he defends. "I would never."

"I said role play, not hurting her."

Oh, this is a great conversation now. "You should give him some pointers. We don't want Delia to be disappointed. Maybe you and Mrs. Garner can stop by and just let him know about the finer points of marriage since he had horrible examples to show him the way."

Her eyes light up. "That's a great idea. I'll talk to Kristy and we'll pop over when we see Delia's at work."

Josh shakes his head. "Mrs. Villafane, I couldn't take up

your precious time like that, not unless I was sure that several people would benefit from your wisdom. Since Oliver here"—he slaps my back—"is a newlywed, I'm sure he needs a lot of help, not just with the sex, which we know he's clearly an amateur at since he pulled a muscle having it."

"I'm here because I did it right," I inform him.

"Whatever you need to tell yourself, asshole."

Mrs. Villafane taps her hand on Josh's forearm. "I'll make a cake and stop by this week."

"Oliver Parkerson." A nurse raises her hand as she calls out my name.

I get up, extremely happy to be leaving this conversation, and wink at my brother. "You enjoy the rest of your chat."

"Enjoy your walk home," he mutters.

I hobble toward the nurse. The swelling in my leg makes it hard to stay upright, but I manage it.

When I get to the back room, I change into a gown that offers very little privacy, and wait for the doctor. I've been coming to Dr. Pang since I was a kid, so it's not like she hasn't seen it all, but still, it's a bit drafty.

My phone dings with a text, and I grab it.

Maren: I just landed, heading to the rental car place now. Are you sure you're fine with coming tomorrow?
Me: Yes. I'll be there tomorrow morning. I'm going to drive so we don't have to worry about delays. I'm at the doctor now.

Maren is none too happy that I can barely walk. I'm not the first man to get a pulled muscle, but she has enough on her plate and doesn't need me fighting her on it.

Maren: Good. Let me know how it goes and light a candle for me—and Linda.

Me: Not sure my light source is what God is looking for, but I'll find someone with a better connection to the big guy.

Maren: Or girl.

Me: You know, it wouldn't surprise me considering what you women are capable of.

Maren: Don't forget it and let me know what the doctor says.

Me: Doctor is going to say something along the lines of, "I hope it was at least good." To which I will say, "It fucking was."

Maren: You need Jesus. Light a candle for yourself too. Also, I talked to Mark.

Now that is some information I was hoping to hear.

Me: And?

Maren: They filed it. So, we are, in fact, legally married.

I shouldn't be smiling. I shouldn't be happy that she's my actual wife, but I am. Maren just makes me fucking happy. While I should be angry, upset, and whatever else, I can't muster it right now. Even if I were mad, Maren is dealing with a lot of shit right now and doesn't need me piling on. So, in a few weeks, we can get this all figured out.

Me: All right. When things settle down, I'm sure you'll share your plan.

Maren: I will. I'll see you soon?

Me: Yes, sweetheart. Very soon.

Maren: Thank God.

Me: You are free to call me that anytime.

I imagine her rolling her eyes.

Maren: You're a mess. Call me later, I'm here now.

I laugh and tuck my phone away when the doctor knocks.

"Hello, Oliver."

"Dr. Pang. It's been a while."

She nods. "Yes, it has. How are you? Happy to be back home?"

"Happy is . . . well, I don't know. We've been busy."

"And you got married." Her eyes brighten as she walks over. "That's wonderful. Congratulations. The town is very excited. I was in Jennie's yesterday, and they were talking about how beautiful she is and wondering what's wrong with her because she fell in love with you."

"There's nothing wrong with her. I am a freaking catch. A big catch," I say.

Dr. Pang's smile widens. "Well, you're lucky to have her and I'm so happy that you found love."

Most people are in love with the person they marry, and by all accounts of this town, we are madly in love, so I give her my most convincing grin. "She's perfect."

"Good. I always hoped you'd find someone worthy. Your siblings have all done well, and it gives me so much joy to see you have as well. Now, what brings you in?"

Is there a delicate way to broach this topic? I decide there isn't and just blurt it out. "I pulled my groin having too much sex on my honeymoon."

"Oh."

I shrug. "We did it . . . a lot. And I mean . . . a lot. I have this bulge here, and I can't walk because I'm swollen a bit."

Dr. Pang hides her face a little and then straightens. "Okay. Let's take a look and see."

I cover my dick with my hand as much as I can and pull the gown over, exposing the enlarged muscle.

"I need you to lie back so I can get a better look." I do as she says. "I'm going to press on this area. Let me know when you feel pain."

We go through the exam, and she keeps moving me around and studying the area. After she's done, I sit up, and she takes a seat on the rolling chair. "Oliver, where you are experiencing the swelling isn't your muscle, it's much higher, you are experiencing an enlargement of the lymph node. When it's inflamed the way yours is, it usually means you're dealing with an infection. Have you had any fevers or fatigue?"

"Not that I can think of. I'm tired, but I just finished opening the resort, got married, honeymooned, and haven't gotten a lot of sleep recently."

She nods. "That all makes sense. What about drinking?"

"Are you asking me out, Doc?" I joke.

Dr. Pang doesn't seem amused. "When you drink, do you feel anything after?"

"Drunk . . ."

She rolls her eyes. "Yes, well that's fine, but sickness or pain?"

I start to say something sarcastic, but then tell Dr. Pang about how I got sick after a few beers while I was in South Carolina. She makes a note of that and then turns to face me again.

"Okay, I'd like to do a blood test to see what shows. I'm not overly concerned, but if we can find an infection, then we can treat it."

"That doesn't make me sound nearly as virile as pulling a muscle during sex."

She laughs. "You can keep your story, but I think it's important to run the test."

"I have to drive to Georgia tomorrow. Maren's father isn't well, and I need to be there."

"Not a problem. We'll start you on an antibiotic and do the blood work here. Since you're going out of town, I'd like to do a biopsy as well. Sometimes the blood tests aren't as definitive as I'd like, so I'd feel better if we covered all the bases just in case. Once we figure out what's causing the lymph node to be inflamed, we can treat it. Sound good?"

"Absolutely."

She stands and heads to the door. There's one thing I meant to ask, and it's really the most important question.

"Hey, Dr. Pang?"

"Yes?"

"Can I still have sex?"

Her head shakes as she lets out an amused sigh. "Yes, but maybe go a little less aggressively."

I would argue, but going slow, torturously slow, is just what the doctor ordered.

The drive to Columbus feels like it takes forever.

I pull into the driveway of her father's ranch-style home, and the door flies open. Maren rushes out, and I barely have enough time to react before she jumps into my arms. I hold her to my chest, savoring the feel of her again. Nothing else matters but this—her. The woman who turned my world upside down and I drove for hours just to see.

I've missed her.

Jesus, has it only been three days? What the fuck is wrong with me?

"Ollie," she says with so much reverence that my knees buckle and I sink to the grass.

With her hands on my cheeks, she pulls my head back so she can look at me with those beautiful green eyes I want to get lost in. "Hi to you too."

She giggles. "I missed you."

"I was just thinking the same thing. How are you? How's your dad?"

Her lips downturn. "He's weakening by the day. Yesterday, he had some energy, but today, he hasn't gotten out of bed."

"I'm sorry, baby."

"It's okay. I know it's coming, but I'm just glad you're here."

"Me too."

And I know that this is exactly where I need to be. Maren leans in, pressing her lips to mine.

"Really, Maren? Do you think we don't have neighbors?" Linda's chiding voice comes from the door.

"Sorry, Linda, I missed my wife."

"*You* didn't go running and leaping out the door."

Maren rolls her eyes. "We'll be right in, Linda."

The door closes, and I grin at her. "Looks like we're in trouble."

"Not you. I'm pretty sure she thinks you walk on water. It's just me who is the hellion."

"Has she been bad?"

Maren climbs off me and gets to her feet. "Bad? No. Normal is the better word. I'm the horrible child who didn't come until it was pointed out. I don't have great manners. I don't know my father's needs like she does. Blah, blah, blah. It's fine. Once Daddy is gone, I am rid of her."

214

I kiss her forehead. "Always a bright side."

"My bright side is that you're here and you can tame the shrew."

"For you, I'll try."

twenty-five

MAREN

I should not be this excited about him being here, but I am. I feel like a sixteen-year-old girl who just had her first date. Butterflies are swarming in my belly each time I look at him, which is crazy, but it's how I feel.

Daddy woke for a few minutes when Oliver came in. He smiled, gripped his hand, and then fell back asleep. Oliver agreed to stay in the room while I started dinner before Aunt Eileen got here for the night shift.

"What are you making?" Linda asks as she enters.

"Roast beef, potatoes, and corn."

All three of my father's favorites.

She scoffs. "He can't eat this."

"I know that."

"He's dying, Maren. He can't eat steak."

I bite back the sarcastic response that wants to come out and focus on cutting the potatoes. I'm well aware he can't eat it. I know that he's dying, and her pointing it out every fucking minute of the day is wearing me down. My heart is breaking into a million pieces because I can't help him. There's no amount of planning that will change the outcome, and I don't really know how to live with that.

So instead, I'm cooking his favorite dish, hoping that just maybe the smell of it will make him feel comfort.

"He can't, but we can, and it makes me feel a little bit of peace."

Linda pours herself some coffee. "I'm not trying to be cruel."

It just comes so naturally.

I put the knife down—no one needs me to kill her if she says something stupid—and take this opening as a chance to make her understand that I love my father.

"I don't believe that's your intention. I don't think you purposely set out to make me feel bad, but sometimes, it's the outcome regardless. There is nothing in the world I want more than for him to get better. My father is all I have left, and I'm trying to do whatever I can, but it's as though nothing I do is ever good enough."

She places the mug down. "He loves you more than you will ever know, and there were so many nights he would tell me how he wished you'd come."

"I came when I could." *Or when you allowed it is more accurate.*

"I was here always," she says.

Yes, because she is his wife and because they moved here. The fact that it was her choice to move them from Virginia to Georgia, which is the whole reason I can't be here as often as either of us wish I were, isn't something she will ever admit. She refuses to admit fault in herself. No, she just plays the victim in the tragedy she created.

"Do you think that makes his love for you different?"

Linda scoffs. "I know he loves me. More than he will ever love anyone else. Our love was for the ages."

"Then why would you not embrace me? Love me the way he did? I had no mother. I had only him, and I wanted so badly for you to fill that role for me."

"I can't have children. Did you know that?" I shake my head. "I wanted them more than anything. Your father didn't want another kid, but I thought he might change his mind after we got married. Then he got sick." I'm not sure what this has to do with me, but I stay quiet because she's never said anything like this to me before. "All I wanted was for you to be my daughter, but you couldn't be. Your father reminded me often that you were Abigail's. You looked like her too, the spitting image. But your father didn't want me to be your mother. He wanted me to be something else, something he couldn't name. So, I stood back, trying to see what my role was. When he got sick, it was clear you hated me, as did the rest of your family. So, yes, I push you away because everyone vilifies me, never understanding what I gave up for your father. The trips I didn't take, kids I never had, jobs I couldn't keep because of your father's health."

Leaning against the counter, I let the words settle around us.

After a few seconds, I say, "I am truly sorry for the things you had to give up to care for him. It couldn't have been easy. When you decided to move here, it broke my heart because I knew I couldn't be there for him—or you—the way you'd want. Daddy knew that travel was difficult when I was with the agency, which is why I left. I came when I could, but I wasn't really welcome to just pop in."

"He would never complain to you. He is so proud of you, and all he wants is for you to be happy. I was the one who was made to suffer."

"You could've asked for help."

She shakes her head. "No, I couldn't. Patrick is my husband, and it is my job to be there for him."

So, she refused to ask for help but then gets upset that she didn't have it? It makes no sense. She can't blame everyone else for the problem she created.

There's a throat clearing, and we both turn to see Oliver standing there. "I'm sorry, but Patrick woke up and he's asking for you, Linda."

The only sound is the mug hitting the counter before

she's gone. Oliver makes his way over to me. "Are you okay?"

"Years of pent-up bullshit won't be solved in one conversation, but maybe I have a small amount of understanding into her psychosis now."

"I know it's not easy."

"No, it's not and I don't agree with any of it." He wraps his arms around me, and I sink into his embrace. When Oliver has me in his hold, it is easy to believe I can tackle the world—or, at least, Linda. I draw on his strength, staring up in his gaze. "But I know my father would want me to be kind to her. He'd hope that his family would treat her with respect, regardless of whether we're afforded the same courtesy."

He kisses the top of my head. "You are a far better person than I am."

That statement is so untrue. Oliver is an amazing man who does things for others without any hope of reciprocation. He has a huge heart and I am falling hard for him.

He moves and winces a little. Oh, damn. "Oliver! Shit. I didn't even ask. How was the doctor?" I ask, remembering that I haven't mentioned it.

"Fine. They did some blood work and routine tests. She said she'll call me this week with the results."

"For a pulled muscle?"

"She doesn't think it's that. She said it's most likely just an infection."

I tilt my head, not having such a good feeling about that. "What kind of infection?"

Oliver sighs. "It's not a big deal. She didn't seem concerned and put me on antibiotics. I'll be good in a few days."

Relief floods me. "Okay. Good. I'm glad you went."

He sways a little, a grin painting his lips. "She also said I have no restrictions."

"All men are the same."

"Not *all*."

"No, not all, but when it comes to that . . . ."

"Hey, I just wanted to inform you of what the doctor said. I didn't say anything else. It's your mind that's in the gutter."

I laugh, which is something I haven't done much of since I got here. "Maybe it is, Mr. Parkerson."

"I'm not complaining."

My finger grazes the skin right below his neck. "As soon as my aunt gets here, we can go to our hotel."

"Yeah?"

I nod. "Where I know you'll find a very inventive way to make me forget all about the hell I'm currently in."

Oliver tilts my head up. "I will. I'll make you forget everything other than my name."

I can't fucking wait.

～

There's not much in terms of luxury in this town, but the hotel is ten minutes from my dad's place, is clean, and has breakfast, so it works. I put my uncles and aunts in a rental house where they can all have their own rooms and it didn't cost a fortune. Plus, they can cook and drink wine without having to squeeze in a room.

Of course, my uncle John had to point out there was a bedroom for me and Oliver, which led to them all ganging up on me on why I needed privacy.

Once inside the room, it feels like our wedding night all over again. There's this strange tension in the air. We both know what's going to happen, but we're being cautious.

I smile at him, and he grabs my wrist as I pass. His blue eyes are filled with an unnamed emotion.

"What's wrong?"

"It's stupid, but . . . your uncle made a joke about your ring, and he's right."

221

"Right about what?"

"You should have an engagement ring."

I'm only wearing the plain gold band that matches Oliver's.

"Oliver, I don't need one. A ring doesn't show love or commitment, I would know." I try to ease his mind.

"It's more that . . . if we had dated and I had the opportunity to do all this the right way, I would've gone to your dad, gotten his permission, and bought you something that you'd be proud to wear."

I smile softly, resting my palm on his cheek with my free hand. "We didn't do things that way, though. We did it our way, and I am perfectly happy without a diamond. One day, if things are different and we can do this the right way, then, yeah, I'd love a ring that you picked out."

He sighs heavily, pulling me closer. "One day, huh?"

I want that one day to come, but not now. Not because we were thrust into this relationship that became a marriage. "You'll know when it's right."

And so will I, but for that to happen, I'm going to have to fix this so we can start over and do it the right way. I want Oliver to know, without a shadow of a doubt, that I want him. I care about him, need him, crave him, and it's not because we're already married.

I would choose this man every day of the week and not think twice.

"You know it's crazy, right?"

"What?"

"That we're here. That I feel this . . ."

"This what?" I ask, my heart pounding out of rhythm.

His eyes are swimming with an emotion I can't name. "Strong."

"I feel it too."

I lift up, pressing my lips to his. All the pain and struggles from today disappear as his tongue delves past my lips.

We hold on to each other, giving and taking each other's

struggles. Oliver lies back, taking me with him. "I want all of you, Maren. The good, the bad, all the parts that you've kept to yourself. All of it, I want . . . fuck, I swore I'd never feel this again."

I felt the same way. Afraid of what would happen if I trusted someone with my heart again. This time, I couldn't stop it if I wanted to.

"It's different for me."

His big hands push the hair back off my face. "How?"

"I want to give all of it to you. I've never wanted to do that before. No one has ever made me want to take that chance before. My heart is yours, Oliver. The good, the bad, the entire thing is all yours."

He kisses me again, and I pour my emotions into kissing him back. His hands skim down my back, gripping my shirt before releasing it. We move together, pulling at the barrier of cloth between us. One by one, items go flying to the floor until we're naked, and I feel more vulnerable than ever before.

This time is different.

It feels like . . . love, not just sex.

Oliver lays next to me, staring into my eyes before his finger moves from my throat to my breast. He slowly circles my nipple, our gazes locked the entire time.

"You're so beautiful. So soft, sweet, and fucking perfect. I could stare at you all night and never get tired of the view."

I blush, unable to help it. "I don't feel beautiful."

In fact, I'm a damn mess. My hair is in a two-day-old ponytail, my makeup is nonexistent, I forgot to pack my contacts, so I'm wearing my glasses, and I'm splotchy.

Emotionally and physically.

"I don't think you could be anything but beautiful." He shifts down my body. "I don't think I could ever look at you and not want you."

"I feel the same."

"I made you a promise," he says as his lips press against my belly.

"You did."

"Do you remember it?"

"I'm pretty sure it was about forgetting . . ."

He grins and then goes lower, pushing my legs apart. "It was indeed. Do you want to forget, sweetheart?"

"Not everything."

Oliver slides his tongue against my clit. "What do you want to remember?"

"You. Only you," I say breathless as he rewards me with another swipe.

"Good answer. Lie back and let me take away your worries."

My fingers grip the sheets as Oliver takes his time with his mouth. He alternates between licking, sucking, and flicking. My body wars with wanting to sink into the bed and needing to buck my hips. His hands grip my legs, pushing them up even higher, and I moan as he finds a new angle.

Everything feels so damn good.

This is heaven, but it's also hell because I know, once my orgasm comes, the ecstasy stops, and I never want that. I hang on to the pleasure with both hands, not allowing myself to let go. He buries his face even more, pushing his tongue against my clit in a merciless rhythm. No matter what I want, there's no way I can keep my orgasm at bay much longer.

"Oliver," I pant. "Please . . ."

His finger enters me at the same time he sucks hard on my clit, and I fall apart.

Wave after wave takes my breath away as I'm washed away in him.

He keeps going, drawing out every bit of bliss, and when he relents, I'm spent.

My fingers move to his hair, stroking as the last of the aftershocks fade.

He moves up so we're face-to-face. "You didn't forget."

I grin. "Did you think I would?"

"I hoped not."

To the women before me who broke this man's heart, you're stupid, and I thank you for it. Thank you for giving me the chance to love him and show him that I will never take him for granted because he is my first choice.

"Make love to me, Oliver."

He leans down, kissing me tenderly. "I want nothing more."

My legs part for him, not wanting to waste any time. I ache for him to be inside me. I want him to know, without a doubt, that it's him I need.

Oliver pushes against my entrance and slides inside me. Tears prick at the corners of my eyes when he's fully seated.

"Did I hurt you?" he asks quickly.

I take his face in my hands. "No. You're saving me, and I've never been as complete as I am now."

He doesn't say anything, just moves slowly, making love to me with so much tenderness that I know I have no chance of not falling madly in love with him. If I'm not already there.

twenty-six

OLIVER

Today has been incredibly hard. We're all sitting at Patrick and Linda's home, waiting for the end to come. These people, who are normally full of laughter and jokes, are somber. Maren is in the room with him and Linda, both refusing to leave his side.

Eileen gets to her feet. "Someone should call Jimmy. This isn't right."

Jimmy is the uncle that Linda forbid Patrick to speak to.

"I already did, but he won't get here in time," John says.

"He should still get to say goodbye."

Marie wipes at her cheeks. "He's never going to forgive himself."

John looks to me. "Oliver, would you be able to see if Maren would call him?"

"Of course."

I get up and knock on the door. Maren opens it, and her eyes are red and cheeks are stained with tears. "Hey, any changes?"

She wraps her arms around her middle. "No, it's minutes at this point."

I don't have much time to word this delicately. "Would

227

you consider calling your uncle Jimmy and letting him say goodbye?"

Linda, who I hadn't thought was listening, looks over. She wipes her nose and then nods. "He should get to hear his brothers and sisters before he goes."

Maren grips my hand. "Thank you."

"I'll bring you some coffee."

I don't know why I say that, but it seems like something she needs.

I head back out, let everyone know that Maren is calling now, and then grab coffee and something to eat for her and Linda. When my grandmother died, food seemed to be all anyone wanted. Stella, who had been the closest to her, was always putting some tray of something out. She baked, cooked, and constantly made us all plates of food. So, I'm going with that same logic.

Before I can bring it in, Maren exits. "You should take a turn going in and saying goodbye."

Everyone gets to their feet, and as they file past Maren, they make physical contact with her in some way. Either kissing her cheek, gripping her arm, or patting her back.

"Here, you should drink this and try to eat something."

She looks at the plate and lets out a sob. I put it down and grab her, pulling her in my arms.

"He's dying. He's really dying, and I'm not ready."

"Of course you're not."

"I'm not ready to lose him. He doesn't know how much I love him, and I hate that I lied to him." She looks up at me. "I lied to him, and I hate myself."

This is what I'd been worried about. "You did nothing wrong. We're not lying anymore, sweetheart."

She pushes out of my grasp as her tears fall. "It doesn't matter. He was so happy just a few weeks ago, and now . . . now he can't open his eyes. What if I made it worse for him? The wedding . . . it took too much."

"Maren," I say, holding her shoulders. "That made him

happy. He told you that. He needed that. You didn't lie to him to get away with something or gain in any way. What you did was selfless, and he loves you for giving him that gift."

Another tear falls. "I sat there, alone in that room, debating if I should tell him, but I couldn't. I was so afraid they would be the last words he heard from me."

"Oh, baby," I say, wiping the tear. "Your father knows exactly how you feel about him, and I've never seen a parent love their child the way he loves you. You didn't rob him of anything."

Her arms are locked tight around me, and I do nothing but hold her. I'm not sure what else I can do but offer her whatever comfort I can. There's a deep ache in my chest as I feel her tremble against me, making me wish I could do anything to take it from her. I would carry her burden if I could.

Eileen enters the living room, her watery eyes meet mine, and she approaches. "He's fighting to hold on."

Maren releases me and looks to her aunt. "Linda won't tell him it's okay."

"It's hard to do, but he needs to let go."

They cry soundlessly, and slowly, more people trickle back into the living room after having said their final goodbyes.

Maren looks to me. "I know it's a lot to ask, but I don't want to be alone. Will you come in with me?"

My comfort doesn't matter. She could ask me for anything and I wouldn't hesitate. "Whatever you need from me."

We walk into the room, and it's impossible not to feel the difference in energy. It's darker, colder, and the air feels heavy.

"He doesn't want to leave me," Linda says from her spot at the head of the bed. "It's why he's still fighting."

Maren goes to her stepmother's side and takes her

father's hand. "He's tired, Linda. We have to let him go."

She shakes her head. "I can't."

Maren's chin wobbles as she stares down at her father. "He loved with his whole heart. He gave without question. He deserves to have peace."

His daughter, the girl who loves her father enough to do the most outrageous thing to make him happy, is being so strong. My heart breaks for her as she grapples with letting go of someone she doesn't want to. For the love of him, she'll let go so he can be without pain.

If that's not unconditional love, I don't know what is.

"Daddy." Maren's voice cracks. "You have been my rock in this world and I am going to miss you so much. Know that you have been the best father any girl could ever ask for, but it's time. It's time to be with Grandpa. Go see Nana and ask her to make you some tea, but make sure she hides the sugar lumps because you're only allowed one. Go to heaven where there's no pain and you can breathe again." Maren sniffs and drops to her knees, still holding his hand. "Tell Mommy I love her. Tell her all about me and how much I wish she could've seen me grow. I'll be here, Daddy, making you proud, and I'm sorry if I ever gave you a reason not to be." She stands, leans over and kisses his forehead. "I love you. I love you so much."

She looks to me, her tears a constant stream down her face.

Linda clears her throat. "I don't know how to live without you, Patrick, but I'm going to have to learn." Maren gets up, putting her father's hand in both of Linda's. "I have loved you more than I ever knew I could. It's okay, Patrick. I'll see you soon, my love. Wait for me in Heaven."

Maren makes her way over to me and I wrap my arms around her. The room is silent, save for the slow breaths that Patrick takes. Linda stays at her husband's side, and even

230

though she's not very kind to my wife, it's clear she loves her husband very much. I can't help but wonder if Maren will still be at my side when it's my time to go.

Is that what I want?

I've fought against the idea of it.

But standing here now, holding Maren, I know I have enough hope to dream of it.

Not the dying part, but the love.

I could love her so easily. I can see a future where we're happy and live the lives my brothers and Stella are currently living. Kids, happiness, love, and family matter, but how can I trust this?

I'm not sure I can. I've allowed myself to think this was possible before—twice. Both times ended with me being a fool who walked away to make them happy. I don't want to walk away this time.

I want her to stand here and want me. Not because it's easy but because she can't imagine her life without me.

The fear of losing her grips me so tightly that it's hard to breathe.

I release her and Maren walks over to her father. She and Linda speak to him softly, holding his hand as his chest rises and falls a little slower with each pass. The sounds of their quiet cries echo around me.

She's going to lose him and my heart is breaking for her.

"You are so loved," Maren whispers.

I close my eyes and tell him what I wish I could say aloud.

I'll take care of her. I won't fail your daughter.

They start to cry a little harder. "It's okay, Daddy. It's okay."

And then he exhales and doesn't draw another breath.

"The service was nice," Aunt Marie says to Maren for the third time.

"Yes, it was."

"And the casket was too," Eileen follows up. "I've never seen that marble detail on the sides before."

Maren sighs heavily and nods. Today has been incredibly hard on her. The funeral was yesterday and today, and we just said our final goodbye at the cemetery. While one might think that, after the moments that Linda and Maren shared prior to Patrick passing, some healing had taken place, it hasn't. I've been stunned at every turn by the way Linda has purposely set out to exclude Maren.

Instead of allowing Maren to speak, Linda did the eulogy and spoke only about her time with Patrick. There was a brief mention of him having a daughter, but that was it. Maren wasn't seated in the front row. She'd been directed to sit off to the side with the rest of her family. Linda's nephew, sister, and cousins sat up front.

With every slight from Linda, Maren sank deeper and deeper into herself. Each little thing wounded her further.

We're at her family's rental house to get some space so she doesn't choke her ex-stepmother, which I've also come dangerously close to doing.

John comes up behind us, placing his hand on Maren's shoulder. "She's a bitch."

For the first time since we left the cemetery, Maren looks alive as she turns to her uncle. "How could she do that to us?"

Marie sighs. "Because some people are just vile, honey. We can't explain it because it doesn't make sense. Don't you let what she did to you diminish anything. Your father loved you more than anything."

"I have tried."

John shrugs. "She doesn't deserve another minute of your thoughts."

Maren gives him a hug. "Thank you."

"Now, no more tears. Your father would want us to eat and talk about how wonderful he was."

She laughs a little. "Yeah, he would."

"Well, we can handle the food part," Eileen says.

For the next few hours, we all sit around and just talk. Maren holds my hand most of the time as she talks about her father. They all tell stories, remembering his love of his permed hair in the 70s and how, when Marie got breast cancer, he shaved his head in solidarity. According to them, he sobbed the entire time.

We laugh, drink wine, and eat.

When I die, I hope this is what my siblings do.

Let them remember with joy instead of sorrow.

My phone rings, and the number is from Willow Creek Valley. "I need to grab this," I say before kissing her temple and standing.

"Hello?"

"Oliver, it's Dr. Pang, how are you?"

"I'm . . . doing okay. My father-in-law passed away four days ago, so I'm still in Georgia."

"I'm so sorry to hear that," she says sincerely. "I hate to do this now, but I got the test results and wanted to call you right away."

I had completely forgotten about that. "Great. Do we have any answers?"

"Yes, and . . . I need to refer you to a doctor who can handle this."

"You can't prescribe me some drugs?"

I turn, looking through the window. Maren's head is thrown back, her hands are clasped in front of her, and she's laughing without restraint. She looks so beautiful, so happy, and I will do anything to keep her happy.

My sister was right, I needed to be here. Not just for her but also for myself. I needed to see how stupid it was to think I could close myself off and be okay.

I love this woman.

I love her, and I'm married to her, and I never want to be without her.

"Oliver, the blood work came back irregular, and the biopsy shows that you have cancer. You need to come home and see an oncologist—immediately."

twenty-seven

MAREN

I pull into the driveway of my beach cottage, feeling as if I could sleep for days, and when I move to open the door to my car, Devney is there, opening it for me.

"Hey, Mare," Devney says, backing up so I can get out.

"What are you doing here?"

"I thought maybe you could use some girl time."

I start to cry again, which I swear is all I do, and hug my best friend. "I could. I so could."

She wraps her arm around my shoulders and we go inside. She already has three bottles of wine and cookies waiting for me.

"This is perfect."

She grins. "Good. I had very clear instructions."

"What?"

"Your husband called on his way home from Georgia two days ago."

"Wait," I say with shock. "Oliver called you?"

"He did. Almost caused me to drop Cassandra when I heard his voice."

This man continues to shock me. He called Devney, his ex and my best friend, because he couldn't stay the extra days in Georgia with me. He had something urgent at home

235

that he had to take care of immediately. He hasn't said what, but I assume it has something to do with the resort.

I miss him, but I understand the pressures of work, so I've been trying to let him focus on that without bothering him too much.

"I can't believe he called you . . ."

"He was very persuasive, not that it took much to convince, but it was very sweet." Devney pours us each a glass of wine before sitting down. "So, tell me the truth, are you okay?"

I sink down, feeling like I can let it all out. "No, I'm not."

"I didn't think you would be. Hell, after my brother and sister died, I wanted to crawl into that hole with them, but we can't."

"You had Sean and Austin."

"Yes, and you have Oliver."

I sigh. "I do, but I worry."

"About?"

"With my father gone, there's no need for pretense anymore. He could end things, and I wouldn't blame him. I keep thinking about how he should, even."

Devney takes a sip of her wine and watches me. "You don't believe that. If he only cared about maintaining the lie, he wouldn't have been there with you for a week right before the resort fully opened. He sure as shit wouldn't have called me to ask if I would come see you so you wouldn't be alone when you got home."

She's right. "Okay, so, maybe it's that I worry we won't work for other reasons."

"Such as?"

"Is this not incredibly strange talking about Oliver?"

Devney raises one brow. "Not any stranger than watching you marry him."

"Point taken."

"We don't have to talk about any of this, Maren. I came

236

here to be a shoulder to cry on or the friend who holds your hair back if you get obliterated drunk. Either one works."

I rest my head on the back of the couch and shrug. "I don't want to talk about Georgia."

"I understand."

"I should. I know I should."

"Says who?" Devney asks. "There are no rules for grieving, Mare. You can talk or not or cry or not, there's no wrong way or timeframe on it either. I don't care what people say, some days you're going to be in the shit and other days won't hurt."

"Do you still cry?"

The last thing I want is to make her sad, but I don't know what to expect. I was so young when my mother died that it's hard to remember how I felt or how I endured it.

"I do. I miss my brother. He was my best friend, and . . ." She looks into her wine as she slowly swirls it around the glass. "I hate saying this, but there are times I feel so much guilt that it can choke me. My brother was supposed to raise Austin. That was the agreement. Yes, he is my son, but that wasn't supposed to be my role, you know? Then the accident happened, and I was a mom to this kid who thought I was his aunt. I shouldn't have him. I shouldn't have the life I have."

I reach over, taking her hand. "I think we all have the lives we have by design."

"Maybe, but then how the hell do you explain your love life?"

"I can't. I'm married to your ex—actually legally married—for now, but we're dating, which is strange."

Devney smiles. "It's also amazing. Wait, what do you mean for now?"

I place the glass down on the coffee table. "I'm filing for divorce."

"What? Why? What?" She sits up straight.

"I spoke with a divorce attorney the day before I left,

237

and she is drawing the paperwork up. She's not sure if I can do an annulment since I kind of tricked him into it, but she thinks he would have to file it. Either way, I'm going to let him out of it."

"What does he think about this?"

"I haven't told him."

Devney's jaw opens and closes. "I'm going to assume you were of sound mind when you came up with this plan?"

"Obviously."

"I'm not so sure. Why would you divorce him without talking to him first?"

I release a heavy sigh. "Because I love him."

"Makes total sense. I would want to end the marriage to the man I love too."

I shift my weight forward, needing to explain. "No, it does make sense. Oliver has always been the guy who was second choice."

"Mare . . ."

"I know you didn't think of him that way, but it's how he feels. You left him to marry Sean, and no one is saying that was the wrong choice, but it is how it went down. Then there was the girl he was with before you guys met."

Devney sits back. "I forgot about her."

"He was engaged to her, I think."

"But she met someone else . . ."

I nod. "Exactly. He told me how he didn't want a relationship. He had no intention of falling in love again."

"But he did, Maren. He fell in love with you. The fact that he was in Georgia for you proves that."

"It does, which is why I have to do this."

I have to give him up so I can prove to him that he's my first choice. He needs to see that we are together because we love each other, not because of some mistakenly filed paperwork.

I want him to know that I love him. I want him. And we

238

can take whatever time we need to get to know each other and be together.

Devney raises her glass to me. "Here's to hoping it goes the way you want it to."

I grab mine and tap it against hers. "I have a plan."

She laughs before taking a sip. "And we see how well that went last time."

This will be different. It's being done the right way.

~

"When will I see you again?" I ask Oliver.

"Soon, I hope."

"How is the issue at the resort?"

"Issue?" Oliver sounds confused. "Oh, the issue I had to leave for? Yeah, it's being handled."

I wipe a spot on the floor a little harder before plopping to my knees. Hearing his voice makes me eager to see him. I don't want to waste time. It's precious and goes far too quickly. What we have is worth making the effort for, so we're both going to have to bend. I'm more than willing to go first.

"Good that you could help. I was thinking that I could come there this weekend?"

Oliver doesn't say anything for a few seconds. "I'd like that, but I'm going to be working the front desk. I have to make up for the time my siblings filled in for me."

"I can help," I offer. "I may not know how to run a resort, but I'm sure I can answer the phones or whatever you need."

"I'm good. We'll get it figured out. Just stay there."

"I don't mind hanging out in your cabin while you work," I tell him.

"If you're here, I'll want to be with you the whole time. We'll see each other soon. Just not this weekend."

We may already be hundreds of miles apart, but it's as if

I can feel the distance growing. Something is different. He doesn't sound right, and my instincts are telling me that I should proceed with caution.

"Is everything okay?"

"Yeah, why?"

I sit back on my heels. "I just feel like something is wrong and you're not telling me."

"That's not the case, sweetheart. I want to see you, but this weekend is my first one back after being gone for weeks. I need to get caught up and let everyone else take a breather too. Plus, I have a possible wedding booking that I need to meet on Saturday. How about I come to you the following week?"

All of that seems completely reasonable. I'm being silly, and he doesn't deserve me being a nutjob. Well, more of a nutjob than I already am.

"Are you sure?"

"Positive. I'd love to come out there and spend the weekend doing nothing but naked snuggling."

I laugh a little. "Naked, huh?"

"Definitely."

"All right. That is a plan I can get behind."

Oliver and I talk a bit more, catching up on the changes his siblings have made and updates at my job. We saw each other six days ago, and I still feel as though the ground is shaking. When he is near, it's steady. I miss steady.

I miss him.

I've always heard that long-distance relationships were hard, but I never truly knew just how hard. It's like a part of you, the one you like and need, is missing. I can't do anything but wait for it to be returned.

"Anything from Linda?" he asks.

"Just a text yesterday saying she needed time to process before she'd be able to speak to me again and that her lawyers would be in touch regarding my father's will."

"She's something else . . ."

He isn't wrong there. "I've been reaching out each day, wanting to see how she is."

"I will never understand why," Oliver muses.

"My father would've wanted it. Even though she didn't hold to the same beliefs, I have to do what feels right. I want him to be proud of me, even now."

At least that's the line of crap I'm feeding myself. I don't know why I'm being nice to her. She and Aunt Marie got into a huge argument after I left, and I doubt they'll ever speak again. It's as though Linda can be as ugly as she wants to the people who loved him now that he's gone.

"He is. He has to be."

I smile. "Cancer stole so much from him, but it never took his kindness. I watched his life fade away bit by bit and rob him of a future he should've had. It was impossible to understand or accept, but my father did it with humility. He was always good to people around him, even when they didn't deserve it. I wanted to rage at everyone because it wasn't fair. It's never fair, and I don't ever want to hear that word again, you know?"

"I understand."

I sit on the kitchen stool. "I pray that no one in my life has to deal with it ever again. I know that's unreasonable, but I just can't handle it. I can't watch it again, but I know at some point, I will."

Oliver goes silent.

"Ollie?"

He clears his throat. "Sorry, phone cut out when I moved across the room."

I had forgot how shitty service is on Melia Lake. "No worries. So, next weekend?"

"Next weekend."

I am so looking forward to it.

twenty-eight

OLIVER

I t's pizza night at Grayson's, and while I really didn't want to come, I couldn't come up with a good reason to skip. I haven't seen Amelia in far too long, and if there's anything in the world that can cheer me up, it's my nieces and nephew.

So, tonight, I'm putting on my best smile and faking it.

"Uncle Oliver, do you believe in ghosts?"

"Not really," I say to Melia as she brushes her doll's hair.

"I do. I think they like to hunt people."

"That's . . . disturbing."

Amelia puts the brush down. "On this one show I watched, the ghost tried to take over a little girl's uncle's body."

"I don't think they'd want mine."

Hell, right now, I don't want mine.

"Ghosts aren't picky."

There are multiple directions to take this conversation, and being that I am the asshole of the family, I stay the course.

"I think ghosts only like little kids. They want girls especially."

Her head lifts. "Why?"

"Because they have long hair, and all ghosts really wish they had long hair so it flies in the wind as they float."

I catalogue this as something Grayson will make me pay for later.

Amelia jumps a little and pats her hair. "Do you think they like little sisters?"

This is why Amelia is one of my favorite people in the universe. She'll sacrifice a sibling if it means she survives. If we have a zombie apocalypse, I'm totally keeping her on my team.

"I know my ghost would like Aunt Stella's hair."

"She has really long hair."

"She does."

"I wonder if we could tell the ghost to take her instead."

I chuckle. "I like that plan."

Melia leaps forward, catching me off guard. "I love you the most, Uncle Oliver. Don't ever leave me."

"Leave you? Where would I go?"

She sits back down on the floor. "With your wife. Daddy said you love her and that he thinks you're next to leave."

Did he now? "I'm not planning to go anywhere."

"Okay," she whispers. "You're my favorite."

While I'd like to revel in this little declaration, my niece is a master at this game. She says the same thing to each of her uncles whenever they say something to make her happy. I may be the favorite right now, but if Josh gets her a doll or Alex sends her presents, then I'm back down in the pecking order.

"For today," I say with a smirk.

"Just don't die."

My head jerks back, and my pulse spikes. "What?"

"That way you won't be a ghost that takes my hair."

My heart rate starts to return to normal. "I . . . okay." I glance at the kitchen, needing to get some air. "I'm going to get some pizza, did you eat?"

Amelia sighs dramatically. "Dad made me eat."

"Okay, I'll come back later."

She nods once and goes back to her dolls.

That one statement has me on edge. While I may be able to breathe again, I keep hearing her words: don't die.

That's the goal here, but what if? What if I do? What if I am sicker than I am prepared to be? I can't . . . I can't go there.

My hands grip the counter, and I focus on breathing. I need to rein myself in before I go down a hole I can't escape.

"What is up with you?" Stella asks as she grabs a slice of pizza and tosses it onto my plate.

"What is wrong with you?" I toss back.

Stella leans against the counter. "Mature."

"I always am."

"No, you never are, but that's beside the point. I'm serious, this week you've been sulky."

"Sulky?"

"Yeah, moping around, whining about everything. You snapped at Jack and just ran away from Melia."

"Jack was tracking mud in the damn foyer after the cleaning crew finished."

She shrugs. "He's a wilderness guide. Apparently, that means nature can follow him. Fuck if I know, but my point is that Josh is the moody one, not you. You're always laughing, smiling, having a grand ole time with life. This week . . . you're moody as fuck."

"Funny coming from you since you're . . ." I look at her belly.

"I have an excuse. You are worse than Josh."

"I think Grayson may have him beat," I add.

"Right!" Stella puts her hands on her hips and looks out toward him. "He's been a bear lately. Last time he was like this was after he found out Jessica was pregnant."

"Maybe our brother procreated again," I suggest,

245

hoping my sister will take the bait. Stella is amazing, smart, and easily distracted by shiny things. Like a baby.

She bites her lower lip. "Man, if that's the case, we're in trouble because after Jess's last pregnancy, he said no more. Plus, Ember is only a year old, but it would be cool because with me *and* her . . . oh, do you think?"

"You should ask him."

"Why would—" Stella's eyes narrow. "I see what you're trying here. You think that if we talk about Grayson then maybe I'll forget about the fact we were discussing you."

So much for shiny objects.

"I'm fine. Things have been stressful, and I won't see Maren for another week."

"You love her."

"I could."

"No, I think you *do*," my annoying sister says with a grin.

"Whatever. That's what's bugging me."

Oh, and I have cancer. Yeah, that too.

I saw Dr. Pang yesterday, and she informed me that she was able to call in a favor with one of the best oncologists in Charlotte and I'll see him in two days. In the meantime, I get to sit around with this impending cloud of doom over my head.

Until I have answers, I'm not going to bother my siblings with this. Josh and Delia have a baby, Grayson and Jessica have their kids, Stella and Jack have their own stuff to deal with, and Alex is in Egypt. So, I'm alone in my head. If I'm being a dick, well, everyone is going to have to deal with it.

"Have you talked to her?"

"Almost every day."

"I know it's hard, believe me, I understand what it's like to stay away from the person you love, but it'll work out. You and Maren will figure it out."

She has no idea what she's talking about.

Once I find out more and start treatments, everything will change. Maren has her career in Virginia, and I'm here.

246

I can't go to her. I can't ask her to take care of me. She just buried her father who died of cancer.

No, Maren isn't going to have to suffer through that pain again. I won't do it.

I'll find a way to get through this on my own.

"Thanks, Stell."

"Something else is wrong, Oliver. I feel it in my bones."

"Your bones? Wow, that's deep. Do you think it's contagious?"

She glares at me. "I think you're an idiot and lying to me."

"Is this your twin osmosis shit again?"

"Sure. Let's call it that, but I know you, which means I know when you're trying to hide something."

Of all the days for her to be a pain in the ass, she had to pick this one. I smile as authentically as I can and lean against the counter. I'm close enough to her that it's as though I'm going to impart some amazing wisdom.

"You know I love you, right?"

"I do."

"You know I am always saying that you're too smart?"

Stella grins. "It's true."

"You got me this time."

"I knew I would."

I want to laugh at her for thinking I'm going to tell her shit. "Well, I feel like I should tell someone, and since you know me so well, you should be that person."

She moves closer, waiting for the secret. "I can keep a secret."

"Good." I drop my voice to a whisper. "I can too."

I straighten, walk away, and laugh when the paper towels hit me in the back of the head.

"Thank you for seeing me on a Friday night," I say to Dr. Dowdle, the oncologist I was referred to.

"Janet is a good friend of mine, so I was happy to fit you in on her behalf. How are you feeling?"

I want to flip the fuck out right now because I'm feeling an array of things and none of them are good. I vary each day from hateful to hopeful to ready to terrified. I don't know which end is up.

Each time I talk to Maren, I have to pretend as if I'm not scared out of my fucking mind.

But I am. I have cancer.

The thing that just robbed her of her father and might possibly rob her of me.

"I'm not doing great, as you can imagine."

"I can empathize even if I can't understand fully. How is the lymph node swelling?"

"It's gone down, but . . . I mean, I don't know if it really has. I want to think it's smaller, but yesterday, I would have sworn it doubled in size and grew eyes."

He smiles at that. "Your mind can do that to you. What helps is information and we'll go over the test results from yesterday first, and then we can talk about the lymphatic system and Hodgkin's Lymphoma specifically, which is the most common and treatable type to have."

I could give two shits about the system or anything. "Honestly, Doc, I just want to know what the results are and then the plan to get rid of the cancer."

He nods. "I understand. Please, have a seat."

I do as he says, taking the chair from the desk. Dr. Dowdle rubs his chest as he looks over my test results. Yesterday, he had me go for a CT scan, more blood work, and a biopsy in another lymph node.

I got home, curled into a ball, and passed out. I'd never felt so exhausted in my life. Between the constant worrying, trying to pretend that I'm fine, and working twelve-hour days, I just don't have much in me.

"I agree with Dr. Pang's diagnosis of Hodgkin's Lymphoma, which is very treatable, so I want you to feel a little relief there. The scan indicates that it has *not* spread past the lymph node in your groin, which is another good thing. As far as staging goes, you are Stage IA."

"I don't know what that means."

"It means that it's the best kind of cancer staging we have, if you can call any of it good. You're young, overall healthy, and the only real symptoms you've had are intolerance to alcohol and a swollen lymph node. Sometimes, we'll see severe fevers, unexplained weight loss, or night sweats, and that would mean you'd be IB. Your stage number and letter determine your course of treatment."

Yeah, I'm still lost. I've gathered that this is the better of the stages and letters, but I still have cancer. "What's my prognosis? How long do I have?"

Dr. Dowdle shakes his head. "Oliver, you caught this extremely early. You'll need two rounds of chemotherapy over the course of two months to start. Most likely, that will be enough to put you into remission. If it isn't, we will reassess and make a new plan. I want to assure you that Hodgkin's Lymphoma is treatable."

The weight that's been sitting on my chest eases the slightest bit. "You think I'll be okay?"

"We've seen exceptional rates of remission with this course of treatment. As I said, you're in optimal health, and there is no sign that it has started to extend into the lymph system."

I let out a huge sigh. "Okay. So, I'm not dying."

"Not today, no. I'd like to start treatment next Friday. Who do you have as far as caretakers or family?"

"I haven't told anyone."

"No? Do you have a spouse or family member who can help if you experience side effects from the chemotherapy?"

"My wife doesn't know. Her father just died from cancer last week, and I . . . well, I can't really burden her with it."

His eyes fill with sympathy. "I'm sorry to hear about that, but you're going to need someone to at least check in on you."

"I have my siblings," I explain. I had hoped I could keep this to myself and deal with it quietly. I hate being a burden and like to think I can tackle my issues without help. This doesn't seem as if it will be that type of issue.

Dr. Dowdle nods once. "All right. Let's get things set up for next week."

We spend the next thirty minutes going over the treatment plan and making sure I understand the risks and possible side effects, but all I keep thinking about is Maren and how the hell I'm going to get through this and lie to her for the next few months.

twenty-nine

MAREN

"Hey, Stella!" I say as I answer the phone.

"Hey! I wanted to call earlier, but I have been super busy at the resort and time got away from me. How are you?"

I sent her a text this morning, needing some sister-in-law help to prepare for when Oliver gets here in a few hours.

"I'm doing better," I tell her honestly.

"There are probably good days and then bad ones."

"A lot of sad ones too."

"I bet. I'm really sorry about your dad. He was such a sweet man, and our family is truly honored to have gotten to meet him."

I push back in my chair and look out my office window. Directly in my view is a pair of wind chimes that are hunter green, my dad's favorite color. Natalie and Liam hung them so I can see and hear them faintly. Each time the wind blows, I feel my father here. It's crazy, but I swear that I only hear them when I really need to.

"Thank you. He loved all of you."

That is the truth. My entire family fell in love with the Parkersons. They were warm and caring when we needed that more than we knew. I will always be appreciative of the love they showed that week.

"What's not to love?" she asks with a lilt in her voice. "I would love to catch up, but with Oliver on his way to you, I'm a little frantic here. Is everything all right?"

"Yes, of course. I was actually calling because I want to surprise Oliver and do something he really loves, but I'm not sure if he'd like seafood on the beach or dinner at my place. Last thing I want is to make this trip stressful."

She sighs. "You know, I would normally say that Oliver would just do whatever and be great about it, but have you noticed that he's been . . . off recently?"

I shift in my chair. A few days ago, I had a feeling that something wasn't right with him, but I brushed it off. It's back now, reminding me that my gut doesn't usually steer me wrong. Only I've been not myself lately so I don't know if I'm correct.

"Yes, but I've been off too," I confess.

"Maybe it's just what you two went through that is coming to a head. I don't know. Ollie isn't usually this moody and prickly. He's just not, but all week he's been. Even to his nieces, which is a cardinal sin to him. The sun shines out of those girls' asses. I could be crazy, but it's just not sitting right with me."

Now it's not with me either. "Did he say anything?"

Maybe it's me.

Maybe now that my dad is gone, he's having all these regrets.

Maybe he wants out and the annulment will be the relief he needs. I'm doing it because I want to show him that I choose him, but what if he doesn't want to be chosen?

My heart starts to pound harder, and my mouth goes dry as I wait for her answer.

"Nothing really. Just that he's working hard, tired, misses you—a lot. As a girl who was madly in love with someone

252

and couldn't be with them, I get it. Maybe this weekend is what he needs?"

The tightness in my chest eases. He misses me. Maybe it's not regret, but longing and fear. I am dealing with the same thing. This long-distance thing is going to be impossible, but I have a plan. A good one. One that affords us both a path through this.

"I miss him too. Okay, if he's been stressed out, then the last thing I want to do is make this any harder. We'll stay in, and it'll be perfect."

We'll spend tonight relaxing and hopefully reconnecting, and tomorrow, we'll have dinner at home where I'll start my big plan by proving to him that he's who I want.

Always.

I get through the hour of work I have left and head home, where I clean and then walk through the house fluffing pillows and making sure the throw over the couch is at the right angle. Then there is nothing left to do.

It's been two very long weeks without seeing Oliver, and while I don't think he cares how clean my house is, I want this weekend to be perfect. We have a lot to discuss, and I think that everything is going to go smoothly.

My home is a beach cottage a few blocks away from the Chesapeake Bay. I bought this little fixer upper and spent the first two years doing nothing but renovating. It's adorable with board and batten siding, black framed windows, and a porch swing that's more of a bed off the deck. The whole house has a beachy vibe, but it's still very clean and classic. I spent a lot of time making every inch of this space what I wanted.

I hear a car pull up, and I rush to the door, not caring that I have zero chill. The door opens wide, revealing Oliver walking toward me.

I smile.

He smiles.

Then he drops his bags on the walkway and pulls me in his arms.

All the fears I had are gone. He wants me, and when I'm against his chest like this, I know it's exactly right.

He tilts my head back, pressing his lips to mine. "God, I missed you." His deep voice echoes in my ear.

"I missed you more."

"Not a fucking chance."

I grin and kiss him again. We kiss, long and sweetly as he lifts me, my knees bending as he spins us.

My laughter makes me feel a billion times lighter. "Let's go inside before my neighbors get suspicious."

He kisses me again. "Good plan. There's a bed in there too?"

"There are two beds."

"Two beds, two days, too many options to make you orgasm."

I roll my eyes and giggle. "Let's go, Casanova, I want to show you the inside of my home."

He grabs the bags and brings them in, dropping them just to the side of the door. "Wow." The approval in his voice makes me grin. "This is amazing. Seriously."

I'd already told him about the renovations I'd done. Since he had gone through it with the resort, it was nice to have someone to talk to about the trials of dealing with contractors. One-point-oh was never interested. He couldn't have cared less and didn't think the place was anything worth discussing.

"You like?"

"I love it. It's really perfect."

"I think so. When I bought it, I had planned to flip it, but I couldn't dream of it after a week. It was just too perfect for me."

Just like you're perfect for me.

I don't say it, but it feels as though he heard it. Oliver comes to stand in front of me, my face framed by his strong hands as he leans down to kiss my forehead. "Show me the rest," he says with an edge to his voice.

We walk through together, holding hands and smiling at each other as I show him the various projects. When we're done, we head onto the back deck and lie together on the swing. It's not a normal swing, which is why I love it, it's almost the size of a twin bed. It's also the most comfortable place ever.

"I missed you," Oliver says as I listen to his heartbeat. "I didn't know how much until I saw you."

I lift my head, resting my chin on my hand. "I know how you feel."

"I've been a dick to everyone at home."

"I doubt that." Even though his sister said as much, I don't want to betray that conversation.

"I have, but . . . I'm so stressed, and there's just so much . . ."

"You don't have to explain it, I get it. My head has been such a mess. I keep saying I'm going to snap if I get just one more bad thing."

"What do you mean?" Oliver asks.

"We had some issues with a mission this week. I was so overwhelmed, and I kept wishing I could talk to my dad. I wanted to call him, but I can't anymore, you know? I'm alone."

Oliver's hand moves up and down my spine. "You're not alone."

"I have you. I know I do, but we're so far apart."

"We knew this would be hard."

"It's been two weeks, and I want to scream," I say with a smile. I'm only half joking. I have wanted to get in my car and go to him so many times.

He makes me happy and safe. "You make it so that I don't think of cancer and death and sadness. In your arms, I'm okay."

Oliver shifts and then closes his eyes.

"What's wrong?"

"Nothing. Long drive, and I'm already dreading leaving."

"Then no more talking about leaving and sadness. Tonight, we have pizza, and tomorrow, we'll go exploring. I want to take you to my favorite places, and Mark would love to see you."

Oliver hugs me tighter. "No sad for tonight."

I lie back down, closing my eyes as I, once again, settle into the steady beat of his heart. "Just us."

"Just us."

256

thirty

OLIVER

A ll weekend I've had ample opportunities to tell her. On the ride down, I promised I would when I got here, but I couldn't, not after what she said while we were curled up on the swing.

Now, I leave in the morning, and I've yet to find a way to say it.

I have cancer.

I have cancer. It's not going to kill me, but I have it and I'm going to be okay.

Maren looks up from her plate and smiles.

Say it. Just tell her.

"The food is good, right?"

I haven't tasted a damn thing. I nod. "Definitely."

She went through a lot of trouble to make this weekend fun and light, but there's darkness hovering over me.

The next few months are going to suck, and I'm not going to be able to come here. I'm going to be sick and dealing with treatments. While it's beatable, Dr. Dowdle was clear that I will still have a few months of hell.

I thought I could just go through it without Maren knowing, but that's not right. I don't want to keep this from her or lie and make excuses as to why we can't see each other.

No, I have to be honest and trust that we'll figure it out. From everything I know about her, I can't see her walking away.

"Oliver, there's something I want to talk about . . ."

"Me too," I say, putting my fork down.

"You do?"

I nod. "Yes, but you go first."

She gives me a soft smile. "Are you sure?"

"Absolutely."

I'm in no hurry to ruin the rest of the small amount of time we have left together. I really wanted to do it after we made love, when she was sated and maybe a little less likely to be upset, but those moments came and went without the words coming from my lips.

She lets out a huge sigh. "Okay. I'll be right back." Maren rushes out of the room, and returns with something that looks like an envelope, before placing it on her lap as she sits. "I first want to tell you how much I care about you. I didn't know that I could feel this way about anyone. I thought I had my life all figured out. I had plans, and those plans weren't this, but then they became this, which is great and perfect. I know you wanted to be alone and didn't plan this either."

Her rambling has me going in circles, but it sounds like she needs me to agree. "I did."

"That's what is so perfect about us. We were completely okay with the plan to walk away at the end of this charade. We never had plans to be together past our fake wedding."

"Which changed," I say carefully.

"Yes, but not by choice, not really. Not in the end."

I lean back, trying to decipher what she's saying. It's impossible, so I just nod.

She grabs the envelope and hands it to me. "Here."

I grab it, open the flap, watching her as I do it. She looks nervous. When I slide the paperwork out, my vision goes red.

She filed for a fucking annulment.

An annulment. After everything. This whole weekend of us being together, saying all kinds of bullshit, she had this planned.

I can't believe this.

Once again, I'm not what the woman I love wants.

I'm fucking done.

I look up at her, and instead of sadness or regret, she looks hopeful. "You want an annulment?"

"Yes, but . . ."

"But what?"

Her head jerks back at the bite in my voice.

"Well, I just thought . . ."

"You thought what?" I ask, anger in every syllable. She didn't think. She just fucking went off on her own.

"I thought this is what you'd want?"

What part of me driving here and spending time with her made her think this is what I want? Nothing.

No, this is what *she* wants.

This is exactly what I wondered about. Her father is gone, I'm no longer required for her scheme, so she's cutting ties. Unreal.

Well, this time, I'm not going to go quietly into the night. I'm done with being used by women, and she is the worst out of all of them. I'm married to her, and she *still* doesn't want me.

"No, you thought . . . hey, my dad is dead, I don't need to keep up with this, never mind the fact that my husband has shown me in every way short of screaming it from a rooftop that he's falling in love with me. I think I'll file for an annulment."

"That's not what—"

I slam the papers onto the table. "What was this weekend, Maren? Just one more weekend where I fuck your brains out before you end it all? A chance to get what you need before you walk away as though you're the victim?"

"Oliver, wait, I'm doing this for us."

I laugh because that's the most ridiculous fucking thing I've ever heard. "Spare me. I have the goddamn paperwork in my hands." I scan the document and shake my head. "On grounds of false pretenses. Well, isn't that sweet? I tricked you into this now?"

"No, of course not," Maren says quickly. "The lawyer and I agreed . . ."

"I don't fucking agree!" I yell and get to my feet. "I can't believe this. I can't fucking believe this!" I run my fingers through my hair. I must be the biggest idiot who has ever lived. Here I was, ready to tell her that I needed her, that I was falling apart, and all the while, she was planning on leaving.

I grab the envelope, head into her room, and start to throw my shit into my bag. Fuck this. I'm not going to stand here and listen to this crap. I have enough on my mind, and this annulment is the last thing I need.

No, I need to go and get my chemotherapy, go back to my fucking miserably lonely life, and be the second choice that no one even wants.

"Oliver, stop," Maren says as I sweep the room, grabbing whatever is lying out.

"For what?"

She goes to touch my chest, but I move away. "Listen to me, please."

"You know what? I won't. I won't listen to another speech about how I'm a great guy but you want something else."

I've already heard this story.

"I want to be with you."

"So much that you want an annulment?"

"Yes! Don't you see? I don't want to be married because we can date."

"That makes no sense. I came here because I needed you. I . . ."

"I love you," she says quickly, causing me to rock back on my heels. If she loves me, then what the hell is the annulment for? No, she doesn't love me. She's grieving and has found a way out that will make her look good. Now, she can tell her family that I somehow tricked her into a marriage and she walked away.

She probably came back here, talked to the first Oliver, and has a plan to make it work with him. Just like every other woman I've loved.

Always good but never good enough.

I laugh once. "You don't know what love is."

She rears back. "I do know what love is, and I love you."

She's unreal. "You don't. You orchestrated lies. You lied to yourself about the first guy. You're lying again about me. Well, I'm done lying and going along with your insane plans that only hurt people."

Her breath catches, and she steps back.

"I knew it was a bad idea when you showed up at my resort, asking me to go along with your insane plan. I said no, but then I felt bad, thinking how hard it must be to love someone and lose them the way you were. Against my better judgment, I went along with it, but I always wondered . . ."

Her eyes fill with fake tears. "Wondered what?"

"How you could have feelings for me so quickly. You didn't love the first Oliver, yet you were going to marry him. You didn't love me, and you actually did marry me. Now you want to say you love me enough to end the marriage?" I shake my head in disgust at myself. I knew better, and yet, here I am, the fucking fool who thought she was capable of being in a relationship after her last attempt. I came here, ready to tell her I'm sick and needed her. Thank God I didn't make that mistake. I toss the rest of my shit into my bag and tuck the annulment papers under my arm. "You can spare me whatever excuse you have. You got everything you wanted—your job, your family farm, and the happiness of your family."

"Please stop," she begs quietly with tears running down her cheeks. "I'm not a liar and I'm not trying to hurt you. I was trying to fix this!"

"I won't listen to another woman feed me the bullshit lies. I've heard it twice before, and I'm not in the mood to hear it again."

I walk out of her room and throw the door open. "Oliver, wait!"

I don't. I just get into my car and leave.

It's time to go back to my home.

Back to my life.

Back to my family.

Back to being alone, which is exactly how it should've been.

Fuck love. Fuck cancer. Fuck it all.

~

I drive through the night and pull into the resort a mess. I'm exhausted and hollow.

Jack and Stella are walking toward the main entrance, smiling as she holds his hand. The people in this town are going to make me sick. I'm happy for my siblings, but I really don't want to be reminded of all I just lost.

I exit the car and head inside. At least my job makes sense. Today is an owners' meeting I had planned to skip, but . . . here I am.

When I enter, Grayson and Josh study me, look to each other, and then back to me. "What?" I snap.

Josh clears his throat. "Nothing, just surprised to see you."

"You all right, man?" Grayson asks.

"Do I look all right?"

"You kind of look insane," Josh answers.

Stella's voice comes from behind. "Who looks insane?" Our eyes meet, and she nods. "Oh, he does. Why are you here? I thought you were having a romantic weekend with your wife?"

No time like the present and no patience left to give a shit.

"Maren and I are getting our marriage annulled, and I have Stage I Hodgkin's Lymphoma. I start treatment on Friday, and they're hoping for a full recovery."

Stella's mouth falls open before she covers it with her hands. "What?"

"I have cancer."

Jack's arm goes around her shoulders. "You saw a doctor?" he asks.

Grayson and Josh are on their feet. Questions come in rapid fire from all four of them.

"When did you find out?"

"Why didn't you tell us?"

"Did you get a second opinion?"

Stella moves toward me. "Who is taking care of you?"

"Where is treatment?"

"How long?"

Stella wraps her arms around me. She lets go, tears swimming in her eyes. "Maren left you because of this?"

I put my hand up, not willing to listen to this anymore. "I found out when I was in Georgia. I didn't tell you because I didn't know anything. It's Hodgkin's Lymphoma and in a lymph node in my groin. I'm very, very early in detection, which means I won't have an overly complicated treatment plan. The oncologist is in Charlotte, so that's where I'll be going through treatment. I should need two rounds of chemo, and then they'll do a PET scan to see if I need more or if they need to remove the lymph node." I turn to my sister. "As for taking care of me, I'll do it on my own, which is how it's meant to be, and no, she didn't leave me because of it. She doesn't know."

263

"You didn't tell her? Seriously?"

"No, Stella, I didn't tell her because right before I was going to, she gave me annulment paperwork. I really didn't feel inclined to say anything about my current situation given she was ending things."

My sister turns to Jack. "It doesn't make sense."

"Yeah, it makes perfect sense," I say, drawing her attention back to me. "She got what she wanted and left. However, I don't have the time to give a damn, I have other things that need my attention."

With that, I walk out of the room and head to my cabin to take a nap and get my shit together for Charlotte.

thirty-one

MAREN

There's a knock on my office door, and I wipe away the tears that keep falling to see my ex there.

"Can we talk?" he asks.

I haven't seen him since before we ended things. "Now isn't a good time," I say and go back to staring out the window.

"Look, I'm sorry."

"I don't want to hear it."

I am not mad. I don't even care. I'm heartbroken, and he reminds me of the Oliver I want. The one I love. The one whose voice I can't stop hearing tell me that he's never anyone's first choice.

He doesn't stop, he walks in. "Why are you crying?"

I sigh heavily. "Why are you here? You left me, Oliver. Didn't care when you walked away, so you don't have to pretend to be now."

Oliver left me. He refused to listen, called me a liar, and stormed out. He doesn't care about why I filed for the annulment any more than the man in front of me cared about why the wedding was so important to me.

No, that isn't fair. The Oliver I love isn't uncaring. He

was there for me, doing whatever he could to make me smile and stay strong. He didn't run away until I pushed him.

"I heard about your wedding. When I got back, it was all anyone could talk about."

"What do you care?"

"I always cared about you. It wasn't like that. We were rushing into things."

"I have a knack for that."

"No you don't," he says, taking a seat. "You're a planner, and you never do something without knowing the possible outcomes."

I laugh once. "Clearly, I'm broken then. I didn't see this coming, that's for sure."

"What has you upset?"

"He left me," I say, not sure why the hell I'm telling him. "I love him, and he left me. I really love him, though, with everything inside me. He saved me when you deserted me."

"I'm sorry I hurt you."

I shrug. "I'm not. If you hadn't called off the wedding, I never would have fallen for him, and you were right, I didn't love you. We should have never gotten engaged."

Oliver looks away. "Still, I could've stopped it sooner."

What-ifs are wholly irrelevant.

What's important is that I know exactly what love is now. I have felt selfless love at the core of my being. He was willing to sacrifice for me, without any expectations, and I've never had that before.

"I appreciate you saying that, but it's unnecessary. I'm not upset about it anymore."

"So, who left you and has you crying?"

"The man I married instead of you."

One-point-oh and I spend the next fifteen minutes talking as I pour over the events of the last month and a half. I tell him about the wedding, Mark marrying us, Oliver and his past. It is nonstop talking, crying, and explaining my thoughts through the entire thing. It's a little insane that he's my sounding board, but I let it out with ten tissues, lots of tears, and a bottle of water on my desk I don't remember getting.

Oliver leans forward and puts his elbows on his knees. "It's a lot to process and also very unlike you."

"I know!"

"I think you need to talk to him because it sounds like he loves you and you blindsided him. Give him a day to calm down and then call him."

"I thought he'd see the gesture as something good."

He stands, giving me a thin-lipped smile. "He'll come around."

I don't think that's true. Not with how angry and hurt he was when he left.

"And if he doesn't?" I ask, grabbing another tissue.

"Then he's not worth taking a chance on."

Oliver leaves, and I sit at my desk, feeling raw and upset. I grab my notebook, draw a line down the middle, and start my list to see if I should call him.

PRO:
FIXING IT.
TELLING HIM ALL THE THINGS I WANTED TO SAY.
GETTING THE LOVE OF MY LIFE BACK.
PROVING I'M NOT A LIAR AND I MEANT HOW MUCH I
LOVE HIM.
BEING HAPPY.

CON:
HE HANGS UP.
HE SAYS MORE HATEFUL THINGS.
HE LISTENS TO WHAT I HAVE TO SAY AND STILL
SAYS NO.

I LOSE HIM FOREVER.
REMAINING MISERABLE.

Great. It's even.

My mind is too fragile to see a way through this. I need a little more time to get my heart and head reconnected.

I grab my phone from my purse to text Devney, only to find a text from Stella.

Stella: Hey, can you call me? I know you guys aren't in the best place, but . . . well, I got your wedding photos back, and also, I'd just like to talk.
Me: Sure, can you talk now?
Stella: Give me five minutes, and I'll call.

I watch the clock, seconds seeming to take longer than normal, and then the phone rings.

"Hi," I say, my throat scratchy.

"You sound as good as he looks."

"Thanks. Listen, I don't know what happened, but it didn't go as I planned," I explain. "I love your brother, and if you want to yell at me, all I ask is that you please give me another day or two, at least until I can stop crying for more than twenty minutes."

"Oh, Maren, I wasn't going to yell." Stella's voice is full of sympathy. "I would if you didn't sound like you've been crying for days, but . . . you do. However, I don't understand what in the world is going on."

"Oliver made a few comments about being second choice and never being the guy, but I love him. He's my first choice. So, I figured if we ended the marriage and dated instead, he would see that it was my way of choosing him instead of us being together because of a series of insane events."

"Right . . ." She inhales quickly. "*Oh*, no. You were giving up the fake marriage to have a real relationship."

See, she gets it. "Exactly!"

"But the execution of it . . ."

"Was bad," I admit.

"Have you . . . called him?"

I chew on my lower lip. "I can't. What he said, maybe he's right. Maybe I am a liar, and I don't know what love is."

Stella huffs. "He said that?"

"I hurt him," I say with the tears pooling again. "I think that maybe . . . we need time. Time to be apart and to see if this is real or if we were caught up in the fantasy. Maybe the end was inevitable."

Stella sighs. "I'm not sure what the right thing is, but you love each other, and I hope you can work it out."

The sad part is, I don't know if that's what should happen. Love doesn't mean a relationship can work. We have distance, mistrust, and hurt between us, so can we even get past all of that? My heart wants to say yes, but my head is telling me I'm wrong.

All I've done is listen to my heart, and look where that got me.

"Time will tell, I guess."

"I guess. Do you want to see the wedding photos?" she asks.

"You can send them over, and I'll look at them when I feel emotionally stable," I say with a laugh.

"All right. Listen, I'm going to just say this and then never bring it up again. You two need to talk. I think a lot of this can be resolved, and . . . he needs you."

"He made it clear he doesn't."

"He's a man and dumb."

There's a knock on my office door, and I lift my finger. "I

have to go back to work. Thank you for everything, Stella. Truly, you became a part of my life and a sister when I needed one. If you ever need anything, please call."

"I will, and . . . well, goodbye."

"Bye."

I hang up, blink away the tears, and turn to the person waiting in my doorway.

thirty-two

OLIVER

Jack is sitting on my couch, watching me pack and drinking a beer. One that I can't have because it makes me sick.

Thanks, cancer. I'm not even allowed to numb the hurt of heartache thanks to you.

"You head out in three days?" Jack asks, knowing exactly what I'm doing since my annoyingly overprotective sister is coming.

"Yup."

"And you're staying for how many days?"

I roll my eyes. "Six."

"Yeah, Stella said as much."

"Yup."

Jack makes a low grumbling noise and then walks over toward me. "Did you decide anything about Maren?"

Tossing the shirt I was folding onto the bed, I turn to my brother-in-law. "Is there a reason you're here, Jack?"

"Yeah, apparently, it's my damn job to fix all the broken Parkerson men. Trust me, it's not a job anyone wants."

"I don't need to be fixed."

He laughs. "Yeah, sure, you're the pillar of strength and perfectness."

I grin. "Thanks for agreeing."

"That was sarcasm."

"This is me not caring," I toss back.

Jack shrugs. "Care or not, I was sent here to fix you because your sister thinks you're a mess, and while my beautiful wife is meddling and frustrating, she's often right. So, here I am."

Stella is a pain in my ass. "And as I said, I'm fine, so you can go and tell her you did a good job and get your reward."

"If it were only that easy . . ." He walks over to the table and grabs the large manilla envelope. "Did you sign them?"

I fucking hate my family. "No, I didn't sign them."

"Why not?"

Is he stupid? Yes, he is because he married my sister. Or maybe that makes him smart—whatever. "Because I've been busy."

"Too busy to sign your annulment paperwork? It takes like, what? Three seconds to scribble your name?"

"I'd rather use the next three seconds to toss you out of my cabin."

Jack smirks. "You can try."

This is going one way, and since I doubt he'll leave me the hell alone until he gets what he wants, I give in. "I love Maren, she doesn't love me back, she filed for an annulment, and I have cancer. All of this adds up to disaster and the end of the relationship. I'm fine. She's probably happy this is done so she can live her life according to her plan. Now, can you let me have some peace?"

"No, because you're an idiot if you think Maren doesn't love you. We all saw it."

"She might have thought she did."

"No, dude, she does. I know she does."

"Oh, now you're a mind reader, awesome, can you imagine what I'm thinking now?" I focus hard, and Jack laughs.

Great. He missed that message.

"Go back over the fight, Ollie."

I sigh heavily and replay the events again. Over and over, I see her face, hear the words, and hate her fake tears. The ache in my chest is so bad it feels as if I'm right back in her house going through it all over again.

I was concerned about telling her about the cancer, hopeful she would stand by me and fight, but she had already given up.

"Did you ask her why?"

"Of course I did."

Jack raises one brow. "Really? It sounds like all you did was flip out and leave."

"I'm about to flip out on you."

"I don't care," Jack says and then leans forward. "Seriously, you didn't get an explanation."

"I got served with the end. I don't need the why."

"Then let's settle it before you go in for treatment." He gestures to the envelope still in his hand. "Sign it, and I'll send it in. Then you can be done and move on with your life of being the weird dude who lives out here alone. It's cool. Chicks will totally like that. Or you can just fuck the guests who come to escape. That way, they leave and you never have to worry about falling in love."

I walk over to the desk and grab the pen. "Sounds good to me."

He extends the paperwork and then pulls it back. "Giving up is kind of your thing, so I guess this fits."

When he puts the envelope back in front of me, I grab it and yank it away from him, tossing it on the table. "What the fuck does that mean?"

"What?"

"The giving up thing. I don't give up."

"No?" Jack asks, pursing his lips. "Really? Because there was the girl you were engaged to in high school . . . what was her name? Janelle? Janice?"

I huff. "Janie."

"Ah, that's right. When that ended, you went to college, to a school that you weren't planning to go to but was clear across the country, which looked like running away to me, but what do I know?"

"Not much."

"Then there was Devney. You met her in college, followed her out to Pennsylvania after begging your dad to let you take over that resort, and then let her go without even a fight."

I clench my fists, wondering if Stella would forgive me if I broke his nose.

"You're one to talk. You've loved Stella since you were, what? Twenty-two? And it took you until a year ago to get your shit together?"

"So, you'd rather spend fifteen years wishing you could be with her, love her, hold her, and give her everything than actually getting to do it?"

"I was with Maren for a month and a half."

"And I kissed Stella once and spent years wishing I could do it again." He throws his arms up. "Don't make that same mistake, Oliver. Don't let your pride or fear of being hurt again stand in the way of what you want. Don't run away. Don't refuse to fight for her. Go to her. Talk to her and find out what the hell you can do to make her see how much you love her."

"I'm tired of it!"

It's not that easy. She wants out, and I'm not going to beg someone to stay with me. I won't be like my mother, taking the scraps of whatever is offered. I won't be like my father, forcing someone to stay when you wish they'd leave. If she wants her freedom, then that's what she'll have.

"Then there's nothing I can say other than this, if you have even a sliver of doubt that you misunderstood her motivation, then you owe it to yourself to call her and find out. Let her tell you, in no uncertain terms, that it's over."

Pretty sure her stance was clear the second she asked a lawyer to draw up the paperwork. That's the part that no one seems to understand.

"I'll take it under advisement."

Jack chuckles. "I swear you are the most stubborn group of people I've ever met."

"Maybe so, but I'd rather be that than a fool."

"I think you're both, but . . . no matter what, you're still my brother."

I walk over, and we clasp hands. "Always."

"Sign it before you go, Oliver. Have one less thing on your mind before you start your treatment. Okay?"

He's right. I need a clear mind and to be wholly focused on my fight and getting healthy.

"I will."

When Jack leaves, I grab the envelope and sink onto the couch. It's been four days since I stormed out of her house, and I'm in absolute misery.

I miss her voice. I want to ask her about her day and tell her the funny stories about the guest requests we got for next week. I want to tell her how fucking terrified I am about starting chemo, and how, despite knowing we caught it early and my prognosis is good, I'm worried treatment won't actually work.

It's her I want by my side, not my sister.

I pull out the papers, reading over the legal jargon that will officially end this if the judge grants it.

It lays out all the ways the marriage was formed under false pretenses, and I want to laugh.

It was a lie. All of it. The memories of us that I cherished are fabrications and worthless.

I get to the last page, seeing her signature already there, and then I hover over the signature line, hating that I will be ending what never should've been started.

I can't do it. I can't sign it. Not now.

275

I grab the envelope to put the paperwork back in, only to find a folded paper jammed in the bottom.

I pull it free and open it, finding a handwritten list. A list that changes everything.

A list that tells me I really am a fool, and I hurt the woman I love.

thirty-three

MAREN

Today sucked.

Every day sucks if I'm being totally honest.

But today was especially sucky. The mission went sideways, causing every contingency plan I had to fall to shit. I'm off my game, and it almost cost someone their life.

After a very long conversation with the two owners, I'm taking the rest of the week off to clear my head.

Only, being home—alone—isn't really helping. Everything reminds me of Oliver.

I'm going to burn the house down and move. It's the only option.

Since my flair for the dramatics is in high gear, I decide to do only mundane things, so I grab the phone, hover over his name for the millionth time, and then fail to actually call him.

No, I am following my ex-fiancé's advice and giving it time.

Who cares that it's been four days of absolute hell? What does time matter when your heart feels as though it's been ripped from your chest? Wounds heal, scars fade, and you learn to move on.

I just need that part to kick in.

I throw my clothes into the dryer, go to slam the door, and close the door on my freaking fingers.

"Damn it!" I scream, clutching my hand as I bounce around. "Great. This is just what I needed. Thank you universe!"

After I grab the ice and wrap it around my possibly broken finger, I sit out on the back deck.

"If I get stung by a bee, I'm seriously going to lose it." I speak directly to nature, hoping it heeds my threat and stays far away from me.

I rest in the swing, letting the rustling of leaves and the faint sounds of the ocean a few blocks away be my companion.

The throbbing in my hand keeps me from falling asleep, but it does give me a reprieve from the ache in my heart.

"Maren?"

I hear Oliver's voice, but I know that's not possible. I wonder if pain can make you hallucinate.

"Maren, are you here?" I hear him again. I sit up so quickly that I fall off the swing.

"Ouch!" I complain, rubbing my tailbone. That freaking hurt too.

There's a banging on the door.

Hallucinations don't knock, do they?

Probably not, so it seems he's here. I push to my feet and limp to the door while I cradle my hand and the ice pack.

When I open it and see him, I can't breathe. He looks better than I remember. His dark hair is falling slightly over his eye, and the stubble on his chin is now a full beard. He looks worn, miserable, and broken, which is probably what I look like.

He looks at my hand. "What happened?"

"I closed it in the dryer door and then I fell off the swing when I heard your voice. If you're here to tell me how much you don't love me, could you just finish me off?"

Oliver shakes his head. "I'm not here for that."

"Here to tell me how much of a liar I am?"

"I deserve that."

Yeah, he does. "Why are you here?"

He reaches into his back pocket and pulls out a piece of green notebook paper similar to the kind I use when I'm writing my lists.

"I came to go over this with you, but I'm not as good at this as you are." He steps closer. "I could use some help."

Words escape me so I just nod.

"Reasons not to sign the annulment," he reads. "Pro: I love her. I want to kiss her. I want to give her my heart and soul. I don't want an annulment. I want to spend my life with her. I need her."

Tears fill my eyes as he glances at me and then keeps reading.

"Con: Blank."

My lip trembles.

"See, I couldn't think of one reason to sign it. Not one." Oliver moves closer so we're toe-to-toe. "I kept trying to convince myself that it would be better if I did, but I can't. Give me a reason, Maren. Tell me why I should sign it, why did you want me to?"

Finally, he's asking me. Finally, I'll get to explain. "Because I want to choose you. I want you to know, always, that you're the only man I want. Not because we were trapped or some sort of chivalry but because I want to choose you, Oliver Parkerson. Every day."

He shakes his head. "I choose us."

He leans down, kissing me tenderly, and I can taste the salty tears. My arms wrap around his neck, holding him where I need him—with me.

When he leans back, his hands frame my face. "I was a dick. I said things . . ."

"I screwed up. I never should've told you that way. There were a million better ways to handle it. I'm sorry that I hurt you."

"We both did that."

When I push up on my toes, I kiss him again. "I have been so miserable."

His hands drop to mine, and he's careful of my injured finger. "I have to tell you something." There's a slight tremble in his voice. "One that may change this whole entire mood."

"Okay?"

We sit on the couch, and his eyes don't leave mine. "I'm sick, Maren. I got my test results the day we buried your father, and they said I have cancer."

My heart stops. I can't breathe or think or move. No, not him. Please not him.

"Wh-what?"

"I'm stage IA, and the doctor assures me that we caught it early, but I start chemotherapy on Friday. I didn't tell you sooner because you were dealing with everything and I didn't know much. Just that the biopsy came back cancerous. I was going to tell you the weekend I was here, but . . ." He flinches, clearly not wanting to finish that sentence. "It's only in the one lymph node, and they're very optimistic that I'll only need two rounds." He sighs heavily. "If you don't want to go through this, I understand. You just lost your—"

"We will fight, Oliver. We will stand together, and we will fight. I love you, and that doesn't mean only when you're healthy or happy. It means sickness and pain and everything between. I don't choose you only when it's convenient."

As though I would ever let him do this alone. It will be hard, but it won't be so unbearable if we do it together. I love him with everything inside me.

"You want to be there for me, even after just losing your dad?"

"I want to be there because you're my heart. Now, tell me the plan and let's prepare—together."

"Stop being such a baby," I tell him as I tuck him into his bed.

"You know I'm perfectly fine."

"For now, but I am preparing in case that changes."

Oliver grabs my wrist. "I may have no side effects or I may be miserable, but either way, we'll be okay."

My God, I love this man. Even after the first round of chemo, he's worrying about me.

I thought this would be much harder to handle, but I'm actually okay. We spent a good amount of time with his doctor and delayed the start of his treatment by a week. Oliver and his doctor had discussed the possible complications of him having kids, but they never really planned to address it. So, after some consideration, Oliver opted to have a sample, er, frozen. In case we need it down the road, it'll be there.

It also gave us—or me—time to come up with a very practical plan. I spoke with Mark and Jackson, explained the situation, and now have the ability to work from home. The only stipulations are that I will need to go to the office once a month for briefings, and they insisted on sending a team to Oliver's cabin this week to install all kinds of security firewalls and satellite whatevers so our missions won't be compromised.

For the rest of the month, though, I am on FMLA. Being married allowed me the opportunity to be here and care for him. More than that, it gives us some much-needed time to really see where this relationship stands.

My hand grazes his stubbly cheek. "Please rest."

"I will."

"Good. Now, I'm going to see your siblings, give them an update, and let you know what they say when I get back."

He shakes his head. "Godspeed."

I grin. "Go to sleep."

This lake, the nature, peace, and silence does something to me. I feel more like myself when I'm here than I did the last time. It could also be that I'm with Oliver, but even when we were together at my house, it wasn't the same as it is here.

The walk up to the resort takes about ten minutes, and I enjoy every second of it.

"Hey, Maren," Jack says as he meets me on the trail.

"Hi." Kinsley waves with a smile.

"Hey, you guys."

"How's Uncle Oliver?"

I smile. "He's doing really well right now."

She stares up at her father. "Can I go see him since he's okay?"

Jack looks to me, and I nod.

It's not as if he's going to be asleep already, and it'll give me a little peace that she's there in case he needs help.

"I'll keep watch!" she promises as she runs off.

"Those kids have always loved him the most."

"He's the fun one," I say in agreement.

"He also spoils them beyond belief."

Jack and I stay silent for a minute as we make our way up the path. "How is the custody agreement going?"

"It's good. Samuel is a great guy, and ultimately, we all want what's best for Kinsley, so there's no fighting. We are just making it legal in case something happens to any of us."

I know that all too well. "It's smart. My mother died young, and I can remember worrying what would happen if I lost my dad too."

"My mother died in a fire when I was a kid, and my dad might as well have died alongside her. It was the Parkersons who kept me afloat. I want Kinsley to have a family that will always be there for her. Much like you have."

I nod with a smile. "They're something."

"You've had a really rough few months, Maren, and I

hope you know this family is here for you as well. I know I'm the outsider, but trust me, my wife runs these guys."

That's very accurate. "I appreciate it. This family is really special, and I'm honored to be a part of it, especially after watching how everyone has stepped up to be there for Oliver if he needs help. I'm looking forward to spending this time with you all."

All of it is working out the way I hoped it would. Finally, one plan is going right.

"We are all really happy you guys are happy. He's one of the best men I know and deserves to have everything he wants. And this is none of my business, but what did you guys decide about the annulment?"

Ah, the stupid annulment. "We used it for the fire last night."

Jack grins. "Good. I'm glad you guys figured that out before you wasted years being apart."

"Me too." I think about how hard those few days were and know that Oliver is who I want and need. "Me too."

thirty-four

OLIVER

~One Year Wedding Anniversary~

S he's been blindfolded for the last thirty minutes and pissed off the entire time. Maren hates surprises, and I can only imagine how crazy her overactive imagination has been as we drove here. However, today matters more than she can ever know, and I want things to be perfect.

"This is ridiculous," she complains as we approach the farmhouse.

"I know."

"No, you don't because unless you're blindfolded, which I really hope you're not since you're driving, you can see where we are."

"It's called a surprise."

Her head whips toward mine. "I loathe them."

"*Really?* I couldn't tell. You've been such a ray of sunshine this whole trip."

If she could glare at me, I'm pretty sure she would be. "How much longer?" Her voice isn't full of vinegar.

"Just a few more minutes. I promise that this is a good surprise." I lean over, taking her hand in mine. "Trust me."

"I do trust you, I just want to know."

"Hence, the trust."

Maren sighs heavily and leans her head back. I allowed Stella to tie the blindfold on me so I could make sure I couldn't see anything through it. I couldn't, which means Maren can't either, so that has probably been the biggest point of frustration for my wife.

We take the twists in the road and arrive at the farmhouse. It's a beautiful property with green hills, a little bridge that goes over the small creek that cuts across the fields, and a modest house that overlooks it all.

Anyone can understand why this farm was worth keeping. Maren and I came here for a week after my second round of chemo. It was exactly what we both needed—peace and quiet. I love my family, but they've been a pain in the ass. At least once a day, someone from my bloodline came to the cabin.

One of those days was one Stella regretted very much as Maren and I weren't dressed when she walked in without knocking.

The last few months of our lives have been focused on making it work and finding the balance between working and spending time together. I am tired of it. We both are. It's been hard, but in the end, Maren is worth all the hardship. Before her, I never knew love like this, and I am going to hold on to it with both hands.

Today is the start of that. It's a celebration of where we are and what we've overcome. I've been cancer free the last six months, and we got through it stronger than ever before. Maren has been at my side the whole time, never wavering. She has shown me what true love is, and I never want her to wonder how I feel about her.

I park the car, and she smirks.

"What?"

"I know where we are."

"And you couldn't let me think I surprised you?"

She bites her lower lip. "I could, but then that wouldn't be fun."

"You may know one thing, but I promise, you have no idea about the rest."

At least, I hope she doesn't.

Her arms cross, and she harrumphs, which is confirmation that she doesn't.

I help her out of the car and lead her up to the porch. "It smells like the farm."

"Nothing says romance like manure."

She laughs. "I love it here."

"And I love you."

"I love you, babe."

"Good. That makes this so much easier."

I remove her blindfold, and she looks out. Everyone we love is here. Her aunts and uncles, my brothers and sisters, even Alex who flew in from Egypt when I told him I could've died and he wasn't here. I'm not above using guilt to get what I want. They are all here to witness what should've been our beginning.

"What is . . . Aunt Eileen? Uncle John? Devney? I don't understand . . ."

Her eyes meet mine, swimming with a million questions. "Today is our anniversary."

She shakes her head. "I know that, but what is our entire family doing here?"

I take her hands and sink down to one knee, pulling out the ring I should have bought for her a year ago. "Maren Parkerson, the last year has been a rocky road. We didn't start out like most couples. You came into my life, turned it upside down and made me a husband when we weren't even dating. Then I fell for you. I fell harder than I knew I was capable of. Now, I would give up my own life before letting you go. I love you more than any man has loved a woman. More than my heart can even contain." Her tears are streaming, and I can hear others catching their breaths. "I married you one year ago without really knowing that I wanted to spend the rest of my life beside you. So, I'm asking you today, as the woman I love with everything that I am, will you marry me?"

She falls to her knees, taking my face in her hands. "You beautiful, wonderful man, I would marry you every day of my life."

I lean in, kissing her softly, and we both smile, breaking away. I slip the ring onto her finger. "Was this a good surprise?"

"The best."

"It's not over," I tell her.

"There's more?"

I glance at Stella and Devney, who come rushing up. They give us each a hug and then pull Maren toward the house. "Come on, today is your wedding day, too."

I wink and watch the woman I love walk away to get ready for what is our true wedding.

～

"I can't believe you did all this," Maren says as I close the door to the master bedroom.

Today has been a really long day, but seeing her in her wedding dress brought me back to our first wedding. "There's nothing I wouldn't do for you."

"Yes, but . . . it was so sweet, Ollie. I'm so happy, and now we're married without any lies."

I pull her into my arms. "No lies."

Three months after I found out I had cancer, we came clean to all of Maren's family. We felt it was the right thing to do. At first, they were really upset at the level of deceit, but as we kept explaining, they settled on a lot of laughing.

That day, I promised myself that I would make sure her family knew the truth about how I felt about her.

"I wish . . . I wish my father could've seen this one," Maren says hesitantly.

"I do too, but I like to think he was here."

She plays with my collar, which she loves to do when she's deep in thought. "This house was his and my mother's, and when we're here, I like to think they're smiling down on us. Did you invite Linda?" she asks before meeting my eyes.

"I did, but I knew she wouldn't respond."

"Yeah, I don't know why I asked."

I tilt my head, forcing her to look up. "Because you still care."

Linda shut out the entire McVee family from her life as though they never existed. No one other than Maren seems to care, and she still reaches out to the woman once a month, hoping that she'll have a chance to ask for a few of her father's belongings. Linda has ignored every phone call.

"I'm dumb for that."

"No, you're kind, which is never dumb."

"It was great meeting Alex." Maren changes the subject, and since it's our wedding night and I'd rather not talk about Linda, I don't push.

"I'm glad you got the chance. He leaves tomorrow so, who knows when we'll get to see him again."

"Oliver," Maren says, and I wait, knowing she isn't done talking and needs a second to get her words together. "Today was perfect."

"It was."

"You gave us the wedding we deserved, and I love you so much."

I kiss her, and I keep kissing her until we're both breathless. Then I lift her into my arms and carry her to the bed.

Our families have all headed home or to the hotel down the road, which is more like a roadside motel, but not my problem. So, we are in our home, the place where I hope we can raise our kids together, alone.

I lay her on the bed, smiling down and marveling at her beauty. She takes my breath away.

"Why are you smiling?"

"Because I can't believe that you're mine."

"I have been yours since the minute I asked you to marry me."

I laugh. "I think I became yours then too."

She leans up and grips my tie, pulling me to her. "And now we belong to each other."

"Always."

She smiles. "Always. Also," Maren says, her voice changing before she tilts her head with a grin, "I have a surprise for you."

"You do?"

"I do. See, I thought we were going to spend our anniversary at the resort, so I had a cake and all kinds of things made."

"I think my surprise is better," I say before trying to kiss her, but she shifts back a little.

"Maybe, but that wasn't all of it. Are you ready?"

"I'm really hoping you're going to tear that dress off and be completely naked because I'm really ready to see if we can make the house shake tonight."

Maren giggles. "I think you're going to like it."

"Yeah?"

"Yeah. I'm pregnant."

epilogue

MAREN

~Six Years Later~

"I'm not ready for this," Oliver says as he grabs Brynn's backpack.

"We may not be, but she is."

"She's not ready to go to school."

"The state says otherwise."

He rolls his eyes. "Like I trust any of them."

I smile and pat his cheek. "She will be fine and so will you."

Brynn comes running down the stairs, blonde hair flying behind her like a cape. She takes the last four as a jump, causing my heart to falter until she stands with her arms in the air. "I did it."

"Can we not do that again?" I make my way to her.

Brynn has her father's personality with my features. It's a lot of fun for both of us. I look at her, and see myself, but when she talks, all I hear is him. She is funny, smart, and sarcastic at the age of five. All we hear is that it's only going to get worse.

"I wish I could make that promise, Mama, but you said I can't lie. It's a sin."

Oh for heaven's sake.

"Nice try."

Oliver comes over. "How about this, if you do that again, you won't have the television for a week."

Her green eyes widen before she clutches her hand to her chest. "You wouldn't do that to me, would you, Daddy? Not for practicing my gymnastics."

"I would."

She looks to me. "I was told that I don't try hard enough, and that's what I'm doing. I'm practicing."

"Your teacher did not tell you to leap off the stairs as practice. But I appreciate your effort in trying to sell it." I boop her on the nose. "Now, go eat your breakfast before the bus comes."

Brynn rushes off, and Oliver flops onto the couch. "That child is a menace."

"That child is you."

He smirks. "Menace."

"Who you love."

"With every fiber of my being."

Brynn is everything to us. She's truly a miracle. We conceived her naturally, but since then, we haven't been able to get pregnant. After countless visits to fertility clinics over the years, we finally decided to stop trying. The emotional toll it was taking on us was too great, and we are eternally grateful for the child we do have. Still, I struggle.

Ashton Miller is one of the top infertility specialists in the country and a good friend of mine. She explained it wasn't anything either of us was doing wrong or even the chemo treatments Oliver had a few years back. It just wasn't working, even after IVF.

There are days when I swear I can imagine the tiny baby in my arms. I can feel his weight and see his blue eyes that are just like his father's.

"Hey," Oliver says, opening his arms, "come here."

I settle onto his lap, allowing him to once again be my

safe harbor, and rest my head on his chest. "How did you know I needed this?"

"Because I know you."

"I'm a lucky girl."

"You sure are."

I snort. "If you do say so yourself?"

"I think both of us are lucky, so there's that. You know that I love you more every single day, don't you?"

"I do."

"And I am completely content with our life. We have everything, Maren. Everything."

He's right. I know he is. We have a beautiful home on Melia Lake that we built when we found out we were pregnant. It's tucked back so the guests can't see it, but we still have a great view of the water.

Every month, we take a trip out to the farm, check on the horses we bought, and visit with my family. A wonderful couple lives there full time to care for the land and the animals. Thanks to Brynn, what started out as a few chickens and horses have grown into a damn zoo.

Really, it's Oliver's fault since he can't say no to her.

"I know we do. I just can't seem to stop from wanting more."

"If it happens, then it'll be because it was right."

"You always know what to say."

He laughs. "I wish I did. It would make arguing with you so much more fun for me. Instead, I usually end up going in circles."

"Because you're usually wrong in those instances."

He raises a brow. "Shut up and kiss me."

I give him a kiss right as Brynn enters.

"Eww! Kissing boys is gross."

Oliver pops his head up. "It is. You should never do it. Ever. Boys are stupid."

"You just kissed Mama."

"Because I'm stupid!" He pushes me up off his lap. "See? I am going to put myself in timeout."

"Don't do that, Daddy! I'll protect you!" Brynn giggles and rushes over to him, throwing herself into his arms.

Oliver catches her and spins her around and around. "Thank goodness!"

They are a mess.

"Daddy, why did you marry Mama?"

"Because she made me."

I snort. "Yes, the hardship."

"It really is hard being married to her. Did you know that she tricked me?"

"She did?"

Oliver nods. "She did. One day, she showed up at my job and said: 'Oliver, I need you to marry me, but it won't really be a marriage.'" He leans in and whispers. "But the joke was on her because we're married *still* . . ."

"That can be rectified," I warn.

"And you said yes?" Brynn asks with wide eyes, ignoring me completely.

"She's a babe. Of course I said yes."

I sigh. "Don't let him fool you, Brynnikins. He didn't say yes at first."

Now her eyes narrow as she turns back to him. "You said *no*?"

"Well, a man has to have some pride."

Brynn purses her lips, probably not understanding. "But you love Mama."

"With my whole heart."

I walk over to them and wrap my arm around Oliver's waist. "And we love you."

"I'm glad you married Mama."

"Why is that?" Oliver asks with a chuckle.

"Because she's the best."

Who knew? She compliments me. Miracles never cease. "Thank you."

She turns to me. "Because Daddy is the best, and he would only pick the best."

I sigh. "Of course." The man walks on water. "How about you go finish getting ready for school."

She wiggles her way down and rushes off.

Oliver grins. "I love that girl."

"Because she thinks you're the best?"

"Partially."

"Well, what about me?"

He turns, pulling me into his arms. Instinctively, I rest my arms on his broad shoulders, as his hands press against my spine. "I think you're the best too."

I smile. "So, do I get all your heart?"

"Sweetheart, you have had my heart since the day you stepped out of that car. I fell in love with you before you ever said a single word."

Silver-tongued as ever. "And why is that?"

He leans in, his lips grazing mine. "Because when you got out of the car, it was as if the whole world stopped and all I could see was you. I knew it then, and I know it now. You are everything I want in life, and as soon as our daughter is on that bus, I plan to prove it to you. I'm going to enjoy not needing to be quiet."

I grin. "I look forward to it."

"You should."

And I know I will because life with Oliver is one word: perfect.

Thank you for reading Oliver and Maren's story. I truly hope you enjoyed it as much as I loved writing it. It's always bittersweet saying goodbye to a series. My heart is torn between being overjoyed that the family I loved is settled where they should be, and also beyond sad that I must leave them. However, I don't know I really ever do that, as you see in this novel, my characters tend to show up in other books years down the road.

I know many have asked about Alex, and I hope you understand that at this time, I just don't have it in me to write his story. I can't explain it fully, other than, he's not strong enough in my heart or head to write. I never say never, but I know it's not meant to be right now.

After typing The End on this book, I wasn't ready to let go! Swipe to the next page for access to an exclusive Bonus Scene!

bonus scene

OLIVER

"Y ou need to calm down, you're worse than the bride," I tell the mother-of-the-bride in a tone that brooks no argument.

She flips me off. "Shove it up your ass."

"You're still a child. This isn't about you, it's about Kinsley."

Stella shakes her head, mumbling under her breath. "And for her, it should be perfect."

"It is perfect. We went over every damn detail a hundred times because of her neurotic mother."

We all want this wedding to be perfect. Every single one of us. Today, my perfect, still twelve-in-my-mind niece is going to marry a freaking Arrowood. Not just any Arrowood either. No, she's marrying Sean Arrowood's son. The irony that our families will be bound through marriage is hilarious.

"Austin will be good to Kinsley."

"I love that boy. It's not that, it's the whole damn thing."

"I'm not too excited either," I say under my breath.

It isn't that I'm not happy for Kinsley, because I am. It's more that there is no man good enough for any of my nieces or my daughter. But I'm not even going there. She isn't allowed to date until she's thirty—forty if it's left up to me, but Maren says I need to be reasonable.

Stella dabs at her eye. "I still feel like we just got her, you know? Like the time I got back isn't enough. She's only been mine for a little while, and now she's going to be his."

I pull my sister in for a hug. "She'll always be yours. And I'm saying this for my own benefit too because no matter who Brynn is married to, she'll always be mine."

Jack walks by the room we're in, sees his wife crying, waves, and walks past. "Hey, Jack!" I yell.

While Brynn may always be my responsibility, I relish the fact that my twin sister became his problem upon their marriage.

Stella lifts her head. "Jack?"

"I'm right here, love." He enters, glaring at me for a second before walking to her. "I've been looking for you."

"I'm not ready for this."

"Well, baby, she is. So, let's go."

This wedding is literally as far from traditional as we can ever get. My sister is the maid of honor, and Kinsley will have Samuel and Jack walk her down the aisle.

All of her cousins and brother are in the wedding party, and the ceremony is going to be in the woods instead of the wedding venue.

Kinsley and Austin want to be surrounded by only the people and things that matter. I think it had something to do with her being a park ranger who likes trees and him being a baseball player who holds a lot of wood. What the fuck do I know though?

Just then, my gorgeous wife appears in the doorway. "Let's go. We have to hike a damn half mile to the actual ceremony once we get into the woods. Devney and Sean are heading out in the golf carts next."

When she says golf carts, she means off-road vehicles because we couldn't get regular old golf carts out to the site.

And even then, we can't get close enough and still have to hike a bit.

"The ATVs?" I ask.

"Whatever. I'm not walking." Maren lifts the hem of her dress to show me her shoes. "These are my favorite."

"Then maybe you should've picked different ones," I say, which earns me the death stare.

I'm just saying that it would've made more sense, but I've given up on trying to understand women and their fashion choices.

Stella sighs. "I should go to Kinsley anyway."

Jack kisses her forehead. "Yes, you should."

"I just needed to cry a little," Stella explains.

I grasp her shoulder and squeeze. "That is absolutely understandable. Now, let's go see your daughter marry the son of the guy who married my ex."

Maren rolls her eyes. "He's one of your best friends, Oliver."

"Semantics, wife."

Sure, Sean and I have become really great friends since my wedding, but really, where is the fun in calling him that? It's much better if it seems as if I harbor hatred for the man who stole what would've been the biggest mistake in my life. Yeah, I could have . . . and thought I did . . . love Devney, but that was before I knew what love could be with Maren.

I just like being a dick, truly, it's more fun.

"Are you guys going to skip the wedding?" Grayson asks.

"We're just missing Josh and Alex," I say sarcastically.

"I'm here." Josh's voice echoes in the hall.

"And me!" Alex rounds out the Parkerson siblings.

Alex is home for the wedding, but he's leaving tomorrow to go back to his life overseas. He's become one of the top architects for his firm and is now in London doing some weird-shaped building that defies gravity. Whatever that means.

He's also happily married to Nadia, who is an heiress or

princess. I'm not sure, I've heard the story a hundred times, but I fade off when she starts talking about bowing or some shit. She doesn't fly, so I've only met her once when Maren and I went to visit.

Then my sisters-in-law yell. "We're here too!"

Stella sighs. "Let's go. My daughter needs perfection."

We all filter out, still the immature assholes of our twenties and thirties. Grayson punches Jack in the arm. Josh shoves me into the wall before Stella slaps him upside the head. Alex flicks the back of Grayson's ear, which then causes Grayson to try to trip Alex. It's amazing any of us were allowed to get married or have kids.

I'd like to think we were just all smart not to have five kids each.

Grayson has three, so he's close to this level of hell.

We exit the resort, which is booked solid with Arrowoods and other guests. For the last eighteen years, we have operated at maximum capacity every week. There was a period, in the beginning, where we weren't sure it would happen. We'd do well, but then there would be a lull, but now, we're rated one of the top family resorts in the country. The Park Inn closed nine years ago, taking my father under as well.

Grayson debated buying it but chose not to after the rest of us said we wanted no part in that company.

Mom, on the other hand, is doing well. She started a charity for emotionally abused spouses, helping other women find ways to protect themselves from narcissistic and abusive men. Her work means the world to her. It's nice to see that she's finally come out from the hell my father put her through. She is seriously dating someone, which is uncomfortable to watch since she's over seventy and he's a family friend.

"Is Samuel seating Mom?" Josh asks. Jack and Stella give him the evil eye. "What? They're together."

"Can we not talk about that?"

Jessica loops her arm in Stella's. "It's been four years."

"It's really awkward."

"What? You don't like your mom and your daughter's other father dating?" I refuse to let this go. Any opportunity to bicker with my sister is fun for me.

Maren pinches the skin under my arm.

"Ouch!"

"You deserved that."

I might have, but that doesn't mean it didn't hurt. "You forget, you're stuck with me for life."

"How could I ever forget?" my gorgeous wife says while fluttering her lashes. "It's a fact I cherish each morning."

"Cherish? I think you mean regret," Stella says.

"They're interchangeable most days."

"Funny," I deadpan.

We all load up in the off-road vehicles, and the girls get blankets to wrap around their legs and also a sort of poncho. It rained the last four days, almost washing out the trail there and covering it with mud. So, they're doing their best to avoid ruined dresses.

Maren and I are lucky enough to be in the vehicle with Jess and Grayson, which means Josh and Delia got Stella, who I can hear worrying over everything.

"Did we get some sort of flooring down?" Gray asks quietly.

"Yeah, I found the wood pallets that absorb the water. It helped make it less . . . mushy, but, it's still bad. Kinsley would only allow us to use natural products, so I couldn't do much other than use planks of wood for the aisles and logs for people to sit on."

He laughs. "I thought that kid would be an accountant."

"She's doing what she loves," Jess cuts in. "It's all we can ask for as parents."

"You're right," Maren agrees. "Brynn is applying to colleges, and I keep wanting to push her into any other major than hospitality. She has years of knowledge on how to run a hotel from her family, but she is adamant."

Brynn is going to take over this place, mark my words. That girl is the best parts of me and Maren. She sees problems, tackles them, and has had some ideas that greatly helped the Firefly.

We get to the spot, and while we've done everything we can to keep things free of mud, there's no way in hell my wife is going to ruin her shoes. Not after she told me the price.

I grab her, lifting her into my arms.

"Oliver!"

"Those shoes are worth more than my left kidney as you pointed out. You're not walking."

"What about the cost of your right arm?"

"Considering I'm right-handed, I think it's worth more."

She laughs. "Let's go."

When we get into the clearing, which is the same one where Kinsley's parents got engaged, I hear Stella suck in her breath.

"Oh, God."

I don't care what anyone says, this place is lit or whatever the kids are calling it these days.

Stella is usually in charge of everything, but we kept a lot of details from her.

Blake, Stella's son, Everett, and I strung lights from the trees going across and the girls wrapped the wires in flowers and moss. Brynn, Amelia, and Ember worked for hours, making sure it looked as though it was falling from the trees, and they outdid themselves. Then they had a lot of fun bossing my nephews around.

"This is like a scene from a movie," Stella says.

"It is, but she deserves it."

Stella's hand rests on my arm. "You're amazing."

"Yes, I know."

She's not lying.

"I'm heading to the tent," she tells us. "I gave them enough girl time without me listening."

"I'll go find Samuel, and we'll wait until you get us," Jack says.

Stella and Jack embrace before heading in different directions. The rest of the Parkerson party head to their seats.

When we are all situated, I take a second to really look around and smile. My life is pretty fucking fantastic. All of ours are. My siblings are all happily married, we have some of the most amazing kids who exist, and they're all starting to come into their own. Amelia is doing her internship for a law firm in Charlotte. Everett and Ember are in college. Brynn and Blake will be starting soon, which is terrifying but also beautiful. Grayson and Jessica's youngest daughter, Rhian, will be in high school next year, and she is the child we all wished on them. She should've been my kid with her flair for mischief. Today, we're here to watch Kinsley start her own family.

My mother comes to sit with us. "You all look very beautiful."

She grabs Jessica's hand, patting it.

The most unlikely friendship formed between those two.

"You look wonderful, Eveline," I say, and she elbows me.

"I may be old, but I'm still your mother. Don't think I won't take a spoon to your backside for being disrespectful, Oliver Parkerson."

As if she ever did. The nanny maybe . . .

I lean into my wife. "I would like it if *you* spanked me."

Maren huffs. "I can't take you anywhere."

The music starts, and we quiet down. I lace my fingers with my wife's, and we smile at each other.

"I love you."

"I love you," she says back.

Brynn makes her way down the path, and then the rest of my nieces and my sister, who has tears streaming down her face. When the music changes, we stand, and Jack, Kinsley, and Samuel walk toward Austin Arrowood and where

303

she will bind her future to his. It's beautiful to see this family, which has endured so much, make a home in Willow Creek Valley. One that none of us ever thought was possible, but one that none of us would ever trade away. Exactly as it was meant to be.

Thank you again for loving this family! I am already working on my next series that I am freaking out about! Sign up for my newsletter to keep up to date with all that's coming.

http://www.corinnemichaels.com

books by corinne michaels

The Salvation Series

Beloved

Beholden

Consolation

Conviction

Defenseless

Evermore: A 1001 Dark Night Novella

Indefinite

Infinite

The Hennington Brothers

Say You'll Stay

Say You Want Me

Say I'm Yours

Say You Won't Let Go: A Return to Me/Masters and
Mercenaries Novella

Second Time Around Series

We Own Tonight

One Last Time

Not Until You

If I Only Knew

The Arrowood Brothers

Come Back for Me

Fight for Me

The One for Me

Stay for Me

Willow Creek Valley Series

Return to Us

Could Have Been Us

A Moment for Us

A Chance for Us

Rose Canyon Series

Help Me Remember (Coming 2022)

Give Me Love (Coming 2022)

Keep This Promise (Coming 2022)

Co-Written with Melanie Harlow

Hold You Close

Imperfect Match

Standalone Novels

All I Ask

You Loved Me Once

acknowledgments

To my husband and children. You sacrifice so much for me to continue to live out my dream. Days and nights of me being absent even when I'm here. I'm working on it. I promise. I love you more than my own life.

My readers. There's no way I can thank you enough. It still blows me away that you read my words. You guys have become a part of my heart and soul.

Bloggers: I don't think you guys understand what you do for the book world. It's not a job you get paid for. It's something you love and you do because of that. Thank you from the bottom of my heart.

My beta reader Melissa Saneholtz: Dear God, I don't know how you still talk to me after all the hell I put you through. Your input and ability to understand my mind when even I don't blows me away. If it weren't for our phone calls, I can't imagine where this book would've been. Thank you for helping me untangle the web of my brain.

My assistant, Christy Peckham: How many times can one person be fired and keep coming back? I think we're running out of times. No, but for real, I couldn't imagine my life without you. You're a pain in my ass but it's because of you that I haven't fallen apart.

Sommer Stein for once again making these covers perfect and still loving me after we fight because I change my mind a bajillion times.

Michele Ficht, ReGina Kay, and Julia Griffis for always finding all the typos and crazy mistakes.

Nina and everyone at Valentine PR, thank you for always having my back and going above and beyond. I love you all so much.

Melanie Harlow, thank you for being the Glinda to my Elphaba or Ethel to my Lucy. Your friendship means the world to me and I love writing with you. I feel so blessed to have you in my life.

Bait, Crew, and Corinne Michaels Books—I love you more than you'll ever know.

My agent, Kimberly Brower, I am so happy to have you on my team. Thank you for your guidance and support.

Melissa Erickson, you're amazing. I love your face. Thank you for always talking me off the ledge that is mighty high.

To my narrators, Zachary Webber and Vanessa Edwin, I am so honored to work with you. You bring my story to life and always manage to make the most magical audiobooks.

Vi, Claire, Chelle, Mandi, Amy, Kristy, Penelope, Kyla, Rachel, Tijan, Alessandra, Laurelin, Devney, Jessica, Carrie Ann, Kennedy, Lauren, Susan, Sarina, Beth, Julia, and Natasha—Thank you for keeping me striving to be better and loving me unconditionally. There are no better sister authors than you all.

about the author

Corinne Michaels is a *New York Times, USA Today, and Wall Street Journal* bestselling author of romance novels. Her stories are chock full of emotion, humor, and unrelenting love, and she enjoys putting her characters through intense heartbreak before finding a way to heal them through their struggles.

Corinne is a former Navy wife and happily married to the man of her dreams. She began her writing career after spending months away from her husband while he was deployed—reading and writing were her escape from the loneliness. Corinne now lives in Virginia with her husband and is the emotional, witty, sarcastic, and fun-loving mom of two beautiful children.